Praise for Laura V. Hilton
and *Love by the Numbers*...

"Beneath Laura Hilton's clever, engaging love story lies an unshakable theme: God is good, all the time, but before He'll deliver the happily-ever-after we desire, we need to confront the Goliaths of our past and lay them to rest. A good story well told!

—*Charlotte Hubbard*
Author of numerous novels, including *A Simple Wish*
and *A Mother's Love*

"Once again, Laura Hilton has crafted a heartwarming romance that tugged at my emotions. It is sure to delight fans of Amish fiction and tender romance."

—*Kate Lloyd*
Best-selling author of *A Letter from Lancaster County*

"It amazes me how this author can whisk me into a novel and have me captivated with so little effort. Descriptive, enthralling, and with continuity, the plot keeps whirling along seamlessly. Family and love are the epitome of the plot. Relationships spark and sizzle, but always tasteful and pure. Once again, love is in the air, with a unique and exciting flair!"

—*Nancee Marchinowski*
Grand Rapids, Michigan
perspectivesbynancee.blogspot.com

"*Love by the Numbers*, by Laura V. Hilton, captured my attention quickly and I instantly feel in love with the story. Laura does a wonderful job with character development, making Lydia and Caleb feel like old friends."

—*Cecilia Lynn*
Goodreads reviewer

"I appreciate the depth of Laura V. Hilton's stories that reel me into the storyline with a connection to the lives of the heroine and hero from the start. *Love by the Numbers* was a tale I could not stop reading. It brought moments of smiles, laughter, cheering, anguish, tears, and heartfelt emotions as I was in the moment with each scene. Laura's characters are three dimensional, with realistic issues to overcome, and infused with a beautiful knowledge of biblical principles of a loving God providing forgiveness, second chances, and love when individuals seek Him."

—*Marilyn Ridgway*
Goodreads reviewer

"I always enjoy reading any story written by Laura V. Hilton. She has the ability to draw her readers in from the start of her books. The more I read, the more I couldn't put the book down. I laughed outright in some of the scenes. I like this about Laura, too: she knows how to put some humor in just the right places!"

—*Tina Marie Watson*
Amish book reviewer

LOVE
BY THE
NUMBERS

LAURA V.
HILTON

WHITAKER
HOUSE

Love by the Numbers

Laura V. Hilton
lighthouse-academy.blogspot.com

ISBN: 978-1-62911-932-8
eBook ISBN: 978-1-62911-933-5
Printed in the United States of America
© 2018 by Laura V. Hilton

Whitaker House
1030 Hunt Valley Circle
New Kensington, PA 15068
www.whitakerhouse.com

Library of Congress Cataloging-in-Publication Data
Names: Hilton, Laura V., 1963– author.
Title: Love by the numbers / Laura V. Hilton.
Description: New Kensington, PA : Whitaker House, 2018. |
Identifiers: LCCN 2017046020 (print) | LCCN 2017052774 (ebook) | ISBN 9781629119335 (E-book) | ISBN 9781629119328 (softcover)
Subjects: LCSH: Mate selection—Fiction. | BISAC: FICTION / Christian / Romance. | GSAFD: Christian fiction. | Love stories.
Classification: LCC PS3608.I4665 (ebook) | LCC PS3608.I4665 L69 2018 (print) | DDC 813/.6—dc23
LC record available at https://lccn.loc.gov/2017046020

1 2 3 4 5 6 7 8 9 10 11 🔲 25 24 23 22 21 20 19 18

DEDICATION

To the God that healeth, the one that saved me.
To Loundy, my favorite song.
To Michael, my adventurous one.
To Kristin, my darling daughter.
To Jenna, my sunshine.
To Kaeli, my showers of blessing.
And in memory of my parents, Allan and Janice, and my uncle
Loundy, and my grandmother, Mertie, who talked about their
Pennsylvania Amish heritage.
To God be the glory.

ACKNOWLEDGMENTS

I'd like to offer my heartfelt thanks to the following:

The residents of Jamesport and the surrounding areas, for answering my questions and pointing me in the right directions.

My husband and children for going with me on vacation and helping me observe.

The amazing team at Whitaker House—Christine, Courtney, and Cathy. You are wonderful.

Tamela, my agent, for believing in me all these years.

My critique group—you know who you are. You are amazing. You knew the right questions to ask, and when more detail was needed. Thanks also for the encouragement. Candee, thanks for reading many pages within a short time period and offering wise suggestions.

My husband, Steve, for being a tireless proofreader and cheering section.

Jenna, for reading over my shoulder and editing as I wrote (also for naming the horses and the kitten).

GLOSSARY OF AMISH TERMS AND PHRASES

ach:	oh
aent/aenti:	aunt/auntie
"ain't so?":	a phrase commonly used at the end of a sentence to invite agreement
Ausbund:	Amish hymnal used in the worship services, containing lyrics only
boppli:	baby/babies
bu:	boy
buwe:	boys
daed:	dad
"Danki":	"Thank you"
der Herr:	the Lord
Gott:	God
großeltern:	grandparents
dochter:	daughter
ehemann:	husband
Englisch:	non-Amish
Englischer:	a non-Amish person

frau:	wife
grossdaedi:	grandfather
grossmammi:	grandmother
gut:	good
haus:	house
hübsch	pretty
"Ich liebe dich":	"I love you"
jah:	yes
kapp:	prayer covering or cap
kinner:	children
koffee:	coffee
kum:	come
maidal:	young woman
mamm:	mom
maud:	maid/spinster
morgen:	morning
nacht:	night
nein:	no
"off in den kopf":	off in the head; crazy
onkel:	uncle
Ordnung:	the rules by with an Amish community lives
rumschpringe:	"running around time"; a period of freedom and experimentation during the late adolescence of Amish youth
ser gut:	very good
schatz:	sweetheart
special:	referring to individuals with a mental handicap
sohn:	son
verboden:	forbidden
"Was ist letz?":	"What's the matter?"
welkum:	welcome
youngies:	young unmarried individuals in the Amish community

1

*H*e was gorgeous. Simply gorgeous.

Lydia Hershberger reached around the cash register to collect the hard candy sticks that had spilled out of their clear plastic canisters when Aenti Judith's Siamese kitten had dashed past, knocking over the display. But she paid only nominal attention to arranging the candy. Her focus was fixed on *him*. She tried not to gawk, but, *wow*. He was *hot*.

Tall. Sandy-blond hair. Clean-shaven face. Milk-chocolate-brown eyes.

As the door closed behind him, he removed his straw hat from his head, then glanced around the gift shop. His gaze moved in Lydia's direction, and she quickly looked away. It wouldn't do to be caught staring.

But she couldn't resist another peek at him.

He seemed to freeze when his gaze caught hers. Or was it hers that caught his?

And then…he scowled.

What?

This man—someone she didn't even know—was glaring at her. Why? She had every right to be standing behind the counter of Aenti Judith's gift shop while her aent and onkel were away on a mission trip in…um, wherever it was that they'd gone. Any other time, she could've spouted off the information without thought.

But not while staring into the most incredible milk-chocolate eyes ever.

Were there any leftover chocolate Easter bunnies in the store? Lydia needed one. Now. She glanced at the clearance display, but it was devoid of candy of any type.

Her gaze snapped back to him.

"You." His voice emerged as a growl.

How, exactly, was she supposed to respond to that? She could flirt, and try to tease him out of the foul mood he was apparently in. She grinned and slowly scanned him, as if she were interested.

Well, she was interested. Nein, *had been* interested. Not anymore. She didn't need to be getting involved with a jerk. Or with anyone, really.

"Have we met?" She felt certain the answer was a resounding nein. Surely, she would've remembered him if she'd seen him before.

He replied with a noncommittal grunt.

Okay, then. She fought the urge to giggle, though her laughter bubbled up and almost smothered her when she tried to restrain it. She tried to remember the advice Aenti Judith had hastily imparted, about handing difficult customers, as they hugged hello and gut-bye at the bus station on Thursday evening. Nothing came to mind. Except for "Smile a lot." And "The customer is always right."

Maybe she should take the time to read the notes Aenti Judith had left for her, written in her cramped, condensed hand. But reading pages of instructions ranked up there with solving math problems. All about rules. *Ugh.* Not to mention boring.

She pasted on a smile. "How may I help you?"

"I'm supposed to do the books for Judith Zook while she's in Papua New Guinea. She said her niece would be running the store in her absence—ach, nein. Nein." He grimaced as if he'd just caught a whiff of a skunk. What was his problem? Did he see her as incompetent, needing someone else to handle the book-keeping in her aent's absence?

Okay, so maybe she was incompetent, at least in the area of finances. After all, Daed had written his sister, warning her that Lydia didn't have the strongest of math skills. Lydia had assured her aent that she could handle things, but Aenti Judith had said she would try to find someone to handle the daily deposits and the monthly payments to her vendors. To manage the books.

Try being the operative word. Aenti Judith hadn't mentioned having found someone. Unless she'd written it somewhere in her notes.

"You're the niece."

"Imagine that." Lydia immediately regretted her flippant tone. This was Aenti Judith's accountant, and she couldn't afford to offend him. Not when she needed his help during the six months.

It would be a challenge. In spite of his rare gut looks, this man made her want to bare her claws.

He straightened, dropped one hand to his side, and, with the other hand, slapped his hat against his hip, once, twice. Then he forced a smile, revealing what appeared to be vampire teeth. Lydia blinked and took another look. Jah. Vampire teeth.

Weird. Creepy. Jerk.

So much for "gorgeous."

Okay, teeth and personality aside, he was still drop-dead handsome.

The man cleared his throat. "I stopped by to introduce myself, since I didn't make it to church this past Sunday. But… we've already met."

Nope. She would remember.

"Abigail and Sam's wedding. December." He filled in the blank. "I came in late. Sat by my cousin Bethany."

Maybe he was right. Lydia had traveled from out of state to be a side-sitter for her best friend as she got married. It was overwhelming to meet so many people in Abigail's new home. In addition, just before the singing that followed the wedding, Lydia had received the devastating news of the death of her fiancé, Peter Fisher. Back home in Ohio, he had been killed in a freak accident. Struck by lightning, in December, of all times. Nein wonder Lydia didn't remember this man. She'd been in shock, disbelieving everything she'd been told by the well-meaning preacher who'd delivered the news.

"Caleb Bontrager." He started to extend his hand, then frowned and withdrew his arm before she had a chance to react. "Your aenti asked me to handle the books for you."

So he'd said. Lydia nodded. "She told me she would try to find someone. I guess I assumed that if she'd found someone, he would've kum in the evening, at closing." Which—she glanced at the wall clock—was right now. Almost. About a minute till five.

The hour hand made a jerky movement, and the clock chimed five times, simultaneous with the cuckoos of several dozen clocks on one of the far walls.

Lydia really needed to read the notes her aent had left her.

"I was in town. Thought I'd…well, as I said, introduce myself. Need help with anything else before I close out the register and make the day's deposit?"

Lydia wrinkled her nose at the way he talked down to her, as if she were incapable of running the store by herself. *Jah, Lydia can do math. If she has to.* She rolled her eyes, then emerged from behind the counter.

Caleb eyed her warily and stepped aside as she skirted around him and headed for the door. What, did he think she'd attack him? He was the one with the vampire teeth. She flipped the sign around so that the "Closed" side faced outward, and then she locked the door.

He moved behind the counter, sat on the stool, and opened the cash register. "Judith gave me a set of keys, so I shouldn't have to bother you again, unless I have a question."

That would be nice. She could finish up her duties in peace, and never have to see him again. A blessing, beyond the fact that she didn't have to do the math.

Lydia straightened the shelves, returning misplaced merchandise to the proper location—handcrafted cards, quilted pot holders, boppli blankets, fabric dolls dressed in Amish attire, candles, jams and jellies…every type of souvenir imaginable for the Englisch tourists.

To Lydia's dismay, her focus was on the obnoxious man seated behind the counter. The one Aenti Judith had enlisted to handle the bookkeeping after Lydia had said she wasn't sure how she'd do with that task. Mathematics gave her a headache. But she'd assured Aenti Judith that she would try her best.

Apparently, she wasn't even going to be given the opportunity to try. Aenti Judith had gone ahead and arranged for this grump to do it, instead.

Which was the lesser evil: a math-induced headache, or a tension headache caused by the presence of an infuriating male to whom she was irresistibly attracted? Either way, a trip to the medicine cabinet appeared inevitable.

When Aenti Judith mentioned the possibility of finding an accountant, Lydia had pictured a gray-haired geezer with glasses perched on the tip of his nose. Not a handsome young man with vampire teeth…as if he intended to suck the life out of her personality.

～

Caleb could almost see glitter shimmering in the air around Lydia as she glided around the store. With her bubbly aura, she radiated sunshine and happiness. Her blue eyes twinkled—first with joy, and maybe a hint of attraction, but the latter had quickly faded into something else—annoyance, probably, or anger—when he'd opened his mouth. True, he'd gone out of his way to be a jerk. That was because girls like Lydia were Trouble with a capital T. Make that *TROUBLE*, in all caps and italicized.

He should know.

So why was it that he couldn't stop watching her?

Hearing the low rumble of a purr, Caleb glanced down at the kitten winding herself around his ankles in a figure-eight pattern. He reached down and picked her up. She was Siamese, and only a few months old. He'd been there when Judith had kum to take her home after she was weaned. His mamm and Judith had remained best friends when Judith had left the Amish in order to marry a Mennonite.

And, lamentably, Mamm had stated her intention to get to know Judith's niece. To act as a mother figure to her while she was managing the store and living far from family and loved ones.

Caleb studied Lydia as she flitted around the cluttered store overflowing with Amish products. His gaze traveled from her forehead to her jaw to her graceful neck. To her light brown hair with natural blonde highlights. Would it feel as soft underneath his fingers as the kitten's fur he now stroked?

He swallowed. Hard. And put the kitten down.

As much as he may long for what she unwittingly offered, he was used to the way things were. Simple. Uncluttered. Orderly. Starting something with Lydia would be messy and complicated.

He'd been there before. Glitter and glitz—they lured men straight into danger, slipping and sliding the entire way.

As it stood now, his footing was already unsure.

It would be best if he stayed far, far away from Lydia Hershberger.

"So, what's with the vampire teeth?"

Her question came with nein warning. He jumped. Blinked. He'd forgotten that he'd put in those toy teeth earlier, to tease one of his young cousins. That explained the strange looks he'd gotten that afternoon. Including the expression Lydia gave him when he'd opened his mouth.

She messed with the hard candy sticks on the counter again, matching the flavors with their corresponding canisters. There was a wide variety: Peppermint. Root beer. Blueberry. Cherry. Lemon.

She was much too close.

His heart rate increased, and his breaths became shallow. He yanked the vampire teeth out of his mouth and stuffed them inside his pocket. Opened the cash drawer and started stacking the dollar bills in neat piles of twenty, with George Washington facing the same direction.

He needed to get away from Lydia. Find some semblance of sanity.

But Mamm wanted him to invite her to the frolic to-nacht, and to offer to drive her home afterward, if nobody else gave her a ride. *Make her feel welkum, Caleb. She's a stranger in a strange land.*

Right.

She'd said a lot more—how Lydia had been in town only a day or two, and how she needed to make friends. Mamm had even muttered something about it being time for Caleb to start courting, but she'd marched out of the room mid-sentence, and he hadn't quite understood her comment.

"I'm...uh, there's a frolic to-nacht. It's supposed to be at Gizelle Miller's." He shouldn't have added that last bit. In fact, he should've ignored Mamm's request and not mentioned anything. What if Lydia decided to attend?

"Is Gizelle your girl?" Lydia didn't look at him.

He hesitated. It really wasn't her business. But the short answer, the honest one, was "Nein." While they weren't courting,

Caleb had taken Gizelle on more than a few buggy rides. She was safe. Nein sparks, nein glitter. Just what he needed. Wanted. Comfortable. Stable. Routine.

Not tempting enough to lure him into trouble.

"So, you're wearing those teeth to attract the girls?" Lydia quirked her lips.

His mouth worked, but he had nothing to say. Nothing.

Because the only girl he wanted to impress was Lydia, and she was very decidedly off-limits. *TROUBLE.*

"Look, you can kum if you want," he said. "I'll take you." Caleb tried to sound nonchalant as he fulfilled his mamm's wishes.

Against his better judgment.

And, suddenly, he really wanted her to kum.

Lydia somehow managed to unclench her jaw. She finished organizing the candy sticks and straightened, more than anxious to retreat to the quiet haven of her temporary quarters in the apartment above Aenti Judith's store. She didn't want to spend any more time with a man who made her blood pressure rise, much less hang out with a bunch of strangers who did the same. Eventually, though, she would have to make an effort to get to know people. She'd actually looked forward to making friends with the girls she'd met at Abigail's wedding almost five months ago.

"Danki, but nein. Have a gut evening."

He winced.

Maybe she should've tried to sound like she meant it.

He leaned down and scooped up the kitten, Rosie, whose purr-motor resumed running. "Dream about me to-nacht." He immediately reared back, wide-eyed, with a sharp intake of breath.

She eyed him. "Would that be with or without your false teeth?" She knew she ought to focus on him with the teeth, to make herself forget how handsome he was without them. For her own sanity, he should keep the false teeth in his mouth—except then her dreams might be nacht-mares. He glanced up and gave her a slow smile that made her pulse jump. "They're vampire fangs."

Jah, fang-free, he was gorgeous. "Kind of sad you have to use props to get the girls." Her voice shook, lacking the conviction she'd wanted to convey. All thanks to his smile. *Ugh.*

"It's absolutely tragic, ain't so?" His grin reached his eyes. "Be sure to put me on your prayer list."

She stared at him for a long, drawn-out moment. Her pulse throbbed. Her breathing hitched. Suspended.

She mentally shook herself, then turned to go upstairs to Aenti Judith's all-electric apartment where she would spend too much time thinking about the man she'd left downstairs. The one going to a frolic at the home of Gizelle Miller—whoever that was.

The man she never had to see again, if she had her way.

So why did she want to turn around and tell him she would take him up on his halfhearted invitation, after all?

2

*C*aleb watched Lydia retreat, her purple dress swaying. She disappeared through the open door to the back room. A few seconds later, creaking noises sounded overhead. Then, silence.

He looked down at Rosie, asleep in his arms. Judith kept her in the apartment at nacht. Nein gut leaving a mischievous kitten all alone in the shop.

Delivering Rosie gave him an excuse to invade Lydia's dwelling.

And the faster he counted the money, balanced the ledger, prepared the deposit, and locked it in the safe, the sooner he could see her again.

She was definitely trouble. And he was a crazy fool.

The cat could stay in the shop to-nacht. He'd obey his initial instincts and stay away.

Far, far away.

Okay. That was settled. Caleb straightened his posture and grimaced, trying to exorcise the spirit—though he wouldn't call it evil—that still fought for control of his thoughts, his mind, his heart. *Lord Gott…help. She…nein. Just nein. Give me strength. You promised never to tempt us beyond what we are able to endure.*

And she, of the glitter and glitz, was definitely more than he could endure.

Gott knew his struggles with everything bright, shiny, and beautiful.

He swallowed and shook his head. *Nein.* He'd learned his lessons—the hard way.

He wouldn't go down that path again.

As the kitten dozed on his lap, he tried to stay as still as he could while he finished counting the cash, coins, and checks, then made out a deposit ticket, before tucking anything not needed for the next day's business into a zippered bank bag. He'd have to take some time to study the way Judith did her ledgers. He had his own method for his clock-making business, but it was probably too simplistic for managing commissions at Judith's shop, where a long list of Amish artisans sold their goods.

He slid the cash drawer back into the register and locked it, then reached for the ledger. At least Lydia had kept track of the day's sales, even if she hadn't done anything beyond listing the vendors' names, the items they'd sold, and at what cost. Three of E. Miller's quilts. A dozen pints of G. Yoder's home-canned jams, jellies, and preserves. One birdhouse and one birdfeeder made by J. Yoder. Five reed baskets crafted by D. Lapp. And the list went on. He glanced down the long list. She'd had a great day of business—and had even sold two of his cuckoo clocks. He slid his fingers over her neat print. *C. Bontrager.* She probably didn't have the vaguest idea that was he.

Gut thing he knew who was who. He would need to add it all up, figure out how much each vendor had earned, and keep track of the amounts Judith was due. There were also the credit card transactions to calculate.

Caleb shifted, disturbing the kitten in his lap. She stretched one foreleg, giving a halfhearted swipe of her tiny paw at whatever bothered her. Did Judith have a basket, or any type of bed, for Rosie in the store? He gently scooped the kitten into his arms and held her as he would his sister's *boppli*, close against his chest. Then he slid off the stool and glanced around. Surely, there was something suitable in the shop to use as a bed. He headed toward the storeroom.

A loud whirl sounded as the furnace kicked on, followed by the clanging of pipes heating. Rosie jerked awake, glaring at him. She clawed her way onto his shoulder, then jumped onto a nearby shelf holding a display of homemade jar candles. The jars at the front slid off the shelf, cracking as they hit the floor. Then the entire shelf tipped, sending the rest of its contents to their demise on the tiles beneath, the crash accompanied by Rosie's yowls.

He grabbed for the kitten, trying to trap her before she did any more damage.

Overhead, a door slammed. Footsteps pounded down the back stairs. A second later, Lydia burst into the room.

Caleb sent her a brief, apologetic glance, then lunged for the kitten. He landed on the floor in a full-out, chin-scraping skid, sliding to a stop at Lydia's feet as his hand closed around the scruff of Rosie's neck.

He heard a sharp intake of breath, then silence. The bare feet were still in front of him, toenails colored with an intriguing shade of verboden polish that matched her dress.

He rolled over and waved the still-yowling Rosie in the air, like a prize—or maybe a white flag of surrender. But Lydia didn't seem to notice. Instead, she stared over him, her hands pressed to her mouth, her eyes wide.

⌒

Lydia had nein words.

As the cloying combination of scents from the shattered candles filled the air, she stared in disbelief at the colorful array of wax chunks and glass shards. Aenti Judith would have two cows and a conniption, for sure and for certain.

Even though it wasn't Lydia's fault.

If anyone was to blame, it was the man lying at her feet, struggling to sit up. She clenched her hands, placed them on her hips, and glared down at him, while fighting the inappropriate urge to giggle.

Caleb pushed himself to his feet, shoved the cat at her, and backed away as the animal latched on to her apron with its claws. Lydia unfurled one fist and grabbed Rosie, just in case she fell or decided to let go.

"The kitten sleeps upstairs. In the apartment, with you." His breath hitched. He flapped his hand toward the mess. "So this kind of thing doesn't happen." Then he sighed. "I'll clean everything up."

Jah, he would. And he would explain the loss of inventory to Aenti Judith, too.

But it was still funny, the way he lunged after the cat and went skidding. And Lydia was struggling to contain her giggles. She pursed her lips and shook her head, blinking away the tears from the corners of her eyes.

Caleb pressed his palm to his chin, and Lydia focused on the redness there, in an effort to distract herself from the appealing shadow of whiskers on his jawline. *Nice.* Peter's hair had been red and unruly, and his stubble had been auburn. She liked the darkness of Caleb's.

"Are you hurt?" Thankfully, her voice didn't waver.

He hesitated a moment, his gaze flicking over her. Then his lips twitched. "I think I deserve combat pay. Maybe it'll help if you go with me to the frolic to-nacht. I'll make sure you get home safely afterward."

Something inside her jumped in anticipation. Lurched. Then tumbled to the ground, shattering worse than the mess of cracked jars and ruined wax candles.

She *couldn't* enter the dating scene here. Nein matter how appealing the men might be.

Without another word, she shook her head, turned on her heel, and went back upstairs.

～

Once Caleb finished cleaning up the wreckage caused by the kitten, he returned the broom and dustpan to the dark closet where he'd found them, then made sure he'd left everything else in order. The ledger book still lay open on the counter. He'd need to note the broken inventory, but for now, he closed the ledger and put it away. He would kum in after hours tomorrow to tally up the totals and make note of them, the way Judith had asked him to. And to figure in the damage.

He slid the deposit bag into the safe, which he then shut and locked. Tomorrow, when he brought his own deposit to the bank, he would pick up Lydia's—er, Judith's—and take care of that one, as well.

He flicked the lights off, then walked toward the rear of the store. Just outside the door, his horse and buggy were tied to a hitching post.

The back stairs loomed off to one side. He glanced up them and hesitated, then shook his head. He didn't need to extend to her a third invitation to a frolic she had nein interest in attending.

He wasn't going to force his presence on her, either. Not when he'd already determined she was *TROUBLE*, and he needed to keep his distance.

And certainly not when he'd already kum across as a jerk and a clumsy oaf, all when he'd hoped to appear suave and charming.

To be fair, he hadn't expected *her*. Jah, he'd known Judith's niece would be running the store, but he hadn't realized she was the same woman who'd haunted his thoughts, dreams, and visions since he'd seen her at Sam's wedding. Four months—or was it five?—was a long time to obsess over a woman.

Maybe "obsess" was too strong a word.

But not by much.

Dream about me to-nacht.

He cringed again at the unpremeditated plea that had tumbled out of his mouth earlier. He couldn't begin to imagine what Lydia thought of it.

But, ach, if only she *would* dream about him…and in a much more positive light than the one in which he'd presented himself.

Then again, he didn't need her setting her kapp for him. He planned to marry someone who didn't turn his world upside down. One who wouldn't lure him down dangerous paths.

And Lydia had a kind of magnetic power over him. One that drew him in and turned him into a blathering fool. One that controlled his every thought.

One he couldn't resist.

He shut the door behind him. Locked it. And climbed into his buggy.

And then he drove away, resisting the temptation to lift his eyes to the second-floor window for an elusive glimpse of the verboden princess.

3

*L*ydia deposited the kitten in her basket lined with a fuzzy blue fleece blanket. Rosie hopped right out again and sprawled upside down on the back of the sofa, right in front of the window where the late-afternoon sunshine shone brightest. Lydia would love to make herself at home in a sunny spot on the couch, curled up with a book. Not that this was her home, but it was as close as it came to one right now.

She was glad Caleb had accepted her decision not to attend the frolic, but it was sweet of him to ask twice, giving her a chance to change her mind. Still, she couldn't possibly go. Not to the frolic, and not anywhere else, either, until she'd studied the notes Aenti Judith had left. She wanted to be prepared for any more surprises that might walk through the door.

At least the room was beginning to warm up. She'd adjusted the heat when she'd kum upstairs earlier.

But sitting in the sunshine to read was a wunderbaar idea. She could curl up beneath another fuzzy fleece blanket, like the pink one that Aenti Judith kept folded on the armrest. A book Onkel Mark must've been reading lay open on the floor beside his recliner, his slippers beside it, as if he'd just kicked them off and would be right back. But his reading material didn't appeal to Lydia. Science fiction, the back cover said. The front-cover image looked pretty scary.

Supper could wait. Lydia didn't know what she wanted, anyway. Aenti Judith had stocked the refrigerator and freezer, having asked by letter what Lydia liked. That morgen, Lydia had put a pound of frozen hamburger in the refrigerator to thaw. That would feed her for several days, once she decided what to do with it. Of course, if she went to the frolic with Caleb, she wouldn't have to cook until tomorrow. She could fill up on finger foods. Sandwiches. Cookies. Maybe chocolate. And pop.

Okay, maybe she did want to go. A little.

Not enough to make an effort to run downstairs and see if Caleb was still in the store. She would read, instead. She picked up the fat little notebook where Aenti Judith had written her instructions. If only she could immerse herself in a real book. Preferably a romance. But the notes would have to do, because a romance was out of the question.

In more ways than one.

Hearing a horse snort, she glanced out the window and saw Caleb directing his horse out of the back parking lot.

Too late to change her mind now, anyway.

Well, she supposed the buggy driver might not be Caleb. Hard to tell from the small side window. It was an Amish man, though.

Then she noticed the two horse and buggies parked at the hitching post.

Heard the soft patter of footsteps climbing the back stairs.

A second later, someone knocked on the door.

She lowered the notebook and stared at the door. If Caleb had left, then who had gotten in? And how? Surely, Caleb would have locked whatever door he'd exited through.

Tendrils of fear snaked up her back, and she shivered. If only Aenti Judith's door had a peephole.

Another knock.

Maybe Caleb hadn't left, after all, and intended to try to convince her to attend the frolic. In which case, she would…go? Or would she stand her ground and tell him, in no uncertain terms, that she said what she meant and meant what she said?

And state it so forcefully that he'd never invite her to anything ever again? Jah, as if. When word got out about her behavior, she'd be in hotter water than she already was for having Mennonite relatives.

Lydia sighed. She returned the notebook to the koffee table, next to the keys she'd dropped when she came in earlier; pasted a pleasant smile on her face; and opened the door. She caught a brief glimpse of a white kapp and a dark gray dress, before she was engulfed in a bear hug. Something hard dug into her spine. Her nose was buried in a neck that smelled like koffee, strawberries, and pie dough. "You're here, you're here! You're finally here."

Lydia tensed for a moment, but she soon relaxed in the woman's embrace.

It was nice to be hugged.

⟞⟝

Caleb half dashed, half stumbled, up the stairs after Mamm, but he reached the top too late to prevent his mother from smothering Lydia in her embrace. The two women were nearly the same height, but Mamm was considerably rounder. She blamed her figure on having birthed eight children. He was wise enough not to argue the point.

"Mamm, let her breathe." Caleb struggled to keep a chuckle contained.

If only he'd left before her arrival. He hadn't even made it out of the parking lot when Mamm had caught him, and asked him to unlock the store so she could go upstairs and introduce herself to Lydia.

Now Caleb had to battle his runaway heart for the second time in one same day. Of course, he had to if his mamm expected to get into the building. He carried the key.

Well, one of the keys. Lydia possessed the other.

His stomach fluttered, and he pressed his hand flat against it. He possessed the only other key to her apartm…

Nein. He wouldn't go there.

Too late. He already had. Gut thing he had a date with Gizelle to-nacht. She would bring him back down to earth. And gut thing Lydia had said nein, because he wasn't sure even Gizelle would be enough to control his thoughts if Lydia were along.

Mamm stepped back, leaving Lydia's kapp slightly askew. Several strands of her hair had fallen loose, and Mamm reached to tuck them into place. "You poor, dear girl. Judith told me *everything*. Here, I brought you some apple-rhubarb cobbler."

Lydia blinked. Frowned. Stepped backward. "What?"

Jah. Exactly. Caleb stared at Mamm. Well, at the back of her head. "Everything?"

Mamm didn't seem to notice. "Now, you tell me Caleb was a gut bu and invited you to the frolic to-nacht, and to dinner tomorrow at our haus. I'll fix your favorites. Judith told me exactly what they were. Like this cobbler. Here, take it."

Lydia accepted the square baking pan. "Danki." She glanced at Caleb, then turned back to Mamm. "You're…his mamm?"

"Of course, I am. And Judith's best friend. Bethel. Now, Caleb did invite you, didn't he?"

Lydia's eyes were wide as her gaze returned to him. "Um, jah, he invited me to the frolic, but I don't want to go."

"Nonsense. You get your shoes on right now and get out that door. Caleb will take you, ain't so?" Mamm twisted around to look up at him, then turned back to Lydia. "And he won't leave you stranded there, either. He'll bring you safely home afterward. Well, maybe he'll stop by a sparking place first."

"Mamm!" Caleb's jaw unhinged as heat burned his neck, his cheeks, his…well, all of him. "Wow. Just, wow."

If it were possible, Lydia's eyes widened even more. "Uh…."

"Just thought I'd encourage you." Mamm winked at him.

Caleb needed this kind of encouragement like he needed the cow to kick the milk bucket over. What this situation required was discouragement. Seriously.

Mamm wouldn't tease him like this if she knew the temptations he faced. Would she?

"Now, I won't take nein for an answer," Mamm told Lydia. "You are going to the frolic to-nacht, and you'll kum to my haus for dinner tomorrow. I'll make sure Caleb picks you up then, too. You won't have to worry one bit about finding your way in this unfamiliar town."

It wasn't as if she'd have to try. She didn't have transportation, because Judith and Mark drove a car. Unless Lydia possessed a driver's license nobody knew about. It was possible, but Caleb doubted it.

He put his hand gently on Mamm's shoulder. "Kum on, Mamm. Let's go."

She shook him off. "Not without her." She pointed at Lydia's bare feet, complete with her incriminating purple-tipped toes. "Shoes. Now."

With a submissive nod, Lydia set the cobbler dish down on the table and sat to put on her shoes.

Caleb's heart took a traitorous leap, then crash-landed in a tangled mess.

⌁

Five minutes later, Lydia was seated too close beside Caleb. Funny, she'd never minded the confines of a buggy before.

Caleb hunched over the reins and cast his glowering expression straight ahead.

Well, she didn't want to be there any more than he did. Not really. But she'd been taught to obey those in authority over her, and Bethel Bontrager—Caleb's mamm, her aenti's best friend— was definitely her elder.

Maybe Caleb would agree to let her out at the next corner. Lydia twisted around and glanced out the back window.

Bethel waved cheerfully at her from her own buggy, right behind them. So much for that idea.

"She'll follow us most of the way there." Caleb shifted. Straightened. "Might as well accept it."

Lydia faced front again. "It might be a little easier if you stopped acting as if you'd rather have a cavity filled without anesthesia than be with me."

His jaw dropped. Then a chuckle emerged as he glanced at her, a grin forming on his face.

"Look, I'm not in the market for a relationship, either. I don't appreciate the matchmaking efforts of my aenti and your mamm any more than you do. I'm not here to find an ehemann; I'm here to help my aenti. So, can we just…I don't know, declare a truce, maybe? Pretend to be friends?"

His eyes skimmed over her, a slow perusal that heated her blood. His gaze stopped and reversed direction when it reached her feet, then traveled upward again, at the same leisurely pace. "Friends. Jah."

He couldn't have sounded more sarcastic if he tried.

Lydia inhaled a deep breath of resignation and looked away. "Have it your way. But, just so you know, I have brothers. I can give as gut as I get."

"Really." He pulled on the reins and turned down a side street.

Lydia glanced out the back window again. Caleb's mamm was still on their tail.

"We'll lose her when we stop to pick up Gizelle."

"Ach, Gizelle. The one you aren't dating."

A moment of silence. She looked back at him in time to see him nod. "Jah, that's the one. Except…we're dating. Sort of. Not courting, though."

Lydia shrugged. "Same difference."

"Nein, it's not. But that's about to change. I'll ask her to be my girl. To-nacht."

4

*C*aleb's knees wobbled as he trudged up the porch steps at Gizelle's haus. He was still reeling from the announcement he'd made to Lydia. What had prompted him to say he would ask Gizelle to be his girl? Probably an instinctive move born out of self-defense. And she would probably hold him to it.

His hands shook. Before he could get a firm grasp on the knob, the door opened.

There stood Gizelle's daed, Andy. "Gut afternoon, Caleb. Gizelle is almost ready. Kum on in and have a seat. You can try one of the chocolate chip cookies she made for the frolic." He pointed to the table, where Caleb saw a square tinfoil pan filled with the lightly browned, chocolate-morsel-studded goodies and fitted with a clear plastic lid.

"Danki, Andy, but I…uh…." Caleb gestured over his shoulder toward the driveway. "There's a girl…." A beautiful, sparkly, feisty, oh-so-out-of-reach girl that he would really love to date, even if just once.

But once wouldn't be enough.

"A girl, eh?" Andy peered past him out the window. "We should ask her in, too."

Caleb cringed. The last thing he wanted to do was sit there while Andy got to know Lydia under the guise of welcoming her to the community. Anything more Caleb learned about her would only serve to feed his crush. "How much longer do you think Gizelle will be?"

Andy shrugged. "Not too much longer. Do you want to take the cookies out to the buggy and share them with the girl while you wait?"

Ach. That was the only other option. Either way, Caleb would kum across as rude, to Andy or to Lydia. Andy knew him well enough not to feel slighted if he were to go outside, but what if he suspected Caleb of wanting to be alone with Lydia? That wouldn't do at all.

Lydia already thought he was rude. Mamm would have been ashamed of his treatment of her, and he realized his reasons were as inconsequential and foolish as Mamm would have called them. Because there couldn't actually be glitter floating in the air around her. She couldn't actually be shimmery, shiny, and bright. She was just a normal girl. Nein twinkles. Nein sunshine.

He glanced over his shoulder at the buggy. At the girl waiting inside.

Maybe it was his imagination, or just the angle of the sun, but golden rays of brightness shone around about Lydia. Laser streaks of lights glanced off the buggy, the horse, the girl.

Caleb sighed. Imagination or not, he still didn't know how to act. As the infatuated, obsessed man he was? As the rude jerk she'd want to keep her distance from? Or was there a happy, safe middle ground he hadn't found yet?

"Go to her." Andy gave Caleb's shoulder a gentle shove. "But maybe you shouldn't give Gizelle any more false hope. Leading her on when you have feelings for another woman is wrong."

Caleb's gaze shot back to Andy. "I made a decision, and I intend to ask Gizelle to be my girl. Love is a decision. Feelings... they aren't anything to base a relationship on. Lust fades." He cringed, hating that the word *lust* had slipped out, especially to Gizelle's father.

Andy raised his eyebrows. "Always best to be sure, ain't so?"

Before Caleb would muster a response, Gizelle came into the room and picked up the container of cookies. "Hallo, Caleb." She glanced over his shoulder. "Who's that in the buggy?"

"Hallo, Gizelle." Caleb swallowed. Hard. He couldn't look Andy in the eye. "That's Lydia Hershberger. She's Judith Zook's niece, in town to manage the gift shop while Judith and Mark are away on a mission trip."

And she had the power to turn him into a blathering idiot.

Best to be sure.

Andy's words trailed Caleb out to the buggy. Hovered in the air as he assisted Gizelle into the seat.

And then those words climbed up next to him.

~

"Hallo, welkum! I'm Gizelle Miller." The girl gave Lydia a friendly smile as she slid into the backseat.

Lydia grinned. "Lydia Hershberger." She realized too late that she should've moved back to allow Caleb to sit next to his girlfriend.

"How do you like Jamesport so far?" Gizelle asked.

Lydia twisted around and smiled at her. "Almost everyone I've met has been super kind, and my best friend, Abigail, lives here, so that's twice as nice. But I'm not staying here forever. Just until my aenti and onkel return."

And then, she would…what? Not go home. That much was certain.

She'd figure it out later.

"Have you met many people, then?"

"A few." Though she hadn't seen anyone she recognized from Abigail's wedding. Of course, that probably had to do with her living in town, a distance from the local Amish community.

Caleb pulled on the reins and turned down another dirt road, then made a third turn that curved around in the shape of a horseshoe. He pulled into a field and parked in a long row of other buggies.

Lydia waited until Caleb had helped Gizelle out of the buggy before she slid across the seat to get down. Caleb's milk-chocolate eyes rested on her, and he extended his hand with obvious hesitation. She ignored the silent offer of help and hopped out on her own.

As Caleb moved to the front to release the horse, Lydia eyed the tin of cookies in Gizelle's hands. "What kind of a frolic is this?" She should've asked before agreeing to attend. It would be awkward attending the birthday frolic of a complete stranger.

Gizelle shrugged her shoulders. "A regular frolic. Nein special occasion. We'll play volleyball, and maybe some other games." She lowered her voice to add, "Board games, if the chaperones are watchful. And if they aren't, then possibly some kissing games, like spin the bottle. Truth or dare."

Hopefully, the chaperones would be vigilant. Spin the bottle was not a game Lydia wanted to play.

"Those are my favorite games," Gizelle admitted with a giggle. "I can tell you who all the gut kissers are—and who you should avoid." She leaned closer as Caleb led his horse toward the pasture. "Caleb is a very gut kisser," she whispered.

Lydia didn't want to know.

"Kum on. I'll introduce you to everyone." Gizelle grabbed Lydia by the elbow and tugged her around the barn. The sounds of laughter and lively conversation grew louder. "We can probably rotate into the volleyball game right away." She stopped as they neared the others and pointed to each person in turn. "Seth, Nathan, Micah, Susan, Linda, Emma, Suzy, Dory, James, John, Martha. On the other side of the net, there's Menno…."

Lydia smiled and nodded, not that any of the pointing or recited names meant anything to her. She was just as lost and confused as she'd started out when Gizelle finally stopped talking.

"And now you know everyone. Do you want to be on Seth's team or Menno's?"

Which team was stronger? Lydia watched the game for a few seconds.

She must've hesitated too long, because Gizelle shook her head and said, "I'll join Seth's." And she jumped into the game.

At least Lydia's decision had been made for her. But before she could take her place, Caleb joined the game on the other side of the net, making the teams even.

"Hallo, Lydia." A girl who looked vaguely familiar approached her. "I remember you from Abigail's wedding. I'm Susanna Troyer. If you'd like to join me, I was going to get a glass of lemonade. I'm not overly fond of volleyball. Something about the ball flying straight at my face…it's scary. Nobody ever wants me on their team. I'm a definite weak link."

Lydia grinned at her. "Lemonade sounds gut."

The girls headed for the beverage tables. "I heard you're here to manage Judith's Gift Shop," Susanna said. "I wish I could get a job like that, but there's too much work to be done at home."

Lydia could understand. She and her three sisters kept plenty busy on the farm. It was a wonder Mamm and Daed had permitted her to kum here to help Aenti Judith. But they probably knew she needed to get away from the memories of Peter. From the well-meaning yet hurtful advice. From the unwanted attention of…*him*.

Before coming to Missouri, Lydia had asked Aenti Judith and Onkel Mark to make it plain she wasn't interested in a relationship. It seemed doubtful they had honored her wishes, however, since Caleb's mamm hadn't bothered trying to conceal her matchmaking designs. *Maybe he'll stop by a sparking place first.*

A flutter worked through Lydia.

She glanced over her shoulder at Caleb.

His gaze held hers for a second, and his eyes flared with an emotion she couldn't identify. Something dark, dangerous, exciting, promising.

She shivered.

He looked away.

⤳

Caleb slammed the ball over the net, glad that Lydia hadn't stuck around the volleyball court with him and Gizelle but had instead headed toward the haus with Susanna, talking. She would probably get roped into joining one of the quieter activities there, maybe with the special teens. They were desperate to have fun, too, and not so gut at volleyball. But some of them were really skilled at checkers. Of course, the nonathletic and shyer members of the youngies enjoyed board games, too.

"Who's the girl?" Menno asked Caleb as the players rotated positions.

"What girl?" Caleb made a show of looking around, even though he knew, beyond a shadow of a doubt, the identity of the person to whom his friend referred. It was the girl about whom he himself had asked the same question when he first saw her, at Sam Miller's wedding. The same girl he'd hung around at the singing that first evening, as close to her as he could get, in spite of the fact that she never seemed to notice him. The same girl he'd given a second, third, and fourth glimpse, even as he approached Gizelle and asked her if she needed a ride home.

"The one who came with Gizelle. Is she one of her cousins?"

"Her? Nein. She's from Ohio, here to manage Judith's Gift Shop while the Zooks are away."

"I remember now." Menno nodded. "Maybe I'll see if she needs a ride home afterward." He grinned. "I'm going to the haus for a drink. Be right back."

As Caleb watched him retreat, a part of his heart collapsed into a hard lump in his stomach. He didn't know whether to hope Lydia would give Menno a resounding "Danki, but nein" or to hope she accepted his invitation.

The better scenario would be the latter, of course. Then Caleb could tell Mamm that Lydia was seeing someone else already, and that there wasn't a whole lot he could do about it—even though Mamm was likely to scold him for missing his chance.

On the other hand, if Lydia turned Menno down, she would be riding with Caleb. And he'd be obligated to see her to her door. And maybe she would invite him in, and….

Ugh, he had it bad.

She would accept Menno's offer. Nobody ever said "nein" to him. He'd dated more than half the girls there to-nacht. "Serial dating," Daed called it—with a scowl—before he'd launched into a lecture about how courting was preferable to dating, and how you wouldn't find a gut frau if you went from girl to girl as if the female species were so many disposable paper plates. When a dating relationship had brought some terrible things upon Caleb's cousin Bethany last year, the preachers, and all the parents, had really cracked down on the practice and worked to establish what constituted acceptable and unacceptable behavior between the unmarrieds. "Courtship," "respect," and "waiting until after the marriage ceremony" seemed to be the key terms and phrases.

Not that Caleb took issue with these things. Instead, he always sat and listened attentively, soaking up wisdom, as Daed talked to him and his siblings about finding a frau who would be a diligent worker. Who would raise his kinner well, and who would possess a whole host of other admirable qualities. About not judging by looks, because beauty fades. Desire dies. Feelings go away.

Lydia Hershberger, in all her sparkly, glittery beauty, would become nothing more than burnt-out fairy dust. And where would that leave the poor sap who married her? Did she even know how to garden? Cook? Sew? Would she be a gut mamm? A loving, respectful, submissive frau?

Judging by her declaration that she could give as good as she got, probably not.

Daed would be proud of Caleb. Gizelle would be the better choice. She knew how to cook, bake, can produce, and clean. She worked hard, both at home and for a salary, part-time, at the Amish Market.

"Break time!" someone called out.

Caleb ducked under the volleyball net to get to Gizelle. "Walk with me?"

"Let's have a drink first." Gizelle fell into step beside him. "Do you think Menno will ask Lydia out?"

"I know so. He said as much." It actually grated Caleb to admit that.

Gizelle sighed, a little more heavily than normal.

Caleb glanced at her. "You all right?"

"I will be, jah. It's Gott's will, ain't so?"

Caleb nodded, pretending he knew what she was talking about.

But he hadn't one clue.

5

*L*ydia sat beside Susanna, swaying gently back and forth on the pink-and-white-cushioned swing suspended from the ceiling of the Kings' spacious front porch. Soon a shadow fell across the floor in front of them, morphing into a lanky man who dropped down between them with enough force to cause the swing to lurch, and the lemonade in the girls' cups to make a jump for freedom. The man's left arm landed heavily on Lydia's shoulder as the cold, sticky liquid saturated her dress, leaving dark splotches in the purple fabric.

"Seriously, Menno?" Susanna grumbled, jumping up and holding out her dripping glass.

"You give towels with your showers?" Lydia tried to keep her reply lighthearted, rather than show the irritation caused by his proximity and by her sticky, wet dress.

He laughed.

Susanna disappeared into the haus, muttering something about a towel.

"Need a ride home to-nacht?" Menno's arm tightened around Lydia's shoulders, his hand dangling dangerously close to her chest. "I could take you to see a few of the scenic places."

"Danki, but Caleb already promised to take me home." Lydia smiled to soften the blow.

"That Caleb?" Menno pointed in the direction of the refreshment table. "The one with Gizelle? He'd be happy to have his girl to himself. Without a chaperone."

Lydia winced. She wished she could slide farther away from Menno, to get him out of her personal space and dislodge his arm from her shoulders, but she was already pressed against the armrest of the swing. While the forced physical contact was uncomfortable, being an unwanted chaperone on a date would be even more so. Especially if the couple shared meaningful glances with each other and whispered in each other's ears. And especially if the man was Caleb.

"I'm not interested in a relationship. With anybody." She would make her position clear. If her aenti and onkel had done as she'd asked them to, she wouldn't have to explain this to everyone individually.

Menno shrugged.

"Plus, I'm still grieving...." Not entirely true. It had been almost five months since Peter's death, and the initial grief she'd experienced had since settled into a very dull ache. If that. Maybe only a faint shadow across her heart. She still didn't want to be forced into a relationship, even though everyone urged her not to let any more time pass. *You can't afford to wait too long,* the well-meaning older women in the community told her. *Nobody will want you. All the buwe will think you're picky. Besides, you'll lose your looks after twenty-three.*

The words stung, even though she doubted their validity.

"Friends, maybe? One can't have too many friends." She glanced at him.

"We could be friends." Menno scooted away, freeing her from his embrace, and stood. "I could still take you home."

Lydia's smile was real this time. "That would be nice."

"I'll find you afterward. I'm going to get myself some lemonade. Want a refill?" He took her glass and walked away without waiting for an answer.

On his way to the beverage table, Menno high-fived Caleb and added a fist bump.

Apparently, Menno still considered their ride a date, in spite of what she'd said about being friends only.

And Caleb was undoubtedly glad to lose his tagalong.

Would she have to fight off Menno's spaghetti arms the whole way home?

⁓

A heavy weight settled in Caleb's stomach. He'd known Lydia wouldn't be immune to Menno's charms. He glanced at Gizelle. At least she had a level head on her shoulders and wasn't easily swayed by the other man.

Gizelle's smile faded into a slight frown, and she studied the ground as they walked toward the tables spread with trays of finger food and three beverage jugs. Maybe she was disappointed by Lydia's decision, too. Or perhaps she wasn't feeling well.

Caleb inched a little closer to her. "Are you okay?"

She shrugged but didn't look up.

"Do you have a headache?"

She shook her head. "Lyd...." Her voice broke. "It's not important."

Caleb frowned. "You wanted her to ride home with us?"

"Jah," she whispered. She looked up at him, a slight sheen of moisture glistening in her eyes. Then she blinked, and the tears disappeared. The smile that appeared then was too bright. "I was looking forward to getting to know her better."

"You'll have plenty of opportunity for that," Caleb assured her. "Maybe you could invite her to your haus for a meal sometime. Mamm is hosting her tomorrow evening." He wouldn't mention the scheme Mamm and Judith had apparently con-cocted, determining to take matters into their own hands in order to see him married off.

Caleb stopped at the first food table and piled his plate with sandwich quarters, carrot and celery sticks, cookies, and other goodies.

Gizelle filled two glasses with tea. "I've got your drink. What did you want to talk about?"

He looked around, then motioned toward a line of trees, where they'd have some privacy while still being in plain sight. "How about over there?"

She glanced that way. "Sure. I'll carry your drink for you."

"And I'll share the food on my plate." He winked.

Gizelle shook her head. "Not hungry, but danki, anyway."

Funny, he wasn't hungry, either. Probably due to the ball of disappointment that had settled in his stomach. Or maybe a sense of dread over what he was about to do.

Best to be sure.... Andy Miller's comment resurfaced in Caleb's mind. But he didn't know how he could be sure.

Maybe today wasn't a gut time to ask her to be his girl. Then again, would it ever be a gut time, when he wasn't in love with Gizelle, even though he'd made up his mind he would be?

Or maybe that took time, too. Maybe if he reminded himself of the idea often enough, it would become true. Surely, the unset-tled tangle in his stomach would go away as soon as he could check off the imaginary box that put Gizelle in the "my girl" column.

He pulled in a deep breath as they entered the grove of trees, then released it with a hiss as he turned to face Gizelle. "Want to go steady?"

⌒

It seemed as if hours had passed by the time Menno finally drove the buggy into the parking lot behind Judith's shop. At least he hadn't tried any funny business during the ride to Jamesport. Other than making a suggestion to stop and stargaze—which she'd turned down—he'd driven her straight home.

"Danki for the ride." Lydia climbed out of the buggy. "You don't need to see me upstairs."

"You sure?"

"Jah. Danki, again." Lydia waved to Menno as he backed the buggy out of the parking spot.

Before leaving the lot, he paused and leaned out. "Want to go out for ice cream sometime? We could walk to the shop from here."

"Ice cream sounds gut. Jah."

He nodded, waved, and turned onto the road.

Home, sweet home. Lydia reached for the doorknob. Twisted. Locked.

Lydia froze. Had she taken a purse with the key, and left both at the Kings'?

Nein. She had been rushed out the door by Caleb's mamm, and she'd neglected to take a key.

Lydia peered around at the dark, abandoned streets. Her eyes burned with tears, but she shook her head hard. *Nein.* This would work out. A police officer would kum by, eventually. If not, then someone else who would surely agree to call for help. There had to be a locksmith in town.

What would Aenti Judith and Onkel Mark have to say about her lack of responsibility?

She looked up at the star-studded heavens. *Gott, I'm locked out. I really don't want to spend all night curled up on the back step. Could You please send someone to help me?* She rechecked her pockets to make sure she didn't have a key, then picked up each of the flowerpots along the side of the building. Felt along the top of the doorframe and around the exterior light fixture.

Nothing.

She sank down on the back step. Camping wasn't something she'd ever really enjoyed. Musty tents, smoky campfires, loud insects. But right now, any of those things seemed preferable to being out here alone, without as much as a cricket for company.

Unable to endure her pinching shoes any longer, she reached down to untie them, then loosened the strings.

Somewhere nearby, a cricket chirped.

Lydia almost laughed. *Danki, Gott, for some company.*

Another cricket answered the first.

And then, in the distance—the clip-clop of a horse's hooves.

Please, Gott, let the driver kum this way. Let him be willing to go to the police station and find someone to help me. Please, Lord.

At the sight of the buggy, Lydia shot to her feet and dashed toward the vehicle, flagging the driver down. "Help! I need—" She tripped on her shoelaces and fell to her knees as the buggy pulled into the parking lot.

The dark form of a man clambered out of the vehicle and approached her.

"I need you to please go for help." She struggled to stand.

The man reached down with his arm. Lydia wrapped her fingers around his hand, and he pulled her up as if she weighed nothing more than a basket of laundry. Her nerve endings went haywire. She pulled away, wobbling.

His hand settled on her elbow to steady her. "Do you need to go to the doctor?"

Caleb.

"Nein, I—"

"Were you robbed?"

"I'm locked out."

Silence, for one beat. Two.

Then he chuckled. "Right. Of course, you are. That's why I came. I remembered you hadn't brought your purse or anything.

You just put your shoes on and left. I wasn't sure if you had the key on you, and I figured it wouldn't hurt to stop and check."

He released her, reached inside his pocket, and pulled out a key ring. "I'll let you in. Can you walk?"

Her knees burned, but they supported her. "Jah."

"Gut." He unlocked the door and pushed it open, triggering the automatic lights in the storeroom and over the staircase to the apartment. He glanced up the steps. "I'll need to unlock that door, too, huh?" He sifted through the keys and separated a different one. "Lead the way, Princess."

Lydia blinked. "Pauper, you mean."

His lips parted as his gaze roved over her face, but he shut his mouth without comment. Then he turned around and locked the outside door.

Lydia grabbed the railing and used it to support herself as she climbed. Her knees hurt with every step, but at least they were moving. Working.

Caleb followed her up, then leaned around her at the top, and unlocked the apartment door. "There you go, my lady."

"My hero." She grinned at him. "Want to kum in for koffee before you head back? It's the least I can do to thank you for rescuing me."

Caleb hesitated a moment. Then slowly nodded. "Jah." His voice shook. "Koffee sounds gut. Since I'm your hero, and all."

"You are! I'm not sure I could have survived out there with nobody but crickets for company all nacht. I almost prayed for a thief to kum along and break in for me."

He chuckled again. "And you got me, instead." He shut the apartment door. Locked it. Then turned to face her.

"You're much safer than a robber."

Something in his smile made her legs turn to Jell-O.

Suddenly, she wasn't so sure about the truthfulness of her words.

6

Caleb followed Lydia into the tiny, U-shaped kitchenette. Definitely too small for his family. He tried to picture his mamm and sisters working in it, and almost laughed. How did Judith fix meals for herself and Mark in such a small area?

It might be the perfect size for a newlywed couple, though. If he was married, and this was his home, he could imagine coming into the kitchen, pulling Lydia into his arms....

He leaned against the counter and shut his eyes. Best to stop that train of thought right there. He ought to daydream that way about Gizelle, instead.

Or maybe not. They weren't married. Yet.

Caleb opened his eyes and watched as Lydia filled a glass koffee carafe with water from the faucet. She then dumped the water into the basin of a black koffeemaker, inserted a paper filter, and filled it with ground beans. "Aenti Judith taught me how to use this thing. So convenient. I'm going to have trouble returning to the old way when I go home. I'm already so spoiled, I feel like the princess you called me earlier." She pushed a button, and the machine beeped. "It's brewing." Lydia opened a cabinet and reached for a mug. "I should've told you, all they have is decaffeinated. I still need to stop at the store and buy some of the real stuff."

"Decaf is fine." The headiness of having been alone with Lydia, and reliving every word she spoke, every move she made, would be enough to keep him awake on the ride home. And beyond. The memories would probably consume his mind and energize his being for days to come.

He was pitiful. Pathetic, prey to a crush.

Why didn't he have more willpower? More control over his emotions? Why did his heart insist on loving Lydia, even though his brain recognized Gizelle as the better choice?

Love? When had he acknowledged that feeling?

As if he didn't know. As if he hadn't sat up and taken notice the moment he'd seen her at the wedding. As if his heart hadn't stated, loud and clear, "There she is. She's the one."

He'd been thinking of her, dreaming of her, for almost five months now. Had grilled Judith, Mark, and even Sam and Abigail for any little tidbit he might learn about her. Searched *The Budget* to see if she was listed. Eavesdropped as much as possible on the whispered conversations between Mamm and Judith about her. Had prayed, and planned his next step, his next move, if ever he was blessed enough to see her again.

Somehow, even knowing she was Judith's niece, even after he'd interrogated Judith, he'd failed to realize she would be managing the shop in Judith's absence. And then, she'd kum. He'd gotten another chance.

So he'd rebelled and asked Gizelle to be his girl. How stupid could he be? Courting Gizelle, looking toward marriage, when he loved Lydia.

"Gizelle said jah?" Lydia seemed to have read his mind. She didn't look at him, but a small smile played around her lips.

As if she thought his being another girl's beau was a gut thing.

Maybe it was, if it meant he and Lydia would be just friends. Never mind that his heart would insist on involvement. That it would end up broken when he made the wise, responsible choice.

He fought to bring his emotions under control. Once they were mastered, if only for the moment, he nodded. Even though

Lydia couldn't see him, since she'd turned away and now rummaged in a cookie jar.

He cleared his throat. "Jah, she said she'd be my girl." And he should be happy about it. Really, he was. Or would be, if he told himself enough times to feel happy. Instead of focusing on the fact that he might have made a terrible mistake and now needed to rectify the situation.

As if that were possible.

He couldn't exactly turn around and tell Gizelle he'd asked her as a sort of knee-jerk reaction, after being around the girl he wanted but couldn't have. A survival technique that had gone wrong.

"Gut." Lydia nodded. "I'm happy for you."

And she actually sounded that way. Cheerful. As if everything was right in her world.

"You're probably happier Mamm won't try to push us together anymore." He cringed. He shouldn't have said that. Shouldn't have—

Lydia turned to him, clutching a handful of cookies, and grinned. "I'm glad about it, for sure. I don't want a relationship—other than friendship—with any man here."

Disappointing. Because, jah, he still wanted her. He looked down at his ankles, and the purring kitten making a figure-eight around them.

At least the cat liked him. Even if he didn't like himself very much right now.

"Not even with Menno?" He didn't glance up at Lydia. Hated himself for opening up *that* can of worms.

She made some kind of noncommittal noise. A non-answer that translated into…what?

"Gizelle was disappointed you didn't ride home with us," he added, purposely omitting any mention of his own disappointment. "She's eager to get to know you."

"I'd like to get to know Gizelle, too." Her smile widened. "Here, take this plate to the living room, please. We'll sit in there." She handed him a small dessert plate on which she'd arranged five peanut butter cookies. "I'll bring the koffees. Do you take sugar? Cream?"

"Neither, danki." He shook his head.

"Then I'll doctor mine up here in the kitchen. I like a glug of flavored creamer…and a lot of ice cubes. I discovered flavored iced koffee on the trip here. I'm getting so spoiled, I tell you." She prepared her own koffee in a clear glass, then picked up his mug and carried both into the living room. She set the mug of steaming black koffee at one end of the small table in front of the couch, and then she settled onto the cushion at the other end. "Tell me about yourself."

Funny—even though he knew more about her now than he did ten minutes ago, he still wanted to say those same words to her.

And maybe he would. If Gizelle were around.

⌒

Lydia watched as Caleb sat down on the couch, one leg bent at the knee and propped across a cushion, his other foot on the floor, his body angled toward her. "Uh…there's not much to tell."

"Sure, there is. Judith tells me you're a clockmaker. That she sells your handiwork in the shop."

He nodded, avoiding her gaze.

"Those cuckoo clocks of yours that I sold today were so cute! And so intricate. How did you kum to develop that hobby?"

His cheeks reddened. "My daedi dabbled in the craft and taught it to me. My daed used to make clocks, too, but when he received the call as preacher, it became too much for him, between preaching and caring for his 'flock,' even though my brothers and I took on the bulk of the farm work. He said I could make clocks in my spare time—mostly at nacht or in the winter, when there isn't as much farm work to do. Daed still helps me when his schedule allows. And my mamm and sisters help paint them."

"That's so neat!" Lydia smiled. "We have to supplement our farming income, too. I help my daed tie the fishing flies we sell at our roadside stand. I used to run the stand, and I'll probably handle the job again when I return. In the meantime, my younger sisters are in charge."

"How long will that be? Mark and Judith are out of the country until…when? October?"

"Jah, just about."

"Tell me about your family." Caleb leaned toward her. "Do you miss them?"

"More than I thought I would. I have three younger sisters and three brothers—two older and one younger. My oldest brother, James, is married with a boppli on the way. They found out right before I came here. My other brother, Kenan, will probably marry this fall."

Just like Lydia was supposed to, until….

Nein. She wouldn't go there. Wouldn't think about it. About *him*.

"Something wrong?"

Of course, Caleb would notice. He studied her with narrowed eyes.

"Nein." A lie.

It seemed Caleb noticed that, too. His mouth opened, but Lydia rushed on before he could interject with some foolish comment about how a double negative equaled a positive, as Peter might have said. "It's just so gut to be here! I've looked forward to this since January, when Daed told me that Aenti Judith had asked if I would manage the shop while she and Onkel Mark were away. Of course, living near my best friend, Abigail, is a major plus."

"I remember you from her wedding," Caleb said.

Lydia glanced at him, searching her memory for an earlier impression of the handsome man. None. "I don't remember you, sorry. But all my memories from that time are rather fuzzy. I got some shocking news that day. My fiancé...he died. Struck by lightning."

Caleb nodded somberly, as if he'd known all along. He probably had. His mamm was Aenti Judith's best friend, after all. Lydia hated admitting to herself that she'd been the topic of whispered gossip around this community. Had Daed shared her horrible secret with Aenti Judith? And if he had, who else knew about it?

Caleb's mamm. *Judith told me everything.*

Caleb looked down at his lap, then quickly glanced back up at her. "We've talked about my clockmaking. What do you do?"

"Besides managing a gift shop for an aent I barely know?" Lydia shrugged. "I'm Amish. I do it all. Sewing, mending, gardening, canning, cooking, baking, cleaning, helping with the farm work...and other things, of course."

"Of course." His eyes twinkled with his smile. "I meant for fun."

"Fun, huh?" Lydia thought for a moment. Life itself was fun. At least, it was as long as she kept her focus on her blessings. Automatic koffeemakers. Electric heat. A change of scenery. She spread her arms open wide, startling the kitten, who gave her a disgruntled look before settling down again with a flick of her tail. If Lydia had been standing, she would have twirled around. She grinned at Caleb. "I live. Life is fun."

⌒

That was why he loved her. For the way she embraced life.

He studied her, aware that he was probably grinning like a fool. If only he could find her joy. Her apparent unquestioning acceptance of the will of der Herr. Her source of light. What made her seem so glittery?

But her outlook also provided ample proof of her ineligibility to be his frau. "Life is fun"? Since when? His sisters would disagree, at least when it came to gardening and sewing and other work. Farming certainly wasn't fun. It was backbreaking. And there were times when even clockmaking wasn't fun. Especially when Caleb had made a mistake that required a redo. If everything worked perfectly, then it was fun. And his mamm and sisters did enjoy decorating the clocks with their paintbrushes.

A buzzing sound came from Caleb's back pocket, where he felt the vibration of his cell phone. He cast an apologetic glance at Lydia and fished out the phone. A swipe of his thumb across the screen revealed the identity of the texter. *Gizelle.*

Probably a gut thing, because he needed a reminder about his girl right now. Sitting in the presence of the woman he imagined—wanted—to be "the one," and getting to know her in person, had made thoughts of Gizelle few and far between.

Did Gizelle find fun in gardening and sewing?

Guilt coursed through him. He read Gizelle's text message.

Menno asked her out for ice cream. Double date?

Jah, because he really wanted to court his girl while spending time with the "other woman" and Menno. His focus would be on the wrong female. And it would cause problems, with Gizelle and Menno alike.

He typed "Nein," then started to slide the phone back into his pocket.

The phone buzzed again.

Please?

He sighed. He didn't want to hurt Gizelle, and she had said she wanted to get to know Lydia. And Lydia had indicated she wasn't interested in any relationship beyond friendship while in Jamesport. That must mean she wasn't interested in Menno, despite his efforts…at least for the time being. Maybe Caleb should agree to double-date, if only to keep Menno from getting to close to Lydia.

He keyed his response: **I'll ask.**

Danki!

"Something wrong?" Lydia eyed his cell phone. Not as if it were an alien creature, because she had a cell phone, too—her aenti's, for business use—but with curiosity. Maybe a hint of alarm.

"Nothing's wrong. Gizelle wanted to know if you and Menno would like to join us for a double date. Maybe when you go for ice cream?"

Lydia blinked. "Wow. News travels fast in this town. He asked me out for ice cream when he dropped me off to-nacht."

Caleb frowned. Kum to think of it, that *was* quicker than usual. How had Gizelle found out about Menno's invitation, anyway? He shook his head. A puzzle for another day.

But if word had already gotten out about Menno and Lydia's plans, the gossipers would have a heyday with the news that Caleb had spent so much time alone with Lydia in her apartment at nacht. And if they knew of his lustful thoughts, he'd be tried, condemned, and forced to kneel for confession and repentance by Sunday.

Lydia grinned. "Going for ice cream will be more fun with you and Gizelle along. Less like a date and more like just a group of friends, ain't so? Tell Gizelle that sounds great."

"So, you and Menno aren't dating?" And there he went, broaching that subject again, even though he knew he needed to stop worrying about Lydia and Menno. He tucked his phone back inside his pocket without replying to Gizelle. She wouldn't expect an immediate answer. And if he gave her one, she might gather that he was in Lydia's presence.

Lydia shook her head. "Just friends. As I've said, I'm not looking for a relationship here."

"You did say that," Caleb acknowledged. "But the gossips— including my mamm—will have you engaged and married off before your aenti returns."

That was the unfortunate truth. He hated the idea of someone else having her, holding her, loving her. She may think she didn't want it, but she didn't stand a chance. Someone in this town would win the hand of the lovely Princess Lydia.

And it wouldn't be Caleb.

With his mood deflated, Caleb drained his koffee, then rose to his feet. "I need to go. I'll see you tomorrow."

Lydia arched her eyebrows in question.

"Dinner at our haus, remember?" He took three steps toward her, then forced himself to stop. He had nein need to approach her, just an overwhelming urge to pull her close and kiss her until she changed her mind about wanting to be in a relationship. Until she wanted him.

A bad idea all around.

"Dinner at your haus. Right. I forgot." She stood.

A citrusy fragrance drifted toward him. His gaze darted to her lips, then back up to her eyes. He trembled. Shoved his hands deep inside his pockets to keep himself from reaching for her.

"I'll see you out." She moved around him and headed for the door.

He followed her, trying not to look at her skirts as they swayed.

Lydia stepped to the side as she opened the door.

"See you later, Princess." He tried to smile, though the expression probably looked more like a grimace.

She stopped him with a hand on his arm, then stood on tiptoe and planted a quick kiss on his jaw. "Danki, again. My hero."

His heart thudded hard enough to play in an Englisch marching band.

And as the door shut behind him, he raised his hand to touch the place where she'd kissed him. Felt the prickles of his whiskers.

Tomorrow, he would shave before dinner, just in case she decided to do it again.

7

*T*he next morgen, Lydia followed Rosie downstairs to the store. The kitten hopped, skipped, and jumped all the way, as if anxious to resume exploring. If only Lydia had the same energy. Her sleep had been restless, fraught by dreams of Caleb, both with and without fangs. Of the kiss she'd planted on his stubbly jaw. Of all the long-dormant feelings he'd awakened within her.

She would rather have left Rosie upstairs in the apartment, especially after yesterday's jarred-candle fiasco. But Aenti Judith had left a note indicating the locals liked to see Rosie snoozing on the windowsill or trying to catch the sunbeams on the floor.

"You have to behave," Lydia warned the kitten.

With a dismissive flick of her tail, Rosie disappeared around the corner of the sales counter.

Lydia flipped the lights on, then reached inside her pocket and pulled out the paper where her aent had written down the combination to the safe. It took three attempts for her to open it. She smiled at her success as she refilled the register drawer with the cash Caleb had put away for her last nacht. Then she unlocked the front door and switched the sign from "Closed" to "Open."

As she turned away from the door, the wall of cuckoo clocks caught her attention. She approached the display and surveyed the variety of intricate designs. One clock featured a carving of leaves all around the outer casing. Several clocks were painted in a rainbow of colors. Some of them used Roman numerals, while others featured Arabic numbers. Caleb had also made some standard clocks from weathered wood, probably recycled from dilapidated buildings, even old barns. These timepieces had a simple battery-operated clock mechanism on the back, and the fronts featured a hand-painted pastoral scene of a barn surrounded by purple morning glories in full bloom.

Just then, the door of each cuckoo clock swung open, revealing a cute little bird that chirped eight cuckoos in succession.

Eight o'clock. Technically, she'd opened a few minutes early.

A purring Rosie wound her way around Lydia's ankles. Lydia picked her up. "Day two. What do you think it has in store?" She laughed at her own pun, then mentally answered her question. Hopefully, a fun, happy Caleb, like the one she'd hung out with last nacht. The one who'd kum riding to her rescue and called her "Princess." The one who made her laugh. Made her body kum alive with awareness…and left her lips tingling after her impulsive gut-nacht kiss.

Lydia shook her head. She shouldn't be looking forward to seeing him. Shouldn't be dreaming of him. He belonged to another woman.

Besides, Lydia didn't want a new relationship.

The bell above the door tinkled, sending Rosie springing from her arms just before a horde of Englisch tourists stampeded inside.

⌒

"What do you mean, Menno took her home?" Mamm worked the broom harder than necessary. "Why didn't you take her home? I told her you would. Nein wonder you aren't married. You let all the gut girls slip through your fingers." Mamm aimed the broom at Caleb's feet, as if she intended to sweep him outside with the dust.

"I'll get married. Someday." He sidestepped the broom. "Maybe even this fall."

Mamm frowned. "Well, it won't be to Lydia, because you let Menno take her home." Still sweeping furiously, she listed off the names of the local unmarried women, then dismissed them all with her next breath.

"I asked Gizelle Miller to be my girl." Maybe now Mamm would stop choking him under a cloud of dust.

"Gizelle? Your girl?" Mamm huffed. "What's the matter with you?"

"What? You'd rather I jump straight to the proposal?" Nein wonder courtship was often kept secret, even from one's parents. He should've kept his mouth shut instead of letting Mamm wheedle the information out of him.

Mamm shook her head in a show of dismay. "Why Gizelle Miller? Never would've put the two of you together. You know, once a girl flutters her eyelashes at you, that's all she is. Fluttering lashes. You need a woman with substance. A woman who—"

"Mamm." He backed out of the broom's path yet again. "Please. Daed preached from Proverbs thirty-one not too long ago. I was listening closely, and Gizelle is all those things. She's organized, she works hard, and she's someone I can rely on."

"Mmph." Mamm followed up that odd noise with another huff. "And what's wrong with Lydia?"

Nothing. Everything. Caleb raised his hands in surrender. "She just got here two days ago. You expect me to start courting someone I just met?" Ach, how he wanted to.

"Menno doesn't seem to have a problem with that," Mamm pointed out.

"I don't know anything about her."

"Phooey. I saw you follow her around like a besotted pup at the wedding in December. I've heard your carefully veiled questions about her. You can't fool me." The broom got dangerously close to his stockinged feet again.

Besotted pup? Caleb moved to the door and stepped into his boots. "I'll go see what needs to be done in the barn before I go get Lydia for supper."

"And Gizelle. You pick up your phone—the one you think I know nothing about—and ask her to dinner." Mamm gave him *that* look. "And we'll just see how they compare."

Caleb rolled his eyes. "Should I invite Menno, too?"

Mamm planted her fists on her hips and glared at him. "Why would you do a fool thing like that? We don't want Lydia being swayed by his considerable charms."

Had Menno turned Mamm's head, too? Caleb frowned. He could never measure up. Guess that was another gut reason to stick with Gizelle. She was too sensible to fall for Menno Schwartz, unlike 95 percent of the women in their community.

Caleb snorted with indignation as he headed out to the barn. *Invite Gizelle to dinner, indeed.* When he was still lusting after Lydia? He didn't want his future bride worrying about whether he would remain faithful after marriage. He would keep his promises; he just had to get this—*her*—out of his system first, so he could settle down.

And being around Lydia would achieve that, surely. She must be just as human as everyone else. She wasn't really a sparkly princess spreading glitter and fairy dust everywhere she went. Eventually, his heart would realize that, and would turn firmly, solidly, to Gizelle.

He hated that he couldn't get his emotions into a neat, clean, orderly line, instead of wanting a girl based on secondhand knowledge, curve appeal, and bright, shimmery, sunshiny spunk. How was that for an adjective overload? Or were those words adverbs? He'd always been much better at math than language arts. Math made sense. Followed rules and patterns.

And that brought him back to his original problem.

Him and Gizelle. That made sense. He grabbed a shovel and started mucking a stall.

Him and Lydia? Nein sense, but it was all he wanted.

Maybe it was a gut thing Mamm had told him to invite Gizelle. Her presence during the meal would keep his attention somewhat off Lydia. And perhaps he'd fall in love with Gizelle that much faster. He pulled his cell phone out of his pocket and texted her.

Kum for dinner? I'll pick you up at 5.

When five minutes passed with nein response, he sent another message: **Where are you?**

Ten minutes later, a reply finally came. **Sorry, can't make it to-nacht. Plans with friends.**

And that left him right where he'd started. Him and Lydia. With a growl of frustration, he slid the phone into his pocket.

"Sohn?"

He whirled around. Daed stood beside the wheelbarrow, looking at him. Staring, to put it more accurately, as if Caleb had grown a set of horns. Or as if he had those plastic fangs in his mouth again. But he knew those were safe where he'd stowed them on his bedside table. At least, they had been there when he'd gotten up that morgen. After all, he had plans for them, based on Lydia's reaction to them yesterday.

"Is there a problem?" Daed pushed the wheelbarrow off to the side, then came toward Caleb.

Caleb shrugged. There were several problems, actually.

"So, were you growling at the shovel? Or the manure?" A hint of a smile teased Daed's lips.

Caleb sighed. "There's a girl."

Daed nodded. "There's always a girl. Your mamm said you made a decision."

"Jah. The right choice. The smart, sensible, wise one. But…I don't love her. And there's this other girl…." It felt gut to unburden his heart to Daed. He would help Caleb sort it all out and would act as his ally in keeping mamm's matchmaking efforts in line.

An expression Caleb couldn't decipher crossed Daed's face. Then Daed raised one eyebrow. "Go on."

"She's everything I want." Caleb looked away. "And everything I can't have. She's trouble with a capital T."

Daed issued a worried frown. "What do you mean? She got you into trouble?"

"Nein. She's beautiful. I'm…I don't know. Suffering from the lust of the eyes, I guess." Would Daed expect him to confess before the church?

"Ah." Daed stroked his beard. "Sounds as if you aren't as sure in your decision as you should be."

And that was his dilemma, exactly. Caleb waited for the sage advice Daed would surely dispense. He was a preacher, after all. He must have some wise fix-it tip that Caleb could use.

Daed smiled. Patted Caleb on the shoulder. "You need to be very sure."

"That's what Andy Miller told me. But how does that translate, mathematically?"

"Mathematically?" Daed's smile changed into a smirk. And then he walked off.

What kind of an answer was that?

⌒

Lydia peeked out the front door and looked one way, then the other, before returning inside and fastening the lock. Fifteen minutes past closing time. Fifteen minutes she'd spent pacing the floor between the register and the front door. Peering down the empty sidewalks and deserted road. Where was Caleb? Had he changed his mind about agreeing to manage the books for Aenti Judith? Maybe Lydia would get the elderly, gray-haired male accountant she'd imagined, after all. The one with a pencil behind his ear. A drab suit and an ugly tie. He'd be a lot easier on her nerves and emotions, for sure.

Or did this mean she'd have to tally the ledgers and prepare the deposit by herself? A wave of panic washed over her, and her temples throbbed with the beginnings of a tension headache. *Nein, Lord. Please let Caleb kum.*

Nothing. Nobody.

Another five minutes of pacing.

But he was supposed to kum, ain't so? If not to do the accounting, then at least to pick her up. She'd been invited to his haus for dinner to-nacht. Or maybe she'd misunderstood his mamm.

With a flick of her wrist, she turned from the door and surveyed the empty store. Well, empty except for her and Rosie, wherever that kitten was hiding. It wasn't as if the feline would be much help counting money, figuring out ledgers, and filling out those confusing vendor forms.

A click sounded in the back room, followed by a low murmur. Lydia hurried in that direction and found Caleb standing there, cuddling Rosie. He looked up with a grin, and her heart thudded into overdrive.

She resisted the urge to rush forward, fling herself into his arms, and burst into tears. That would have been entirely overdramatic. Instead, she stumbled to a stop and pressed her fingers to her mouth. "You came!"

That reaction was overkill, too. It wasn't as if he'd saved her from freezing to death on the back steps, as he had last nacht. Instead, he'd saved her from a math-induced migraine.

"Did you think I wouldn't kum?" A brow hitched. "I told you I would. And that I'd take you to my haus for dinner." He sighed. "Sorry I'm a little late. Lost track of time while I was mucking stalls in the barn. I, uh, asked Gizelle if she wanted to join us for dinner, too. Mamm's suggestion. But she's busy with friends."

"I'm sorry to hear that." But Lydia felt only relief, not regret. She didn't know why. She didn't want a relationship—not with Caleb, not with anyone. Yet, somehow, knowing he was involved with someone else cut her deep.

8

I'll get started on the books right away." Caleb bent down to set the kitten on the floor, then stood up straight again but wasn't sure what to do with his hands. Not when he wanted to reach out, pull the unsuspecting girl into his arms, and—

Nein. He shook his head.

"What?" Lydia studied him quizzically.

"Nothing."

"Okay." She shrugged. "I've already gotten the store put back in order, so I'm going to run upstairs and refill Rosie's water bowl and food dish. And put on a fresh outfit."

She brushed at the bust of her dress, as if to rid it of a piece of lint, but he didn't dare let his gaze stray from her face. He'd looked downward more than enough. Hopefully, she hadn't noticed.

As she passed him on her way to the stairs, he got a whiff of her scent, fresh and citrusy and delicious. It brought to mind ice-cold, sugary lemonade. Or lemon meringue pie.

"Um."

She stopped. Turned around and looked at him.

He fiddled with his hands again. "I…um…forgot what I was going to say." Then he pivoted on his heel and strode into the main part of the shop, his legs, arms, and hands all shaking. Heat crawled up his neck.

Don't look at a woman with lust in your heart. Preacher David had preached on that biblical mandate last church Sunday. He'd quoted a Scripture, too, but Caleb couldn't remember the reference. Caleb hadn't taken notes. Because, last church Sunday, the topic wasn't applicable to him. Now, it was. Maybe. He didn't know if lust adequately described the attitude with which he looked at Lydia. Felt about her. But love...who would believe that? He didn't even believe it and he was the one who made it his business to learn everything he could about her over the past five months.

"Ach!" Now he remembered what he'd wanted to say. He yelled over his shoulder, "I'll be late again tomorrow. But don't worry, I *will* kum. I can let myself in."

Deliberately late, so he wouldn't have to endure the torture of being around Lydia. So he wouldn't make a fool of himself, not knowing how to act, forgetting what he was going to say. And Gott help him if he gave into his impulses, pulled her close, and kissed her senseless.

Or kissed her until *he* was senseless. That shouldn't take long. Especially considering how quickly his senses left him when she came around.

A shiver worked up his spine, and his belly clenched.

He settled on the stool behind the cash register and made short work of counting the money before he filled out the deposit ticket. He'd take care of the deposit in the morgen. Then he went through the credit-card receipts and started filling out the ledger by seller.

"I'm ready when you are."

He jumped at the sound of the voice from behind him. A squiggly line now ran across the page.

He didn't look up from the ledger. "Okay. Give me a moment."

The only reason he needed one was to collect himself before facing her again. Before riding beside her in the buggy for forty-five minutes. Before sitting across from her at the dinner table, trying not to watch her eat. Before taking her to see the clock shop, and demonstrating the basics of clockmaking.

Well, that last part was optional. If she wanted to see it.

She didn't answer again, but he was achingly aware of her presence lurking somewhere behind him. The lemon scent lingered, tempting him. He might need more than a moment to regroup.

He finished up as quickly as he could. Hopefully, he had gotten everything right. He would go back and check the calculations sometime when he wasn't so distracted.

Maybe it would help if he took the books home with him to work on. And he would. But not to-nacht.

He stashed the ledger in the safe, set the deposit bag on top of it, and topped the stack with the money for the cash register for tomorrow's business. Closed the safe, stood, and turned around. "Ready."

Except that he was alone.

"Lydia?"

Nein answer.

Had he imagined her presence?

Must've.

He checked that the front door was locked, then turned off the lights before climbing the back stairs to the apartment. He knocked on the door. Two seconds later, the door opened, and Lydia emerged, having changed into a coral dress. She held up a pink heart-shaped keychain with her first name printed across it in white script. "Gut thing I remembered these. I don't want to get locked out again."

"I would've stayed to make sure you got inside," Caleb said. "You're robbing me of my chance to be your hero."

Her smile widened. "You'll always be my hero."

If only.

❦

"I'll take the keys along, anyway." Lydia slid the set into her pocket and descended the stairs ahead of Caleb. "I need to work on being responsible. Daed is always telling me, 'People are too willing to take care of you, and you're too willing to let them.'"

"That's because you're a sparkly princess, and everyone knows it."

At least Caleb was kind enough to omit the word "pampered." Lydia shook her head. "I'm not a princess. And I'm not spoiled. Really. One of my reasons for coming here to help Aenti Judith was to prove that I'm capable of taking care of myself. On my own terms, not ones that are forced on me."

He blinked and then frowned, as if struggling to make sense of her comment. Finally, he shook his head as he held out his hand. "I don't understand."

"Never mind." She was just venting—something she shouldn't do, especially to a stranger.

Except Caleb was ceasing to be a stranger.

She accepted his hand and climbed into the buggy. As she spread the faded lavender blanket over her lap, she glanced over at him.

He sat next to her, quietly watching. Waiting.

She frowned at him. "'Sparkly'? Really?"

He blinked. Then nodded. "Jah. As if you comb glitter through your hair." He reached out, his hand grazing her neck, and fingered a few short strands that escaped from her kapp.

She shivered as unfamiliar sensations cascaded over her. Through her.

"I know you don't, but it seems to float around you. The sunshine, it follows you."

Her cheeks burned. "You're too sweet." Why did her voice have to quiver like that?

His brows furrowed, and his face turned an intriguing shade of pink, as he abruptly withdrew his hand. "Sorry. I shouldn't have touched you like that."

"I don't mind," she whispered, but then she straightened her posture and shifted away from him. "Gizelle might."

Caleb pressed his lips together in a flat line. He gathered the reins, made a clicking noise with his tongue, and backed the buggy away from the hitching post. A minute later, they were on the road, heading away from town.

After a few moments, he shook his head quickly, then smiled at her. "So, twenty questions. Favorite food?"

She blinked. "Pizza, of course. I love what my friends called 'garbage pizza.' I'm not sure why. It's loaded with different kinds of meat, cheese, vegetables...."

"Supreme. That's my favorite, too. Favorite dessert?"

"Cheesecake. Plain, with blueberries or cherries on top."

He smiled. "I haven't met too many desserts I don't like. Favorite color?"

Lydia hesitated. "Maybe pink...or purple. Or turquoise. Or maybe yellow."

He glanced at her. "I figured yellow. Like the sunshine." He pulled back on the reins and turned off the main road.

"I do love jonquils and daffodils. They're my two favorite flowers."

"I like blue, I think. Like the sky. And your eyes," Caleb added quietly. "My favorite flowers are the little violets that grow wild in our yard. I think Mamm's are dandelions. Those are the only ones she displays indoors."

Lydia laughed. "My mamm used to keep dandelions on our kitchen table. She always made such a fuss when my siblings and I would kum inside bearing handfuls of them. As if they were expensive bouquets from an Englisch florist."

"Exactly." Caleb pulled closer to the side of the road so a car could pass them.

Lydia leaned forward for a better view of a group of Amish teens standing on the banks of a pond in someone's field. The buwe skipped stones across the water, likely encouraged by the girls—one of whom looked familiar.

"Isn't that Gizelle?" Lydia pointed at the strawberry blonde whose hair was loose, reaching almost all the way down her back. "There, in the light green dress? And that looks like Menno next to her."

Caleb glanced briefly in their direction, then quickly shook his head. "Nah. That couldn't be Gizelle. She's too sensible."

Lydia frowned. "Sensible?" She looked back at the girl. Had to be Gizelle. And that was definitely Menno. Nein doubt.

"She's a gut Amish girl. Pays close attention to the Ordnung. She wouldn't be hanging out with a group of youngies with her hair down."

"She is?" Lydia swiveled in her seat and surveyed the group again. "She wouldn't?"

Caleb grunted.

Lydia shrugged. He knew Gizelle better than she did. But a gut Amish girl wouldn't be whispering about who the gut kissers were, would she? Speaking of which…. "Do you like to play spin the bottle?"

"What?" He whipped his head to the side and faced her, wide-eyed. "Nein. I haven't played any kissing games in years. The next time I kiss a girl, it'll be because I mean it." His Adam's apple bobbed, and he looked away. "Or if you drive me too crazy to resist," he muttered.

Lydia's jaw dropped, and she stared at him. But his expression was impassive. His mouth flat-lined again, and his knuckles whitened as he firmed his grip on the reins. She must've misheard him.

He made a left turn down a dirt road, drove past three or four Amish farms, and pulled into a circular driveway that separated a sprawling white farmhaus from a faded red barn. "This is my home."

Red and yellow tulips and purple grape hyacinths bloomed in the weed-free flower bed along the front porch, where a swing similar to the one at Susanna Troyer's swayed in the breeze. The cushions were dark blue, a slightly lighter shade than navy, with several blue-and-white-checkered throw pillows tucked on each side. Lydia longed to relax there with a gut book. To dig her fingers into the rich black soil of the flower beds. Someday, if and when she married, she wanted to have a home like this.

The door opened, and Caleb's mamm stepped out with a big smile. "Welkum, welkum. Caleb, don't just sit there. Help the girl out."

Red crept up his neck. He clambered out of the buggy, hastened around to the other side, and held out his hand to Lydia. Once on the ground, she stepped a little closer to him than necessary. "I love your home. So beautiful."

"I'll take you on a tour later, if you want." His eyes darkened, and his gaze lowered slightly before it jerked back up to meet hers again. His nod was somewhat brusque as he moved away and began unhitching the horse.

Lydia climbed the porch stairs to greet Bethel. "Danki for inviting me for dinner. Is there anything I can do to help?"

"Nein, danki. It's almost ready. Kum in, have a seat, and visit with me while I finish up. Caleb can show you the clock shop later, if you want to see it."

Lydia glanced over her shoulder, intending to say, "I'd *love* to see it, Caleb." But the words lodged in her throat.

He stared at her with a look of what appeared to be pure longing.

Her heart leapt in response.

As she watched him, his expression changed into one of acute misery.

And then, shoulders slumped, he turned away.

❧

Caleb kicked a rock out of his way as he led the horse, Blackberry, to the barn. He should've asked Gizelle what she had planned with her friends, and tried to get an invitation to join them, instead of mindlessly feeding his crush on the unattainable, much-too-tempting princess.

It had appeared to be Gizelle flirting with Menno by the pond, but surely not. There were a lot of girls with strawberry blonde hair. She wasn't swayed by Menno. And she had assured Caleb she intended to join the church. She would be taking classes this summer. She was ready to become a gut Amish frau.

"So, Lydia's the girl." Daed stepped out of the shadows as Caleb approached the barn.

Caleb's face hurt from trying to school his expression into something neutral. He couldn't quite manage a nod. Instead, he led Blackberry to his stall and pumped some water into the bucket.

Daed followed him. "I saw how you looked at her. She is very pretty, but I'm a bit concerned. How is she 'trouble,' exactly? Or does she remind you of something in your past? Something…or maybe someone?"

Someone, jah. Caleb swallowed hard. He patted Blackberry and exited the stall without answering. He stopped in front of Daed, his eyes downcast. There were nein words. Even after all this time, he still couldn't confess to Daed. *Gott, I'm so sorry.*

Daed sighed and tugged at his beard. "The Gut Book says in Jeremiah that der Herr knows the plans He has for you. Plans for gut and not for evil. Plans to give you a hope and a future. Consider something. What if the future Gott has planned for you is hiding behind your worst failure, or behind your greatest fear?"

Caleb's stomach churned. Would Gott be cruel enough to make him face his past, his failures, his fears, in order to embrace the future? What if he didn't want to?

The answer was just as clear as if Daed had spoken it. *You would settle for mediocre.*

A muscle ticked in Caleb's jaw. *Then I'll just settle for mediocre.*

Silence. But a heavy weight settled in his stomach.

He was trying so hard to be gut. To obey the rules. To follow the advice of the preachers. But....

All your righteousness is as filthy rags.

Caleb cringed. *Why do I bother with You? I know what You think of me. But what if I told You that You're wrong?*

The weight seemed heavier now. Caleb squeezed his eyes shut, wanting to add a plaintive *"Spare me this cup!"* to his selfish-enough-as-it-was prayer. Some gut it did Jesus, praying that. It wasn't likely to do Caleb any gut, either.

He sure wasn't earning any gold stars with Gott by showing Him an attitude. Telling Gott He was wrong. It was a wonder lightning didn't flash from the heavens and strike him dead on the spot.

When he opened his eyes, he was alone in the barn. He saw Daed striding across the yard toward the haus, nein doubt to escape the pending fire from heaven. Either that, or to greet Lydia, wash up, and eat supper. Caleb would be expected to follow.

He'd offered to give Lydia a tour. *A tour!* Which would include the dawdi-haus where he'd imagined—dreamed of—starting out married life ever since meeting Lydia. He was the youngest sohn, after all, and would inherit the farm. The clock business.

She'd called it beautiful.

He pulled in a deep breath. *A little help, Gott?* There was nein way could he perform his assigned role in this saga without it.

Maybe he was being a bit presumptive, telling Gott off and then asking Him for help. Perhaps Gizelle would somehow rescue him.

He took out his cell phone and sent her another text message. Lydia is here for supper. Kum join us?

The reply came right away. Sorry. Can't.

He slid the phone back inside his pocket. Squared his shoulders. And headed toward the haus.

To face *her*.

9

Lydia helped Caleb's ten-year-old sister, Dolly, set the table by placing a napkin beside each plate. The three older girls bustled around the kitchen, helping their mamm with the final meal preparations.

Bethel had gone all out, making porcupine meatballs, creamy mashed potatoes, a medley of steamed vegetables—broccoli, cauliflower, and carrots—and a tossed salad with homegrown tomatoes, mushrooms, and radishes. For dessert, there were five different types of pie: raisin, coconut cream, apple, cherry, and blueberry. "We weren't sure which kind you liked best," Bethel explained.

Lydia liked them all the same, but it seemed a little much, especially considering the apple-rhubarb cobbler Bethel had brought over the previous nacht.

Bethel hugged Lydia again, and Lydia forced herself to embrace her, as well, even though she wasn't accustomed to such displays of affection. In response, Bethel tightened her hold. "We just want to make you feel welkum. Maybe you'll decide to stay in these parts instead of returning home. I know Abigail would be glad to keep her best friend nearby."

Lydia would like that, too. And going home wasn't an option. Then again, neither was staying here.

The door opened, and an older man with slightly graying brown hair came in. "Hallo, Lydia. I'm Preacher Zeke. Welkum to our home." His smile mirrored the relaxed grin Caleb had given her last nacht—the one without the fangs.

"Danki. Very glad to be here."

With a friendly wink, Preacher Zeke crossed the room to the sink and scrubbed his hands and arms. He reached for a towel as the door opened again, and Caleb strode in, shoulders firm, back straight, as if he were about to be graded on his posture. He glanced at Lydia with a grin. "They put you right to work, eh?"

"She insisted," Bethel said. "Supper's ready, so wash up and take your seat."

With a nod, Caleb marched over to the sink.

Lydia hid her smile. He was so much like his father in his mannerisms...and he obeyed his mamm without question.

Bethel placed one last serving dish on the table. "Lydia, you sit here, beside Caleb. We used to seat the buwe on one side, the maidals on the other, but Caleb's brothers are married, and my oldest girl married this past fall, so it's just Caleb and the four girls still at home."

Caleb pulled out a chair. "Here you go, Princess. Uh, Lydia."

His mamm beamed. She glanced at Preacher Zeke. "I told you."

She didn't specify what, exactly, she had told her ehemann. And Lydia didn't want to guess. She probably didn't have to, considering the red that stained Caleb's cheeks.

Bethel had an accomplice in her matchmaking efforts. Didn't Caleb's parents know about Gizelle? If they thought Caleb might be interested in Lydia, they couldn't be more wrong.

But the look she'd seen on his face as she was going into the haus.... Her own cheeks warmed at the memory.

It wouldn't be so bad if Caleb liked her. If Gizelle didn't factor into the equation.

But she did. And Lydia didn't want to ruin their relationship.

Preacher Zeke bowed his head. "Let's pray."

Lydia spent the ensuing period of silence formulating this prayer: *Lord Gott, danki for giving me new friends here in Jamesport. Please don't let me disappoint Aenti Judith and Onkel Mark. And help me not to kum between Caleb and Gizelle. Bless this food. In Jesus' name, amen.*

"Amen," Preacher Zeke boomed. Then he smiled at Lydia. "Help yourself, please. Judith tells me this is one of your favorite meals."

"It is! I always request it for my birthday dinner."

"She didn't tell me your favorite dessert, though."

Lydia glanced at the array of pies lining the counter, and decided to borrow Caleb's line. "I've never met a dessert I didn't like."

Preacher Zeke chuckled.

Lydia heaped a helping of buttery mashed potatoes onto her plate before passing the bowl to Caleb. Then she ladled porcupine meatballs and gravy over top. Her stomach growled. As she hurriedly passed the platter to Caleb, their fingers touched, and her hand shook as she reached for the bowl of steamed vegetables.

Finally, when everyone had been served, Lydia took a bite of the porcupine meatballs. They tasted so gut, she nearly groaned. "Ach, these meatballs are delicious."

Caleb grinned at her. "Aren't they? Mamm is an excellent cook."

The door opened with a bang, and Gizelle blew inside.

⸺

At Gizelle's abrupt entry, the chatter around the table quieted immediately, and Mamm emitted a sharp gasp. Caleb shot to his feet, almost upsetting his chair. His fork clattered to the table and bounced onto the floor. "I...I thought you said you couldn't make it."

"There was a change of plans. So now I can."

As she bent to take off her shoes, Caleb saw that the hem of her light green dress was damp. As if perhaps she *had* been at the pond. Next, he studied her hair for any signs of having been loose recently. But every hair was perfectly in place.

Gizelle was too sensible to chase after Menno. She'd agreed to be Caleb's girl. Would she have done that if her heart was otherwise engaged?

Unless, of course, her answer had been a knee-jerk reaction. Like Caleb's request had been.

If that were the case, they were a doomed couple.

The knot in Caleb's stomach tightened. Pulled.

They were doomed, anyway, if he couldn't get a grip on his emotions.

Gizelle stood upright once more. "So nice of you to invite me to dinner, Bethel."

"Glad you could join us." Mamm didn't quite sound as if she meant it. "Let me get you a plate."

"I don't mean to put you out." Gizelle must've picked up on the insincerity of Mamm's welkum. "But Caleb did text me an invitation. Twice. I assumed you'd okayed it."

"Of course, I did." Mamm said tartly. "It was my idea in the first place."

Daed frowned.

Only Lydia smiled, her eyes brightening. As if she were relieved.

But the hard gaze Mamm shot in Caleb's direction clearly communicated her intent. *We'll just see how they compare.*

Caleb's stomach cramped.

There was nein comparison. He knew it. His parents knew it. Gott Himself knew it.

And yet he'd asked Gizelle to be his girl, and he'd meant it.

Or he would mean it. Eventually.

As soon as he got over his crush on Lydia.

Caleb drew a deep breath. What was it the Englischers said? *Fake it till you make it.*

A man's got to do what a man's got to do.

That meant pretending to love Gizelle until the love was real. Pretending not to like Lydia until he didn't.

He didn't know if it were possible.

He set his jaw, attempting to maintain a neutral facial expression. Again.

Mamm put a plate and some silverware on the table, next to Caleb's place setting. He gave Gizelle his chair, moved his own plate closer to Lydia, and went to retrieve another chair. Then he sat down, between the two women who were tearing his life to shreds. The one he loved but shouldn't, and the one he didn't love but should.

His appetite got up and walked right out the door.

He was tempted to follow it.

Instead, he tried to think of something to talk about. The weather? Nein. He pushed his food around on his plate with his fork, arranging it. Rearranging it. And then re-rearranging it.

Gizelle chattered about her job at the Amish Market and mentioned having seen Caleb's cousin Bethany in town, visiting family. Bethany and her new ehemann, Silas Beiler, had relocated to Iowa.

"Something wrong with your meal, Sohn?" Mamm asked sweetly. Too sweetly. Because the slight smirk on her face told him that she knew what was really wrong.

His sisters giggled.

Caleb didn't dare glance at either Lydia or Gizelle. Instead, he put his fork down. "Nein. Just…not hungry."

"That's too bad. Guess you don't have an appetite for pie, then, either." Mamm must've realized the reason for his appetite's departure, or she would've worried he was sick and started fussing.

More giggles from his sisters. They were enjoying this too much. Their gazes darted back and forth between Lydia and Gizelle.

Caleb nodded. Placed his fork and knife across his plate. Bowed his head for the silent prayer, then looked up, all the while avoiding Daed's gaze. "May I be excused, please?"

Mamm's eyes widened, as if she were surprised by this turn of events. Or maybe she thought he was being rude to his guests. Well, they were her guests, technically speaking. He wouldn't have invited Gizelle if Mamm hadn't suggested it. Had she truly expected him to suffer through this painful experience?

"Go on out to the workshop," Daed said. "I'll send her out when we're done eating."

Her?

Her.

It could be either one. Or both. But he knew to whom Daed was referring.

"Danki." Caleb stood and bolted for the door.

⁓

Lydia finished her dinner, but not without interruptions, as Caleb's family and Gizelle asked questions about how she liked running the shop, and did she think she'd like to stay in the area after her aenti's return? Those were in addition to the tell-me-about-your-family questions and the polite getting-to-know-you questions.

But strangely, the room seemed to have emptied with Caleb's exit.

Hopefully, she wasn't to blame for his sudden loss of appetite. Or perhaps he was nervous, having his girl there with his family. Though, what kind of beau would abandon his girl, leaving her to face his family alone?

After a slice of absolutely wunderbaar coconut cream pie, Lydia bowed her head for the silent prayer, then stood, gathered her dishes, and carried them over to the sink. Bethel and her dochters began clearing the rest of the dishes. "How can I help?" Lydia asked.

Gizelle pushed her chair back. "I don't want to overcrowd the kitchen, so I think I'll go on out to the shop and see what Caleb's doing."

Bethel swung around so quickly, she almost plowed into Lydia. "Actually, Gizelle, I thought we could spend some more time together. It seems like ages since we've seen you. Lydia, don't worry about helping. Go on out to the workshop—it's right across the drive."

Lydia frowned. "If you're sure there's nothing I can do to help—"

"Go." Bethel set her mouth.

Okay, then. Lydia walked toward the door. Bethel probably wanted to spend some time alone with her future dochter-in-law.

Dolly skipped up beside Lydia. "I'm going out to play with the kittens. Want me to show you where the workshop is?"

"Sure, danki." Lydia took the little girl by the hand, and they walked outside together.

"The kittens are in the barn. That's the workshop, right there." Dolly pointed to a shed that looked fairly new. "Caleb and Daed work in there. Caleb, mostly. Daed's gone a lot with church stuff." She led the way to the shop, then pushed the door open. "Go on in. He might be putting a clock together, or just sitting there doing math problems."

"Math problems?"

Dolly laughed. "You'll see." She waved, then turned and skipped off toward the barn. "Kum see the kittens before you leave," she called over her shoulder. "I'll show you my favorite."

"Okay." Lydia slipped inside the brightly lit shed. The room was filled with clocks in various stages of assembly. Some appeared to be finished, and they ticktocked merrily along, while others sat silently, partial pictures painted on them.

Caleb was bent over a desk, tapping a pencil on the wooden surface. A book that looked like a Bible was open in front of him.

Lydia cleared her throat. "Your mamm sent me out to get the grand tour."

The pencil stopped tapping.

"If now's a gut time, that is."

Caleb turned to face her, and she could've sworn she saw a sheen in his eyes.

10

*N*ow's a gut time," Caleb said quietly. He tried not to notice the way Lydia's silhouette against the setting sun seemed to radiate shimmering light.

She glanced at his Bible. "What are you reading?"

"The Psalms." Caleb closed the cover of the Gut Book. She didn't need to know which particular chapter he'd been studying. It would be too revealing.

He took a deep breath and stood. "This is my workshop. Well, our workshop."

Lydia ran her fingertip lightly over the edge of the carved leaves decorating the face of the clock nearest her. "The clocks are gorgeous. You're so talented. How do you make them all keep perfect time with each other?"

He smiled. This, he could handle. He reached for the notebook on the side of the worktable and slid the pencil off it. Flipped the top page so she wouldn't notice the neatly organized columns he'd made just before his Bible reading—"Lydia" as one heading, "Gizelle" as the other. And the two columns under each of those, labeled "Pro" and "Con."

"We calculate the timing by configuring the spacing on these gears." He pointed to a set of gears lying on the workbench. "And in order to do that…." He opened the notebook to a page of scribbled equations, and started explaining the mathematics involved.

When he looked up, her eyes were glazed over. She smiled slightly. "Wow. A lot goes into them. Fascinating, ain't so?"

She was kind. A mark to be added in the "pro" column beneath her name. But her comment about the clocks being "fascinating" was probably a stretch. If so, he didn't appreciate it much. There went a mark on the negative side.

Caleb hitched an eyebrow. "But...?"

Lydia giggled. "But, math...ugh."

"Math, ugh?" He frowned.

She shrugged. "Sorry."

Judith had mentioned that Lydia claimed to get math-induced migraines. Probably purely psychological. "Guess I'd better back off, in case the mere proximity of mathematical equations causes you illness."

She giggled again. And stepped backward.

Caleb ran his fingers over the page of calculations, then pushed the notebook away and pulled open a tiny drawer of the old-time library card catalog file cabinet they'd purchased at an auction. "This is where we keep all the clock parts. The minute hands, for example, are all in this drawer. And the hour hands are kept in the drawer beneath it."

Lydia moved closer again and peered into the drawer. Then she reached out and opened another, wider one, filled with an assortment of knives of various sizes. "Wow."

"We...we use a lot of different knives for the detailed carvings, like the leaves you looked at earlier." He glanced up at a shelf above the cabinet. The clock sitting there was almost finished. He just needed to add the chains for the eight-day setting. He could show her the bird inside the door, and let her hear it made the cuckoo sound.

He lifted his arm but miscalculated the distance, and his calloused finger grazed her jaw.

She shivered and drew back.

He jerked his hand away. But he had to lean closer to her in order to reach the clock. Too close to her curves. Too close to her sun-streaked hair. Too close to....

He pulled in a deep breath.

She still gave off an intriguing scent like lemon, one that made him want to bury his face in the curve of her neck and solve the mystery.

"Caleb?"

"Sorry, I got distracted." He reached for the clock again and lifted it down.

"So, what do you think?"

"I...." Nope. Couldn't tell her the truth. He cleared his throat. "What do I think about what?"

"About the idea I just shared—that you could bring some of your unfinished clocks, maybe some of the simpler ones, to Aenti Judith's shop on a Saturday and do a clockmaking demonstration. The artisans in Ohio do this sometimes. The tourists love it, and it makes them feel more a part of the process—and likelier to make a purchase."

He stared at her, weighing the proposition. "Not sure the preachers would go for it. We're not allowed to have our names on our business cards. Demonstrating would be like showing off. You know the Bible verse about boasting not about yourself? I think it's in First Corinthians. Besides, we don't have a bishop right now. The bishop of a neighboring district is filling in until we draw lots. And he's strict." Or so he'd heard. He hadn't actually met the man. "I could ask Daed, but I doubt he'd agree, especially considering the Ordnung. And even if he did, I don't think he'd give me that long of a break from the farm work. Especially since clockmaking is a hobby, not a business."

"What about a rainy Saturday?"

Hadn't she been listening? Caleb shook his head. "The number of tourists would be down anyway, so it probably wouldn't be worth the while. Besides, I told you, Daed might see it as a way of boasting about my abilities."

"It's so confusing, how much the Amish differ from one district to another. In Sugarcreek, Ohio, we're much more tourist oriented. Mamm told me Jamesport was, too."

"Not to the same degree." Caleb frowned at the clock in his hands. Why had he gotten it down from the shelf? He couldn't remember. "Do you want to see anything more in the shop? Or should we continue the grand tour somewhere else? The dawdi-haus, maybe?" Because he wanted to see what she thought of their—um, his—starter home.

Even though that would be asking for trouble, for sure and for certain.

"The dawdi-haus?" Lydia sounded startled. She glanced out the window. "Won't your großeltern mind?"

"They've gone on to glory." Caleb rubbed his jaw as Lydia made a sympathetic noise. "They've been gone a while." Stubble poked at his fingertips. He'd forgotten to shave. But it wasn't as if Lydia was going to kiss him, anyway. Not with Gizelle there. He sighed.

Where was Gizelle, anyway? Probably with Mamm, who'd be doing her best to keep her away from him. Forcing him to be with Lydia. Not a hardship, in his mind, but it did feed his crush. Did Mamm want him to suffer a broken heart?

Lydia shrugged. "Well, if it's okay with your parents, I don't mind. But I did promise Dolly I'd stop in the barn and see the kittens."

Caleb rolled his eyes. "They're cats. Just like Rosie."

"But I don't want to disappoint your sister. She's a delight."

Caleb smiled. Another mark in the pro-Lydia column. So far, she seemed to live up to all the positive secondhand information he'd gleaned about her over the past five months. "Jah, Dolly was aptly named, for sure." He turned off the gas light in the shop. "Let's tour the dawdi-haus, and then you can visit the kittens before I take you home."

He led her across the gravel drive to the smaller, attached haus, and let her precede him into the kitchen. It was small, but still much larger than the tiny U-shaped one in Judith's apartment. The room smelled of Lysol cleaner, as lemony as Lydia's scent. Caleb liked the smell, though he realized Lysol would always make him think of Lydia. Would always trigger the memory of her standing in his kitchen.

"How nice!" Lydia twirled around once, twice. "I've never seen a kitchen with the cabinets painted white. I can almost imagine yellow curtains on the window, and a vase of jonquils in the center of the table."

And now, Caleb would forever envision the room that way, too. He nodded toward the doorway. "Shall we?"

Lydia led the way into the living room, which featured a plush sofa, a glider rocker handmade by Caleb's onkel, and a small end table with a lantern and Daedi's Bible, right where he'd left it. Well, Caleb's Bible now. As Daedi's namesake, he'd inherited it. He wiped the thin layer of dust off the front cover. "There's a bedroom and a bathroom downstairs, and two bedrooms and another bathroom upstairs. Mamm and Daed plan for me to start my family here when I marry. I'll live here until my sisters are grown, and then I'll move into the big haus."

Of course, those plans had been made when he'd had grand ideas of marrying a woman who never would have fit into his life, his home, his family, or his faith.

A woman like Lydia. A beautiful, glittery princess who swept in and claimed all his thoughts.

All his hopes. All his dreams. All his desires.

All his love.

"Want to see the upstairs bedrooms?" Caleb nodded toward the steps.

Lydia hesitated. Then shook her head. "I'd better not. I've gotten carried away as it is, envisioning the décor of this home, as if it's my future residence. The reality is, it's not. And I don't need to see the room where you and Gizelle will be sleeping."

Another mark in the pro-Lydia side.

A big black mark against himself. Especially since he couldn't imagine Gizelle ever living here.

On the other hand, it was easy to pretend that Lydia was his future frau, getting the grand tour. Especially with the joy in her smile. The excitement in her gait. The twirls she made as she pivoted to see the haus from every angle, happily chatting about quilted throw pillows with sunflowers, and more yellow curtains....

"Gizelle must love this haus." Lydia glided past him.

He'd never showed it to Gizelle. Had nein desire to. Lydia was the only woman he wanted to make a home with.

Andy Miller and Daed were right. He shouldn't have asked Gizelle to be his girl until he was sure.

But he *had* asked. And now he had to live with his decision.

"Want to see the kittens?"

Lydia smiled. "I'd love to."

Seemed all women went cuckoo over kittens, even though the felines all grew up to be the unglamorous mouse-catchers that remained in the barn.

Cuckoo.... That was the reason he'd gotten that clock down from the shelf. To show Lydia the cuckoo bird. Demonstrate how it made sound.

"There's something I forgot to show you in the clock shop. If it's okay, we'll return there before going to the barn to see the kittens. And then we'll say gut-bye to Mamm and Daed before I take you home." Would he need to drive Gizelle home, too? He hoped not. "Shall we?" He almost offered Lydia his arm. Stopped himself in time.

"We shall." Lydia glanced around the room one last time. "Danki for the tour."

He nodded as he opened the door.

Giggles drifted on the air from the direction of the barn. Lydia glanced that way.

Maybe the inner workings of the cuckoo clock would have to wait.

⌒

Lydia hurried into the barn in search of the giggling little girl. She found Dolly in a horse stall with the kittens—beautiful white and gray Siamese.

"They are so cute! They look like Rosie."

Caleb nodded. "Her sisters and brothers."

"Really?"

"They all have homes lined up," Dolly added. "Just waiting for things to get settled here and there before they leave us. The one with the pink ribbon is going to a little girl for her birthday on Saturday. The one with the sailboat ribbon is going to a home where the ehemann works on a riverboat, and his frau thought his mammi would enjoy a kitten. They're coming to pick her up tomorrow. This one, with the ribbon that has road signs on it, is going to a truck driver, to keep him company on the road."

"Ingenious, the way you have them marked." Lydia bent down and scooped up one wearing a blue ribbon. "Who's this one going to?"

"An Englisch pastor. He takes animals along with him to visit shut-ins and people in nursing homes. Says it's the best medicine." The kitten in Dolly's arms batted with its paws at her kapp strings. "Your aenti was in a big hurry to get Rosie home before you came, so you wouldn't be lonely."

Lydia raised her eyebrows and glanced at Caleb. "Really?"

He shrugged. "Sounds like something she'd do. I wasn't here when she decided on a kitten."

"Jah, you were," Dolly insisted. "It was the same day she asked you to do the accounting for her shop, since math gave her niece headaches."

Lydia laughed. "I don't think I'd go quite that far. But I will admit I detest doing math."

Caleb eyed his sister. "So, does Rosie belong to Judith? Or Lydia?"

Dolly shrugged. "Judith, I think. Especially since she and Mamm decided Lydia will marry you, so she won't need the company of a kitten anymore."

Lydia gasped. Her face burned, even as a shiver of excitement shot through her. She didn't dare glance at Caleb. Time stood suspended for seconds, minutes, maybe hours.

Suddenly, Gizelle peeked over the stall door. "Well, that's too bad, because I'm Caleb's girl."

⌒

"Right, Caleb?" Gizelle reached out and gripped Caleb's shoulder, as she sent Lydia a glare that said, *I dare you to make something of this.* A bolder move than he'd seen her make before.

Caleb looked at her hand, still possessively grasping. He didn't appreciate it. He made a slight move away, hoping she would get the hint.

Her grip tightened.

Caleb clenched his jaw.

"I came out to tell you I'm ready to go home. Can you drive me, please?" Her grasp turned into an equally annoying pat, as if he were a small bu. Several new marks on the "con" column beneath Gizelle's name.

"Um, sure. Jah." He dared to glance in Lydia's direction. "You ready to go?"

"Your mamm and daed want to visit with her a bit before she leaves," Gizelle put in. "Maybe your daed will drive her home when they're done talking. But I came over here to spend time with you, not to help your mamm with dishes. If I'd wanted to do housework, I would've stayed home."

Caleb frowned. And mentally made another mark against Gizelle. Not helpful. "I'll get the horse hitched. Do you want to play with the kittens while you're waiting?"

"Nein, I'll kum help you." That would be a mark in the "pro Gizelle" column. Helpful.

Hold it. Didn't the two latest marks cancel each other out? Caleb was getting confused. Maybe he should carry a small notebook and a pen, and make literal marks as he thought of them.

Or maybe he was overthinking things. A tendency his schoolteachers had consistently pointed out to his parents.

He cast an apologetic glance toward his sister and Lydia, but neither girl looked at him.

And then he went after Gizelle.

11

After Caleb had left the stall, Lydia glanced at Dolly. The little girl rolled her eyes but didn't make any unkind comments, so Lydia remained quiet, as well, even though she wondered what had gotten into Gizelle. It was almost as if Caleb's girl felt threatened by Lydia.

Lydia shifted the kitten she held in her arms, and stroked its fur. "Did you put a color-coded ribbon on Rosie until Aenti Judith picked her up?"

Dolly nodded. "A red one. Judith named her Rosie the moment she saw her." She peeked her head over the side of the stall. "I think they've left the barn, but let's wait a few more minutes before going to the haus." She lowered the kitten she'd been holding to the dusty, hay-strewn floor. "I don't like Gizelle. She never pays attention to me. But I like you. I think you should marry my brother."

It seemed best to leave that comment alone. Lydia glanced around. "Where's the mama cat?"

Dolly shrugged. "Hunting, probably. She leaves the kittens more often, now. They're eating and drinking on their own, and are litter box trained, so they're ready to go to their forever homes. The new owners just have to take care of their shots and stuff."

Lydia needed to check Aenti Judith's notebook of instructions for any details about Rosie. Had the kitten gotten her shots already, or did she still need them?

"You should probably go to the haus now. I'll kum in a minute." Dolly took the kitten from Lydia. "It's time for me to tell the kittens their bedtime story."

"Their bedtime story?" Lydia grinned at the girl.

Dolly nodded. "It's about a tuna fish bouquet."

"That's so sweet. Danki for sharing your kittens with me. I'll be sure to take gut care of Rosie." With a smile, Lydia gently shut the stall door behind her, then walked out of the barn.

Bethel and Preacher Zeke were seated on the front porch swing, both holding a glass of lemonade. Bethel waved Lydia over. "Such a beautiful evening. Kum, sit with us." She motioned to a macramé chair as Lydia approached. Another glass of lemonade sat on the table beside it.

As Lydia sat down, Bethel's gaze strayed toward the yard. "I'm thinking of asking Caleb to till the garden tomorrow. We're going to enlarge it a little this year. With a fall wedding, we'll need to put up extra food, ain't so?"

Preacher Zeke cleared his throat.

Lydia nodded, because it seemed the proper thing to do, though she wasn't sure why. Who in the family was getting married in the fall? If Caleb and Gizelle had just begun courting, it seemed a bit premature to prepare for a wedding six months down the road. Maybe the oldest dochter still at home was the one getting married.

Bethel continued studying the yard. "I'm thinking of a flower bed with lots of mums in bloom."

"That'll be pretty." Lydia pictured pretty yellow blossoms with red accents. Not that it would be her choice.

"What colors—"

"Are you planning on transferring your membership here, Lydia?" Preacher Zeke interrupted his frau, with a gentle pat of her hand. "Or keeping it in Ohio?"

"Keeping it as it is. I'm only here until my aenti and onkel return from their mission trip, you know."

The preacher nodded as he studied her. "And how's your heart health? Are you doing okay after the death of your beau?"

Why was he asking? It seemed rather intrusive. But he was a preacher, so maybe he wanted to make sure the community wasn't dealing with a visitor suffering from acute depression.

"I'm fine." Just not ready to risk her heart. And even if she was, there were those who would try to manipulate her and her decisions.

Not unlike the couple sitting beside her—if what she'd noticed, and what Dolly had suggested, was true.

"Do you sew?" Bethel peered at Lydia's garment. "That's a beautiful dress, but the length is a bit short for this district. I could help you lengthen it, if you want."

She didn't say anything about the color, but none of the other Amish ladies Lydia had met in this district had worn coral. "I do sew, I'm just not at all experienced with an electric machine like Aenti Judith has. I'd love to kum over to sew, though, so if you'd like to help, that'd be great."

Bethel nodded. "We'll plan on it. I look forward to spending more time with you."

"I don't think the length matters, since she's a visitor," Preacher Zeke said. "She'll follow her own district's Ordnung."

"Ach, I forgot about that." Bethel nodded. "Are you using the electricity in Judith's apartment? I guess you have nein way around it. You might find it hard to go back to the old ways, ain't so?"

Lydia laughed. "Probably. I'm getting so spoiled here. But I'll readjust. It's what I'm used to, after all."

"It'll be like the way Caleb adjusted when he gave up driving that fancy red car." Preacher Zeke looked at his frau. "He missed it, but plain and simple is best, and he recognized the truth of that. Just as Lydia will."

Caleb had driven a fancy red car?

"We were all so worried about him." Bethel shook her head. "But Gott is gut."

"All the time," Preacher Zeke agreed.

Lydia frowned. They'd worried about Caleb? Mr. Straight-and-Narrow? But those vampire teeth indicated a mischievous side. And there was something about him that excited her.

⌇

As Caleb drove the buggy, he glanced at Gizelle, exercising her thumbs on her cell phone's miniature keyboard. "Let me out at the corner," she said without looking up.

"Okay…." He wanted to ask, *Why the secrecy?* Her daed already knew he'd planned to ask her to be his girl.

Well, if she didn't want to be driven all the way home, that just meant Caleb could race back home and spend more time with Lydia.

"Menno says he plans on taking Lydia for ice cream Friday nacht, after she gets off work." Gizelle spoke without looking up from her phone.

Caleb frowned and slowed the horse to a walk. What was his girl doing, texting another man? He wouldn't be half as bothered if it were anyone but Menno. Maybe Gizelle wasn't as immune to his charms as Caleb had thought. Had she been the girl at the pond, after all? "Are you texting with him right now?"

"Jah. A bunch of us are planning on going into the city to see a movie. Too bad you joined the church already. You could've gone with us."

Caleb shook his head. He'd learned his lesson.

"You could kum along, anyway. Nobody will tell."

Another strike against Gizelle. Encouraging him to sin.

"I need to take Lydia home. And work on the books for Judith's shop, since I didn't have a chance to finish that earlier." He really needed to make that deposit at the bank.

"You're such a stick in the mud sometimes," Gizelle grumbled. She keyed something else into her phone.

Another con.

Caleb grunted and glanced again at Gizelle's thumbs flying over the tiny buttons.

Texting was quite the finger workout.

He wasn't very gut at it. Preferred calling, actually. But since he and Daed owned a business, they were permitted to use cell phones, and the devices had kum in handy on several occasions. And the clockmaking enterprise was a business, even if Daed did call it a hobby. It generated money. Especially since they now had a website—set up and managed by Judith—for online sales.

Who was handling the web sales now? Not likely Lydia, with her aversion to numbers. She was probably scared of computers, too.

He pulled up to the corner and stopped the buggy. Gizelle climbed out, still clutching her phone in one hand.

"Do you want me to wait?"

"Nein, I'll be fine." Gizelle waved him off. "He—they'll be here in a moment."

A cloud of dust rose in the distance.

Gizelle glanced in that direction. "I bet that's him now. I mean, them. See you Friday when we double-date with you and Lydia. I mean, with Menno and Lydia." She laughed.

That was an awful lot of slipping up. Caleb arched an eyebrow but nodded. "Friday, jah. If you're sure you want to join them."

"Jah, jah, I'm sure. Bye!"

"Tell Menno it's dangerous to text and drive." Caleb clicked his tongue and turned the buggy around toward home. Hopefully, he'd get there before Daed drove Lydia home.

He wouldn't feel guilty about looking forward to spending time with her—not when Gizelle was in such a big hurry to go to the movies with Menno and whoever else was going. *If* anyone else was going.

Caleb's stomach knotted. Jah, he and Gizelle were doomed. She wasn't his girl. Not as much as he'd thought.

Things just weren't adding up.

⟱

Lydia finished her lemonade as Caleb pulled up beside the porch in the buggy. He jumped out and took the stairs two at a time. "You ready to go home now, Princess? I can take you in a minute, I just need to run upstairs for something. Be right back."

Lydia was happy he'd ditched Gizelle so quickly and would drive her home, after all.

His parents were clearly happy, too. His daed tried to hide his smile, while his mamm openly beamed.

"Okay, but you promised to show me something else in your shop," Lydia reminded him. She wouldn't comment on the "Princess" nickname now.

Caleb nodded, his eyes widening. "Jah, I did. Sorry I didn't do it earlier." He opened the door and went inside.

Lydia glanced at Preacher Zeke and Bethel. "Danki again for inviting me to dinner. It was really nice visiting with you and getting to know my aenti and onkel's closest friends."

Bethel's smile grew even bigger. "The pleasure was ours! Please don't be a stranger, Lydia. I realize you're busy with the shop, but I hope you can plan to kum out again next week for dinner. In fact, let's not wait that long. Amish and Mennonite businesses are closed on Thursdays. Kum spend the day with us. I'll have Caleb pick you up bright and early."

A day with Caleb and his family. Lydia considered the suggestion, then shook her head. "That sounds lovely, but I need to write my parents and Aenti Judith, and I really should try to figure out the washing machine. I also need to peruse the instructions my aenti left about how to run the store. I hate to admit it, but I haven't given them much more than a glance."

Bethel's mouth flexed into a frown that quickly disappeared. "Well, it can't be that hard. Judith didn't have an instruction manual when she started the store, and she did fine. If you change your mind, give Caleb a call. We'll get you his phone number. And I'll pray you'll kum."

It was nice to be wanted.

The door opened, and Caleb came back outside. "Ready?"

"Jah." Lydia turned back to Bethel. "I'd love to kum out on Thursday. Give me a few hours in the morgen, and Caleb can bring me out here in time for lunch. If he isn't too busy."

"Lunch?" Caleb hesitated on the porch.

"Thursday." Bethel stood, took Lydia in her arms, and hugged her. "She's joining us for the afternoon. Isn't that wunderbaar?" She released her and stepped back.

Preacher Zeke chuckled and slapped Caleb on the arm as he went past. "Don't stay out too late, Sohn."

"I won't." Caleb gestured for Lydia to go ahead of him down the porch steps. "I guess what I was going to show you could wait until Thursday, then. Unless you'd be in too much suspense. I wanted to show you how the cuckoo is installed inside the clock, and how it makes its signature noise."

"I'd like to see it now."

They crossed the yard side by side to the shed. Caleb held open the door for Lydia, and once they'd entered, he flipped the gas lights on, then moved to the worktable and carefully opened the back of the clock.

Lydia leaned next to him on the tabletop, her chin resting on her palms. "Your family is so nice. Being with them makes me feel less homesick."

Not that she'd really started feeling homesick. Yet.

Caleb looked over at her. "Dolly loves you. She was getting ready for bed when I went inside and came into my room to say gut-nacht and gave me a hug."

"She is so sweet. She reminds me of my youngest sister, Phoebe."

He angled the clock to give her a view of the interior. "See how the bird is attached to this lever, here? When these gears get to a certain point, they trigger the lever, and the door opens. The noise is caused by air being forced out of the bellows." He pointed to two white rectangular blocks. Then he moved his hand, touching something inside the clock.

"Cuckoo, cuckoo," the clock obliged.

Lydia grinned. "I really hope your daed lets you do a demonstration at the shop. I'd love to see you work."

He glanced up. "Did you mention the idea to him?"

She shook her head. "We were talking about weddings, and gardens, and sewing, and…." She shrugged. "All kinds of stuff."

"Weddings?" He shook his head, then put the clock back together. "I'll ask Daed and let you know what he says when I see you Thursday. But don't expect him to agree."

"Then that's what I'll expect, so I'll be pleasantly surprised if he does."

Caleb lifted the clock and returned it to the shelf. "I still need to add the weights to this one, and then it'll be ready to sell." He glanced around. "Let's get you home. Unless there's something else you want to see in here."

"Just you, working." She bit her tongue for having let that slip. "But maybe Thursday. You can show me how to add the weights." She started for the door.

Caleb turned off the lights.

Neither Preacher Zeke nor Bethel was on the porch when Lydia reached the buggy. She climbed in while Caleb unhitched the horse. Then he got in beside her and released the brake. He made a clicking sound with his tongue, and they were off. The horse moved at a faster pace than a walk, maybe a canter. Caleb was probably in a hurry to drop her off and get back home again.

She wouldn't invite him in. Shouldn't.

But she wanted to.

Especially when his hand came to rest next to hers on the seat. His pinkie brushed against hers.

Even though the touch was innocent, tingles shot through every cell of her body.

12

As Caleb followed Lydia up the stairs to the apartment, he rubbed his hand over his smooth jaw, thankful he hadn't nicked it in his haste to shave before driving Lydia home. It was shameless, his hope that Lydia would invite him in, or at least give him another gut-nacht kiss.

At the top of the steps, Lydia stepped aside so he could insert his key into the lock. He fumbled with the key a bit, his hands trembling, until it granted them entry. He removed the key and swung the door open. "Here you go, Princess. Home, sweet home. Want me to check around inside?"

Her glance was quizzical. "What for?"

His cheeks warmed. He shrugged with feigned nonchalance. "The boogeyman? The big bad wolf? The Abominable Snowman? Or maybe the Loch Ness Monster?"

She giggled. "I think I'm safe from fictional characters, but danki for offering."

"Maybe so. But what about nonfictional characters?" He reached into his pocket for the vampire teeth he'd grabbed off his bedside table, and slipped them into his mouth when she entered the apartment ahead of him.

When she turned to face him, her gaze rested on his mouth. "Seriously? You brought your fangs?"

"You said yourself they attract girls." He winked. "Am I the man of your dreams, or what?" He flexed his muscles and grinned.

She blinked, but a smile played on her lips. "Maybe the man of my nacht-mares." She started to close the door.

Wait. He would be on the wrong side of it. How was he going to get a gut-nacht kiss if he was shut out?

"I mean, I'm irresistible, right? Don't you want to kiss me?" Caleb smiled broadly, baring his fake teeth, even as he felt humiliated for begging. Maybe she would play along.

She hesitated. Tilted her head. Eyed his fangs, then met his gaze again. "Nein."

Should he laugh her off? Treat her rejection as a joke? He removed the plastic teeth. "How about now?"

"Nein!" But at least she giggled. Her cheeks turned pink.

He swallowed. Couldn't she have hesitated for even a second? Thought about it just a little bit?

He held out the fake fangs. "I'm afraid that if I don't get a kiss from you, I'll go crazy."

Now he was certifiably off in den kopf. He'd be ashamed to face her again after this.

She laughed. *Laughed.* And opened the door wider. "I thought you were in a hurry to spend more time with Gizelle. Take a walk or something."

A walk sounded gut. But not with Gizelle. "She went to the movies with some friends." Maybe he should explain further. "She's still in her rumschpringe. I'm not."

"Do you want to kum in for a bit, then?" She stepped aside.

Finally. "Danki. Maybe I will stay a bit. If you don't mind." A bit. Because he did have the ledgers to take care of downstairs.

"I don't mind. I would've asked you in from the start, but I didn't know Gizelle had plans."

He stepped inside. "I don't want to talk about Gizelle." Mainly because, well, he wanted to focus on Lydia. Not on the mistakes he'd made when she entered his life a second time. Not his fears—his fear of his own desires, or his fears of making a mistake big enough to rival the first.

She shrugged. "Okay. Do you want something to drink?"

"Water would be gut. Danki." He shut the door. Locked it. Then turned and followed her into the kitchen.

She took a glass tumbler out of a cabinet and held it beneath the automatic ice and water dispenser in the door of the refrigerator/freezer. "Isn't this the coolest thing? Like I told your daed, I'm going to be so spoiled by the time Aenti Judith returns."

"You said that to my daed?" *What must Daed think?*

"Jah, I did. And your mamm told me about your fancy red car." She grinned at him. "I think my temporary enjoyment of electricity is pretty minor, in comparison."

They'd told her about the car? His face heated. He stared at his feet. "Did she mention…anything else?" He gulped.

"Nein. Only that Gott is gut."

Gott is gut. All the time. If only Caleb could find his place in the goodness of der Herr, instead of trying to earn his way into His forgiveness.

Time to change the subject before Lydia pursued the topic further and threatened to uncover what he never wanted her to know.

"Here you go." She handed him the glass of water.

"Danki." He accepted it. What to talk about? Her deceased fiancé? Nein. If an unknown, unnamed man had won Lydia's heart, there was nein way Caleb could compare. And how could one ever dream to compete with a memory?

"So, tell me about your ex-beau. You must miss him terribly." So much for controlling his runaway tongue.

Lydia dispensed ice and then water into a second glass. Shrugged. "It's been five months since Peter died. I've had some time to get over the shock." To relish her freedom. And to develop a healthy dislike of being manipulated into a relationship.

Never again.

Which was strike one against Caleb. His parents and her aenti were clearly pushing for a match between the two of them. Gut thing Caleb courted Gizelle. He and Lydia were free to be friends, free to spend time together, and nobody could force them to be anything more.

Too bad Caleb was so appealing. Tall, handsome, and sexy, even with those toy teeth. And he did haunt her dreams. Likely because he was verboden.

"Don't you want to kiss me?"

Ach, jah. Her gaze darted to his well-shaped lips. Not too full, not too thin. Just perfect. She resisted the urge to touch her own mouth. It tingled at the memory of planting a tiny kiss on his jaw the other nacht. A real kiss? Jah, she could be persuaded. Gut thing he only teased, because he was not hers to kiss, anywhere other than on the cheek.

And while she didn't know whether she and Gizelle would become friends, she wouldn't make a play for Gizelle's man.

Especially since it would be just that—playing. A relationship was out of the question.

Caleb turned and headed for the living room. She watched him go, her gaze lowering to his narrow hips and attractive backside. He settled on the middle cushion of the couch, one arm stretched out along the back.

Would it hurt to sit in the curve of his embrace?

Seemed she had nein other choice, unless she sat on the floor. Because the only seat in the living room was the couch. Except for Onkel Mark's recliner, and it just seemed wrong to sit there. Especially with Onkel Mark's book lying open beside it, as if her onkel might return at any moment.

Lydia's stomach clenched. She forced herself to carry her water glass into the other room. Set it atop a plastic coaster, cut in a star design, on the koffee table. And settled next to Caleb. Stiffly.

His arm trembled, but otherwise he didn't move. Gut thing, because she likely would've bolted if he'd lowered his arm around her shoulder.

An uncomfortable silence filled the room. Caleb stared straight ahead, at the black screen of the TV, which Lydia didn't know how to activate. She glanced at him out of the corner of her eye, then looked down at her lap.

She wanted to kiss him. More accurately, for him to kiss her.

"So…Peter." He cleared his throat. "What was he like?"

What could she say? The memory of Peter Fisher fled into nothingness around this man.

"He…uh…he was a farmer. And, uh—"

"You know, I should go." Caleb withdrew his arm and brought it to his side. "I need to leave. Now." He bolted to his feet. "I'll see you Thursday. You don't need to see me out."

She reeled, surprised at his sudden departure. What was wrong?

He opened the door and stepped out, then hesitated. Turned back. "Remember, I'll be late tomorrow. If you hear someone downstairs after hours, it'll be me. Don't worry."

Lydia nodded. Stood. And walked toward him. "Danki for taking me home, Caleb. You truly are my hero. But…is something wrong?"

⌣

Is something wrong? Jah. I want to kiss you. Caleb couldn't keep his gaze from lowering to Lydia's lips. They were slightly parted, with a moist, inviting sheen, possibly due to a coating of verboden lip gloss. Her greenish-hazel eyes looked up at him. Trusting, and also inviting. Or was that just his imagination? Had to be.

Nein way he could—or would—admit his desire to Lydia. It was wrong. Sinful.

He reached out, letting his thumb graze her jaw, the way it had earlier in his workroom. But this time, the touch wasn't an accident.

She leaned into him. Trembled.

Or maybe those reactions were only what he wanted to see, and not reality. He forced his feet not to move toward her. "See you Thursday morgen, Princess."

She nodded. Moved forward.

His senses went into overdrive. Then stalled as her hand came to rest against his chest.

She stood on tiptoe, and—

His cell phone rang.

She lowered herself to the ground and backed away. "See you Thursday. Danki again for the ride home."

The door shut.

The lock clicked.

And he was on the wrong side of it. Again.

13

*L*ydia had thought she heard Caleb in the shop Wednesday nacht. Heard the door shut and a horse snort. But he never came up to her apartment. And by the time she decided he probably wouldn't, and went downstairs, the lights were off, the store locked up. The money she'd moved to the safe had been taken, the bag gone.

An empty bag rested on the counter beside the register, a note propped against it.

I'll be by in the morgen, around 11. See you soon.

—C

Disappointed, she'd gone back upstairs and gotten ready for bed.

Thursday morgen, Lydia awoke and bounced off the mattress, startling Rosie, who'd apparently planned to sleep in. The kitten rolled over with an indignant swish of her tail and an angry bat of a paw in Lydia's direction.

"I'm going to the Bontragers' for lunch today," Lydia sang.

"Meow." Another swish of the tail that seemed to indicate, *"So what? I was born there."*

"Whatever." Lydia lifted the protesting kitten off the bed, straightened the covers, and then hurried to the kitchen for a glass of her latest caffeine fix: iced koffee with white chocolate raspberry creamer.

She opened one tin of the cat food Aenti Judith had left in the cupboard. Turkey. Seconds later, Rosie purred as she winded her way around Lydia's ankles.

Her own breakfast eaten, Lydia opened the closet doors off the kitchen to reveal the washing machine, with a clothes dryer mounted above it. Aenti Judith had left handwritten instructions on how to use it—and the laundry soap, which was nothing like anything Lydia had ever seen. Mamm used homemade detergent. Aenti Judith had pods. Squishy things that were ever so cute. Probably wouldn't work in a wringer washer, though.

Once the washer was churning away, Lydia sat at the table with her second glass of iced koffee, picked up her favorite lavender pen, and started writing.

Dear Mamm and Daed,

How are you? I miss you and hope you'll write soon. Four days here, and I think I've done okay running Aenti Judith's shop thus far. Thankfully, I don't have to mess with the book-keeping; Aenti Judith found someone else to do it—the sohn of her best friend, Bethel.

She glanced at the note Caleb had left last night, now lying about ten inches away from her on the table. She reached over to drag it nearer, and with her fingertip, she traced the simple C he'd left as a signature. Simple and straightforward, like the man. Nothing at all like the curlicues she always added to her autograph.

She glanced at the digital clock on the microwave. Still a few hours to go before he came. Plenty of time to accomplish what she wanted to.

Aenti Judith's apartment has been a big learning experience. I figured out how to use the electric washing machine this morgen. I've had to learn to cook all over again on the electric stove and in the microwave oven. After burning my supper on Sunday evening and my breakfast Monday morgen, I've decided, for the time being, to live on boxed cereal, canned soup, and sandwiches. Not much I can do to ruin those. But Aenti Judith's best friend brought over a dessert and has already invited me twice for a meal. She seems very kind and has gone all out to make me feel welkum.

And to play matchmaker with her sohn.

Not that it would be such a hardship, if she were to be courted by Caleb.

Nein point in following that train of thought.

She shook her head and returned her attention to the letter.

I haven't seen Abigail yet, but I hope to soon. I'm going over to Bethel's again this afternoon, and will write again soon to tell you about it.

Take care.

Love,
Lydia

She put the letter in an envelope, which she addressed, affixed with a stamp, and tucked inside her apron pocket. Then she ran downstairs, exited the shop by way of the back door, hurried to the end of the block, where the post office was located, and slid the letter into the drop box. For the walk back to the shop, she maintained a more leisurely pace. Once there, she dug inside her pockets. Nein key. Nein cell phone. Nothing. She was locked out. Again. And she was barefoot. Bareheaded, too. At least her hair was braided. But she hadn't grabbed a sweater, and it was chilly. Hopefully, Caleb would show up early.

Whenever she finally got inside, the first thing she would do was write "Keys?" on two pieces of notepaper, and affix one to the inside of the apartment door, the other to the inside of the back door to the shop.

How embarrassing. Worse, this time, she couldn't pray. Nein kapp.

Filled with despair, she slumped onto the back steps to wait for Caleb.

When he came...well, he deserved a kiss. That's all.

On the cheek, of course. Because he was Gizelle's man.

⁓

Was it too soon to break up with Gizelle? Caleb slowed the buggy as he approached her haus. He'd spent two days second-guessing his decision. Two days worrying he'd done the wrong thing, instead of feeling the relief he'd expected. Two days of torture.

But she'd cheated on him with Menno, if she'd been at the pond with him. Though maybe not, since there'd been a group. But if she'd gone into town with him to see a movie, just the two of them, it counted as cheating. Right? Well, again, that hadn't been verified. And with Caleb's thoughts the way they'd been recently, he'd cheated on Gizelle with Lydia. He grimaced.

Probably should give it more than two days. That wasn't enough time to determine whether a relationship would work. Especially if he was wrong about Gizelle and Menno. And even more especially if he were right about Lydia being a sparkly, glittery princess, and not future Amish frau material. She'd want bling. Diamonds. Sapphires. Emeralds. Like....

He growled deep in his throat.

He would stop in and see Gizelle, anyway. Not to break up with her, but maybe to solidify his belief that she could never be seriously interested in Menno. His belief that she wanted boring. Plain. Unexciting.

Make that dependable. Solid. Trustworthy.

Even those positive words did nothing to bolster him. Because, the truth was, they probably meant the same thing. *Dull.*

Jah, that was sure to win her over. Plain, old, uninteresting Caleb. In fact, why was he worried so much about Lydia? The thought of a girl like her loving a man like him…? There were better chances of a snowflake falling in Florida. And the kiss she'd brushed on his jaw would be the only one he got from her. Ever.

Her hero. Right.

Maybe just that once. But never again.

He succumbed to the temptation to touch the place where she'd kissed him. Remembered his thumb brushing over the curve of her jaw.

Maybe he should confess his lusting over Lydia to Gizelle.

Nein. Besides, it was attraction. Not lust. Right?

He shut his eyes. Briefly, but long enough for Blackberry to decide to turn into Gizelle's driveway, out of habit.

Andy Miller came out of the barn, trailed by Gizelle's brother William and her brother-in-law Josh, also a close friend of Caleb's. Andy opened the buggy door. "Hallo, Caleb. What brings you by?"

"Thought to visit with Gizelle a bit before I ran an errand for Mamm." Because picking up Lydia and driving her to his family's farm for lunch and an afternoon visit counted as an errand for Mamm, ain't so?

Andy shook his head. "She's working at the Amish Market today. You could probably see her if you stop there, but she won't have much time to visit."

"Oh, that's alright. I don't want to get her in trouble with her boss. Just tell her I came by, and I'll see her tomorrow evening." For ice cream. With Lydia. And Menno.

"Gut enough." Andy stepped back. "I'd invite you in, but we're right in the middle of a project. Unless you want to stay and help."

"Another time. I have that errand for Mamm." He really shouldn't have stopped. He clicked his tongue at Blackberry, and the horse pulled the buggy around the circular driveway and out to the road.

The ride to town gave Caleb plenty of time to pray. About his feelings for Lydia. His lack of feelings for Gizelle. His attitude toward himself in comparison to Menno. Because Menno had as much charisma as anyone possibly could, and Caleb had as much charisma as a…. He frowned, then sighed. As a pail of slop for the hogs.

Real attractive.

Why couldn't Gott have given him even a quarter of the charisma He'd given Menno?

When Caleb pulled into the gravel lot behind Judith's Gift Shop, a figure dressed in teal caught his attention. Lydia sat huddled against the door, her arms crossed over her knees, her uncovered head buried in the curve of them. Her long, loose, sun-kissed braid dangled over her shoulder.

Caleb parked the buggy, jumped out, ran over to her, and crouched down. "Lydia?"

"I went to the post office and got locked out." Her voice was muffled. She didn't look up.

"I get to be your hero again, huh?" *Don't milk it.* He stood up straight and reached into his pocket for his keys. His fingers closed around the vampire fangs, instead. He switched hands to check his other pocket. Success.

"Danki." Lydia got to her feet but kept her head dipped. She folded her arms over her chest, as if she were cold.

A glimmer on her chin caught his attention. It dropped, followed by another. Tears? "Are you crying?" Stupid question.

He unlocked the door, then led the way up the stairs and opened the door to her apartment. Followed her inside, then shut the door and trailed her down a hallway to…ach. He stopped and stepped backward.

When she came out of the bathroom, her face looked brighter, but beads of moisture still clung to her eyelashes.

"How long were you locked out?" He shouldn't have stopped at the Millers'. At least Gizelle hadn't been home.

Lydia didn't answer.

"Ach, Lydia." Caleb wanted to hold out his arms. For a brief moment, he imagined doing just that. Imagined her stepping into his embrace. Crying on his shoulder. Him, comforting her.

But with everything so unsettled in his mind, he couldn't. Shouldn't. Wouldn't. He stepped aside.

"Too bad the ice cream date isn't to-nacht." She brushed at her eyes.

Caleb laughed. He couldn't help it. "You were sitting outside shivering, and you want ice cream?"

"Comfort food." She still didn't look at him.

He smiled. "Then I'll make sure you get ice cream, Princess."

She brightened. "I think there's some in the freezer." She hurried past him into the kitchen and pulled open the freezer door. A second later, she held up a small carton of mint chocolate chip as if it were a trophy. "Want a bowl?"

Rosie appeared out of nowhere and jumped up on the counter, meowing.

Caleb smiled. "Looks like Rosie wants some, too."

"Sorry, kitty. Nein ice cream for you." Lydia took two bowls out of a cabinet, then opened a drawer and dug through it until she lifted out an ice cream scoop and waved it triumphantly in the air. She dished some ice cream into both bowls, then peeked inside the carton once more. "There isn't enough left to save." After scooping the rest into both bowls, she tossed the empty carton in the trash, got out a couple of spoons, and handed Caleb a bowl. "I hope this doesn't ruin our appetite for the meal your mamm's preparing."

"I don't think that's possible." Caleb pulled out a chair at the table and sat down. He scooped up a spoonful of the light green ice cream. "Life with you could never be dull, ain't so?"

Maybe he shouldn't have said that. The comment bordered on inappropriate.

Lydia sat down next to him, then took a bite of her own treat. "Peter always called me a ditz. Said my blonde hair took control without warning, making me do clueless things."

Caleb couldn't think of what to say to that. To agree would be unkind. Then again, she *had* run out, hair down, with nein kapp, in bare feet, to the post office, and neglected to take a key.

Her hair was still down. Even in a thick braid, its length nearly reached her bottom. His fingers itched to touch her braid. To feel its softness, its thickness. And maybe use it as an anchor to hold her in place while he kissed her. Deeply, passionately. His body warmed. "You're adorable," he whispered.

That was the safest thing to say. The truth, too. And judging by the big smile that appeared on her face, it was appreciated.

She scooted her chair closer to his, leaned over, and gave him an ice-cold kiss on the jaw. "You truly are my hero."

He could've melted into an ice cream puddle on the floor. Instead, he sat there, grinning. Probably looking every bit like a fool in love.

⌐‿⌐

After the meal, Lydia helped clean the kitchen, despite Bethel's protests, then headed outside with Caleb's sisters to weed the garden. She enjoyed working in the dirt. On the strawberry plants, tiny, hard green berries had already started forming.

Hopefully, Lydia would be invited over for strawberry shortcake later in the spring.

A few minutes ago, Caleb had left with his daed when the Amish grapevine started buzzing about a buggy accident. An Amish neighbor with a phone shanty on his property had delivered the news.

Someone on horseback raced into the circular driveway. Lydia looked up, as did Caleb's sisters.

"It's Caleb," Dottie said, "but that's not Blackberry." She brushed her palms on her apron and hurried out of the garden

Caleb dismounted and ran into the haus. A few minutes later, he came out again, said something to Dottie, and rushed into the barn.

"Kum, Vi." Dottie ran toward the haus. "Mamm might need us."

Nein explanation was offered to Lydia, but she was the newcomer. She didn't know anyone in the community. Should she go inside and see if there was something she could do to help? Or should she continue weeding and stay out of the way?

The weeding won out, until a pair of brown boots stopped in front of her. Lydia shaded her eyes and looked up.

Caleb stood before her, his hand outstretched. "Daed said to take you home. There's been an accident, and…well…." He sighed. "The plans have changed."

"Is there any way I can help?" Lydia brushed the dirt off herself, then reached for his hand and allowed him to pull her to her feet.

"I really don't think so. A motorcycle hit some gravel and crashed about a mile down the road. The bike slid right in front of a horse and buggy. The horse spooked, and the buggy tipped over, injuring the pregnant frau of the driver—and sending her into labor. Daed sent me for Mamm. She isn't a midwife, but she's a doula, and might have to assist with the birth if the boppli comes before the ambulance gets here." He grimaced. "Ambulances, plural. But it's a little late for one of the motorcyclists. The other guy's in pretty bad shape, though."

"I earned my EMT certification in Ohio," Lydia said. Not to brag. She released his hand. "I've even helped deliver a few boppli."

Caleb studied her, clearly thinking. He pressed his lips together. "Okay, then. I guess you could help. But I have to warn you…it's graphic. Kum on."

"I need to wash my hands." Lydia hastened to the pump, Caleb right behind her. He opened a plastic pail and handed her a bar of lye soap. Once she'd thoroughly lathered, rinsed, and dried, she hurried toward the driveway. Toward the readied horse and buggy. But Caleb bypassed the vehicle, going to the horse he'd ridden. He swung up onto the horse's bare back, then reached down and pulled Lydia up behind him.

"I've never ridden on horseback before." She looked down with a gasp. "It's so high off the ground."

"Just hang on tight."

The horse shifted, and Lydia slid a little to the right. She squealed and wrapped her arms tightly around Caleb's waist.

"There you go." He drew in his knees, and they were off.

Lydia squeezed her eyes shut. This was not gut. Not gut at all.

"Hang on. You're perfectly safe."

His chest rumbled with his words. She leaned closer to him, resting her head against his neck. And held tighter, bunching his suspenders, along with his shirt fabric, in her fists.

If it weren't for the tragic accident and the scary horseback ride, she might enjoy this.

14

After Caleb had delivered Lydia to the scene of the accident, he left to return the horse to the farmer he'd borrowed it from, then jogged back to check on things. With every step, he burned with the memory of Lydia's softness pressed tightly against him during the too-brief horseback ride.

As he neared the scene, he looked around for Lydia. She knelt among the weeds along the edge of the woods behind the overturned buggy, where the laboring Ilene rested. Ilene's ehemann, Luke, and an Englisch man who had stopped to help were working to right the buggy again. The vehicle would need some serious repairs. A buggy blanket had been spread over the body of the deceased motorcyclist. Caleb hadn't gotten an identity on him before Daed sent him for Mamm.

The other young man riding the motorcycle was Caleb's cousin Timothy Weiss. A miracle he'd survived. He now huddled on the side of the road, his skin reduced to hamburger, his pants and shirt shredded from skidding on the gravel. Sam Miller, a first responder and paramedic, knelt beside him, checking his vitals.

Graphic. Jah.

Gravel scattered as a truck skidded to a stop behind the overturned buggy. Another first responder jumped from his pickup and raced over to Sam. "Ambulances are en route."

Probably the police, too, but the EMT didn't say that.

Sam nodded as he kept up his quiet conversation with Timothy.

Daed must have driven their own buggy elsewhere, maybe to a phone, to call for a driver, or to notify Timothy's mamm or the family of the deceased. Caleb still didn't know his identity, only that he was a Englisch man. Too young.

Not sure what else to do, Caleb went to help the men trying to right the buggy. The horse, which had broken free, would find its own way home.

Mamm arrived in her buggy. She parked behind the first responder's truck, climbed out carrying a bulging quilted tote bag, and hurried to where Lydia crouched beside Ilene.

They had just gotten the overturned buggy upright again when a police cruiser pulled up, followed by an ambulance. Nothing to do now but step aside. The professionals were here.

Mamm approached Caleb as the EMTs loaded Ilene into the ambulance. "I'm going to the hospital when the driver comes, to wait for news on the boppli. Will you make sure Lydia gets home?" She hesitated. Then frowned. "Wait, that's not necessary. The driver will have to go through town. I'll make sure Lydia gets dropped off."

Caleb looked around for Lydia. She'd climbed into the ambulance with Ilene, and had both of Ilene's hands clasped in hers. Her bowed head told the rest of the story. Caleb's heart warmed toward her even more. She was kind. Loving. Merciful. Given to prayer. Gut with kinner. A gardener. A servant. The "pro" side of her list just got a lot longer.

She looked like a princess, she reigned over his heart, and she didn't act like a spoiled brat.

At least he'd gotten another kiss from her before Mamm had robbed him of the opportunity to take her home. But one kiss— even two—wasn't enough. He wanted more. He still wanted to bury his face in her neck and solve the mystery of her lemony scent. And, if he were honest, he wanted a lot more than that.

He must've hesitated too long, because when his focus shifted back to Mamm, she wore a triumphant smirk. Gut thing she couldn't read his thoughts.

"You don't mind, do you?"

He shook his head. Probably too quickly. But he would see Lydia tomorrow, even if they would be in the company of Gizelle and Menno. Even if Gizelle was his date, and Menno would be the one taking Lydia home. That would have to be enough. "I have things to do. Daed needs me to finish up the chores that were interrupted."

"Are you sure?" Mamm's smirk faded, replaced by a look of concern.

What, had she expected him to argue for the right to be with Lydia? Nein. Mamm was doing him a favor, separating him from a major source of temptation.

"I'm sure. Lots to do. Danki for making sure Lydia gets home."

In his peripheral vision, he saw Lydia climbing out of the ambulance. The hem of her dress slid up a little as she clambered out, showing more leg than was appropriate. Jah, he noticed. She stopped to say a word to one of the EMTs before making her way toward him and Mamm.

"Ilene will be fine." She smiled. "She's in gut care. They might be able to give her something to stop the labor, since the boppli will be premature if it's born now."

"I called for the driver at the phone shanty before I got here," Mamm told her. "She ought to be here soon. I'll have her stop and let you off at Judith's apartment on the way, so that Caleb won't have to take you home."

Caleb shoved his hands into his pockets to keep from touching Lydia's shoulder. The fingers of his left hand closed around the plastic fangs, stored in their sandwich bag, the fingers of his right, around his set of keys to her apartment and Judith's store.

Lydia frowned and looked down at her dress. Slid her hands over her hips, where Mamm sometimes sewed hidden pockets inside her own. She nibbled her lip as her eyes rose to meet Caleb's. "I don't think I have my keys."

A tremor worked through him. He'd be able to take her home and maybe get rewarded with yet another kiss. Two in one day. *Mercy!* And she'd held his hand, too. Snuggled against him on the back of the horse. He'd have enough fodder to keep him awake at nacht for the next two weeks.

Mamm nodded, but her concerned expression had changed into something resembling smugness.

The ambulance holding Ilene drove off in silence, probably because the siren might've scared the horses. Another ambulance had arrived, and Timothy was being loaded inside.

Caleb glanced at Mamm. "Will the driver be coming here, or to our haus?"

Mamm's eyes widened. "The haus. We'd better go."

He'd hitched up the two-seater to Mamm's horse, Shooter.

Lydia sat in the middle of the seat. Okay, he wouldn't argue. Because it meant Lydia would be pressed up tight against his side all the way home.

Lydia sighed in relief when Caleb pulled the buggy into the driveway of his family's haus. Her body burned from such prolonged contact with Caleb—the place where his thigh had pressed against hers, and their arms had touched repeatedly, as he drove. Add that to the memory of her chest being plastered against his back as they'd ridden that horse, and...wow. She was singed everywhere.

An Englisch driver's van waited in front of the haus, and a woman—presumably the driver—stood talking to Vi on the porch. Caleb's mamm jumped out of the buggy. "We'll have you over again soon, Lydia. Hopefully on a less active day. Danki for all the weeding you did. The garden looks wunderbaar." She grabbed her quilted bag.

"Danki for having me," Lydia said as she slid away from Caleb. Finally, a respite from the powerful sensation of skin contact.

Caleb completed the circle and drove out onto the road again, then glanced at her hands, resting demurely in her lap. He opened his mouth, as if to say something, then seemed to think better of it. With a slight shake of his head, he shut his mouth and returned his attention to the road.

Lydia finally collected enough oxygen and space for her mind to function at near-full capacity. "I'm sorry for taking you away from your work. Again."

"I don't mind, Princess." He shrugged. "Time with you is to be cherished."

She glanced at him with wide eyes.

Red crawled up his neck, flooding his face. His hands tightened around the reins.

She looked away as temptation coursed through her. If only she dared to slide closer to him and press herself as tightly against him as she had on the ride to his haus. Maybe he would hold her hand again, or wrap his arm around her shoulders. And—

Gizelle.

Her name had the effect of a bucket of cold water dumped over Lydia's head. She was awful, thinking this way about a man who was taken. Jah, he'd flirted with her, asked her to kiss him. But it was all an innocent joke. He was a tease. And even if she had taken him up on his invitation to kiss him, he never meant it. Because he and Gizelle…

She sighed.

Caleb glanced at her. Then his right hand released the reins and closed over both of hers. Warmth replaced the coldness. She turned her palms upward and clung to him.

Friendship. That was all it could be.

Though she was likely to cry on his wedding day. Because even though she doubted she would ever find herself in the right place or time for another serious relationship, her heart was becoming attached to Caleb.

And he would marry Gizelle, blissfully unaware that another woman had given him her love.

Love? She looked away. Frowned.

But she didn't object when his hand shifted, and his fingers entwined with hers.

Too soon, he pulled into the parking lot behind Aenti Judith's shop. "Wait a second, and I'll help you out." He got down and tied the horse to the hitching post before coming around to her side of the buggy. They held hands all the way to the door. He unlocked it and held it open for her, then climbed the staircase after her. At the top of the steps, he unlocked the door, then turned to her. His hand rose, trembling. Neared her cheek.

"Meeeooooowwwwww!"

The cat's cry was faint but insistent.

Caleb's hand fell away without making contact, to her great disappointment. He turned and entered the apartment. "Rosie?"

"Meeeeoooooooooowww!"

Lydia shut the door, then followed Caleb into the kitchen.

He stopped. Looked around.

"Meeeooooow."

Caleb stepped forward and removed the push-in lid from the trash can. Then he burst out laughing. Lydia came up beside him and glanced down. Inside the bin huddled the scandalized kitten with her tail flicking, a layer of hardened green ice cream plastered to her whiskers and nose.

Lydia giggled.

Caleb reached inside and scooped up the kitten with one hand. He replaced the trash can's lid, then snagged a dishcloth, ran it under the faucet, wrung it out, and used it to wipe at the kitten's fur. Once done, he set Rosie down, rinsed the washcloth once more, and started to wring it out.

Hesitated.

Then turned to Lydia with an impish expression.

She squealed.

And ran.

15

*T*here was really nein choice but to follow her.

Except…except…*except.*

It would end with her in Caleb's arms. With him holding her body against his. Playfully scrubbing her beautiful face, then following it up with passionate kisses, and—

Gizelle.

He tossed the dishcloth on the kitchen counter.

Ach, he wanted Lydia. So much.

A favorite quote of one of the preachers came to mind. "Gott will not allow you to be tempted beyond what you can handle." Caleb sighed. *Lord Gott, give me strength.*

Lydia peeked around the corner. Squealed again. And turned, ready to dash away—a clear invitation to follow.

Gott must think Caleb had nerves of steel. Because he was very close to giving in.

"I need to go." Ach, it hurt to say that. "I'll see you tomorrow." He walked to the door before turning to look at her.

She lingered in the entrance to the hallway she'd disappeared down earlier. The one leading to the bathroom.

To the bedroom.

Caleb's stomach clenched.

She probably hadn't thought anything of it. He hated that he had.

"Do you know what time Menno is coming to take you for ice cream?"

"Um, he didn't say. But sometime after work. I can't leave before then." She started toward him. "Probably about the time you usually kum to do the books."

"I'll have to do them later. Be sure to put the money tray in the safe when you close up."

"I will." She nodded. "But, just so you know...Menno and I, we aren't dating. We're just friends."

"I know." His gaze met hers. "But I am courting Gizelle."

And with that boulder positioned between them, he turned and walked out the door.

⁓

Friday dragged by. Lydia didn't know how she was going to face Caleb that evening, after the way she'd flirted ever so blatantly with him. Never mind he'd flirted back. Her face burned at the mere thought of it. And to-nacht—assuming he showed up—she would be forced to sit across the table from him and Gizelle, knowing she'd held hands with him. Kissed him on the jaw, not once but twice.

All this when she already knew the pain of being the "other woman." Not that she technically was. The Amish man who would ruin her life said she flirted. She'd thought she was just being nice. If she had accidentally misled him, well, sorry. But just because he believed she'd flirted didn't mean she was interested. She wasn't. After all, he was married. With three kinner, and a boppli on the way.

Peter had been her escape. She'd thought that if she married someone—anyone—then *he* wouldn't bother her. He'd have to stop following her. Stop trying to catch her alone, attempting to steal kisses. His frau would have to stop whispering, spreading gossip, about her. And the bishop would have to stop insisting she kneel and confess "trying to ruin" a "happy marriage."

So when Peter asked to court her, she'd agreed. But they weren't in love. Love was supposed to kum. In time.

Then he'd had to go and die on her.

She was left with nein escape.

Until Aenti Judith stepped in.

She couldn't go home again. But once the word got out, she wouldn't be able to stay here. It was just a matter of time. *He* would tell someone, who'd tell someone else, and the rumor would make its way here. Women would eye her with suspicion. Men with raised eyebrows, just like at home—as if she'd been wearing a sign around her neck that read, "*For a gut time, call....*"

Lydia sighed. Now she'd met a man she could care for, but he was taken. She was left the fool.

With nein place to run.

At least he'd had the courage to step back.

What would Gizelle do when Caleb told her Lydia had made a play at him? Would whispers start here even before the gossip from home arrived? Then the flames of suspicion would burn hotter.

Lydia swallowed. Hard.

Her only hope was that Caleb would tell Gizelle he couldn't take her for ice cream, after all. Or that Menno wouldn't show up, because she had nein way of contacting him to call it off. *Gott, please...let nobody kum. I'd rather not have ice cream at all.*

The cuckoo clocks in the store all chimed five. Lydia went to the door, flipped the sign to "Closed," and secured the lock.

Wait. What was she worried about? Menno didn't have a key. If he did show up, she just wouldn't answer the door. She'd go upstairs, figure out how to turn on the TV so she wouldn't hear if anyone knocked, and shut herself in the closet with the doors shut, to read Aenti Judith's instructions by flashlight.

Problem solved.

She quickly straightened the shop and put the contents of the cash register drawer into the safe, then gathered Rosie in her arms and ran upstairs. Locked the door.

And proceeded as planned.

⌒

Caleb assisted Gizelle out of the buggy in front of the ice cream shop. As they approached the restaurant, the door opened, and Menno came outside. "I can't reach Lydia."

Caleb glanced across the square at Judith's shop. "Did you knock?" That seemed like a nein-brainer, but then, Menno sometimes lacked basic common sense.

"Jah, I knocked! I even called the phone. It rings upstairs, ain't so? But she isn't answering." Menno glared in the direction of the shop.

Caleb didn't see any lights on upstairs—or downstairs, other than the security lighting. Had Lydia fallen and broken a leg? Gotten knocked unconscious?

He had to go check on her.

But in so doing, he would have to admit he had a key to the shop. To her apartment.

What else could he do?

Simple explanation—he was the temporary accountant.

For the store, not the apartment.

"Let me go over there. Maybe she just didn't hear your knock."

"Or maybe she's a tease and was leading you on." Gizelle touched Menno's arm. "You deserve better than that."

Caleb bit back his defense of Lydia's character and strode off in the direction of Judith's Gift Shop. Something had to be wrong.

"We'll all go," Menno said, and started off after him.

Gizelle huffed, then hurried to catch up, matching her stride with Menno, not Caleb. But Caleb didn't particularly care. Except that he and Gizelle needed to talk. Soon.

Menno and Gizelle gathered around him as he unlocked the back door of the shop. "I'm handling the bookkeeping for Judith while she's away," Caleb explained, not that anyone had asked. He flipped on the lights long enough to take a gut look around but saw nothing amiss.

He made his way to the back and led the way up the stairs to the apartment. Knocked on the door. "Lydia!"

He could hear the sound of loud conversation, followed by laughter. Was Lydia watching television?

He waited a few moments, then pounded his fist on the door and shouted himself hoarse. Still nein response.

He had nein choice. He reached for the apartment key and unlocked the door.

Menno and Gizelle crowded inside after him, neither one asking how he happened to have a key.

Sure enough, the television blared. Caleb turned it off.

Rosie appeared at his feet and purred as she made a figure eight around his ankles.

But there was nein sign of Lydia. Caleb checked the kitchen. The bathroom, flinging open the shower curtain, with his gaze aimed toward the ceiling. Just in case. The bedroom. Under the bed, though he had nein reason to check there. Menno and Gizelle followed him around, Gizelle picking up items at random and making snide remarks to which Caleb paid nein attention. Where was Lydia? Had she gone out? If so, where? Did she have her keys?

Nein. There they were, lying on the bedside table.

Caleb's stomach roiled.

He flung open the door to the walk-in closet between the bathroom and the bedroom.

Lydia was curled up on the floor against the far wall, sound asleep, an open notebook in her hand, a lit flashlight beside her.

Caleb released the breath he hadn't realized he'd been holding. Went into the closet and knelt beside her.

Someone—either Menno or Gizelle—flipped on the light.

Lydia woke with a start.

Screamed.

Grabbed the flashlight and raised it over her head like a baseball bat.

Swung.

16

*T*he sudden, unexpected bright light blinded Lydia. She was seized with an overwhelming sense of panic. She squeezed her eyes shut and swung at her stalker with the flashlight, her only means of self-defense. Had *he* somehow managed to find her here? In Aenti Judith's apartment?

Wait. This didn't make sense.

The only other person who had a key was Caleb. But he'd never invaded her space uninvited before.

Someone spoke in a muffled voice, and then a strong hand gently encircled her wrist, and removed the flashlight from her grasp. Sparks shot up her arm.

Caleb. It was Caleb. *Breathe. Breathe. Breathe.*

"Turn. The. Lights. Off." Lydia opened her eyes but kept her head ducked.

Another muffled comment.

She reached for her ears and removed the plugs she'd discovered in Aenti Judith's medicine cabinet. Just then, the light went out. Only the dim glow of the flashlight remained. Much better.

She stared at Caleb, who crouched beside her, and then gaped at Menno and Gizelle, standing side by side in the doorway of the walk-in closet. Gizelle smirked and leaned closer to the frowning Menno.

Lydia blinked. Was this a dream? "Where did you all kum from?"

"We were supposed to meet for ice cream, remember?" Menno scowled. "I knocked. Called the shop, too. Why didn't you answer?"

"I was...um, reading." And had purposely left the cell phone downstairs in the shop, so she wouldn't hear it.

Gizelle sneered. "Reading. In the closet. In the dark. With the TV blaring in the living room, and your ears plugged. Jah, most sane people read like that." Could she sound any cattier?

Lydia winced. "I...." But she had nothing to say. Other than confessing she didn't want to go out with Menno and couldn't face Caleb. And both buwe stood here in her closet. Her face burned, and she scrambled to her feet.

"Are you okay?" Caleb stood, too, and rested his hand on her shoulder. His touch singed her skin through the fabric of her dress.

"Fine. I'm...." She rubbed at a spot of moisture on her cheek. "I'm sorry I fell asleep."

"Are your aenti's instructions really that boring?" Caleb bent and picked up the notebook. Thumbed the lower edge, as if he planned to open it.

Her breath caught. *Nein, nein, nein.*

He flicked it open to the first page. His eyes scanned it. He frowned.

Jah, she knew what he read.

Lydia,

There are nein instructions. I am completely confident you'll do just fine running the store if you let Caleb handle the accounting. He will guide you if you have any questions. He has his own business, and my complete trust. The lady who owns the fabric shop, Regina, will handle the internet orders for you. I left her some stock, and she'll tell you when she needs more.

Lydia had read the first several pages, relieved she wouldn't have to worry about remembering a host of detailed instructions, but still afraid she would fail or appear incompetent in front of Caleb. But her fear was tempered with a sense of excitement over having even more reason to spend time with Caleb. She studied his expression, wondering what he thought about the prospect of spending more time with her.

His brow furrowed.

Ach, jah. There was more there, enough to cause the look of concern in his eyes as he glanced at Lydia, then looked again at the fat little notebook.

> *So I will start by saying that I'm glad to offer my home as a safe haven for you. When your father contacted me to ask if you might be able to come and stay, right at the time when we were beginning to make plans for the mission trip, I knew it was God's providence. Your father shared everything with me. Including how he went to the bishop about the married man….*

How much had Caleb read, anyway? Surely, not all that much. Not with him just picking up the book and….

Wait. He was still reading. His frown deepening.

Lydia forced herself not to yank the notebook away from him and slam it shut. She calmly took it. "Danki."

"Shall we go for ice cream?" Menno asked. His expression had evened out to something more accepting. Even hopeful.

Lydia hesitated, searching for a nice way to decline. Found a smile, shook her head, and—

"Comfort food," Caleb whispered. He touched the small of her back.

Right. There was that.

She nodded at Menno. "I need some shoes."

Gizelle and Menno stepped to the side like parting waters, letting her through. Gizelle glared at Lydia as she passed.

Okay, so they wouldn't be friends. Lydia firmed her shoulders. Not like she was going to stay in Jamesport, anyway. It was just a matter of time until the vicious rumors reached this community. Rumors that she ruined secure, wunderbaar marriages.

She cringed, imagining how Caleb would react when he connected what he must've read in the notebook with the gossip he was sure to hear. Matched it with the way she flirted with him. And decided she was indeed what everyone said.

A Jezebel.

She'd known before coming here that she would never marry. Never be courted.

Even so, she'd hoped she would outrun the lies, eventually.

Seemed her fate was sealed.

⌒

Safe haven. The words echoed in Caleb's mind as he settled down in a chair and studied Lydia across the table. He hadn't read all of Judith's note, only enough to confuse him. To pique his curiosity. Why did Lydia need a safe haven? What was the danger she hid from? Try as he might, nothing he could imagine matched up with what he'd observed of her. What he'd been told about her.

Or did it? Because she seemed adamant about not forming any relationships here. Was she hoping that something would work out with a man in Ohio? His heart broke a little. He hated to think she might long for a guy back home. Being attracted to her was trouble for his peace of mind, for more than one reason.

He'd known from the start she was trouble. *TROUBLE.*

Menno dug his spoon into his bowl—a double dip of what appeared to be cookies and cream, or maybe Oreo swirl. Gizelle had ordered a single scoop of strawberry ice cream with chocolate chunks, while Lydia had chosen the chocolate cheesecake swirl.

Caleb had gone with his favorite. Vanilla.

Solid. Dependable. Tried-and-true.

"Vanilla? Really, Caleb?" Gizelle rolled her eyes. "So many flavors, and you get vanilla? How boring."

Caleb merely shrugged.

"Caleb is hardly boring." Lydia pointed her spoon at Gizelle but tempered her defense with her signature smile. "I've never met a more fascinating man."

Never? Not even Peter? Not even whoever it was that she might be holding out hope for?

Caleb's face warmed as Gizelle gave him a speculative glance. Menno raised his eyebrows.

Safe haven. Did Judith Zook consider Caleb to be part of the safe haven she'd planned for Lydia? Funny, because Caleb didn't feel very safe around Lydia. She tied his insides in knots and made him think of sparkles and glitter. Fairy dust. And trouble. Trouble meaning about to upset his well-ordered, perfectly timed gears of a life.

But when Caleb's mamm had first met Lydia, she had said, "Judith told me everything." Lydia had seemed taken aback by the comment. What was "everything"? Would Mamm explain it to Caleb if he asked? Or maybe the answer was hidden somewhere in the fat square spiral-bound notebook whose cover featured a purple dolphin jumping through a sea of colorful waves, The words *To Lydia* written in bold black marker across the troubled waters. The one he could've picked up off the koffee table at any time while visiting Lydia, but hadn't. He doubted he would ever see it again, now that he knew it wasn't what he'd thought it was.

"More fascinating than me?" Menno winked at Lydia.

She laughed. "He uses mathematical equations to build cuckoo clocks."

Menno shrugged. "Caleb always was a nerd."

Ouch. "I had some mint chocolate chip ice cream yesterday." As though that fact somehow made Caleb less nerdy and more interesting. He glanced from Menno to Gizelle. *Stupid, stupid, stupid.* Couldn't he think of anything more intelligent to say? Why was he bothering to defend himself in the first place?

Gizelle leaned across the table to offer Menno a bite of her ice cream.

Caleb frowned. Most people didn't share ice cream unless they were dating, and she hadn't given as much as a taste to him.

Menno shared a bite of his dessert with Gizelle, too. Offered some to Lydia, as well, but she declined with a quick smile and a "Nein, danki." Then her smile flatlined.

Lydia seemed to be making an effort to be friendly and act happy, but something—nein doubt related to the snippet of Judith's note that Caleb had read—had chased away her habitual sunshine. She eyed Menno and Gizelle, who were talking, and Caleb studied her, hunting for a sign she might be jealous of Menno—technically her date—for paying more attention to Gizelle.

He saw none.

But still he scrutinized her, looking for a remnant of her sparkle beneath the dark, gloomy shadows.

Nothing.

They finished their ice cream, Lydia still interacting, albeit with more reserve than usual.

Menno stood up and pulled out Lydia's chair for her. "Are you ready to go home, or would you like to take a walk?"

"Home, if you don't mind. I think I have a bit of an ice cream headache." Lydia stood. "Danki for the ice cream. It was wunderbaar."

Caleb frowned. "Do you have your keys?"

Lydia's eyes widened. She slid her hands over her hips, just as she had done yesterday. She must have some hidden pockets. "Um...nein."

"Then I'll see you home." He turned to Gizelle. "I'll be right back."

"I'll just take her home, if it's okay," Menno offered.

Caleb shrugged, then nodded. He looked at Gizelle. "I'll stop by on my way home. We need to talk." And call the relationship quits. For more than one reason. The top reason being, he didn't need her help figuring out that he was boring. All he had to do was compare himself to Menno.

Or maybe the top reason was simply Lydia.

Either way, Caleb had only been fooling himself, trying to court Gizelle.

Though, he might regret breaking up with her if the worst-case scenario was true, and Lydia wanted to return to Ohio. To someone else. But Gizelle would still find him boring, and who wanted that in a frau?

Gizelle lifted a shoulder. "Don't bother stopping by. I know." She glanced at Lydia with a partial smirk, making her point clear. Then her expression softened as she looked up at Menno.

Wow. Caleb hadn't expected the breakup to go so smoothly. It didn't hurt the way he'd expected it to, either. All he felt was relief.

Lydia started gathering the trash from the table. Menno helped her, and the two headed for a trash can by the exit.

Caleb remained seated next to Gizelle. "I'm sorry," he said quietly. "We're just not suited."

"Nein, we're not."

Caleb hadn't expected Gizelle to agree, but it was the truth.

Gizelle crumpled a paper napkin into a ball and launched it across the room, toward the garbage can. It missed the can. Hit Lydia. Though maybe that had been Gizelle's intention all along, if she thought Menno was interested in Lydia.

Lydia bent down and picked up the napkin. Eyed Gizelle, then tossed it into the garbage can.

"You seriously can't stop staring at her, can you? I don't understand it. She isn't 'all that.' And you're too much of a stick-in-the-mud for someone like her. Besides, Menno finally noticed me, and it's a bit awkward being seen by two buwe at once." Gizelle offered him an apologetic smile.

Caleb only nodded. He wouldn't bother pointing out that when someone agreed to be someone's girl, exclusivism was implied. Because, well, he could turn that reminder on himself. And…wait. She'd noticed him staring at Lydia?

His grossdaedi always said, *If you do a thing, do it right.* Now, Caleb would do it right. With the woman he was attracted to. Not the one he'd misread. And he'd thought Gizelle was too sensible for Menno.

Lydia flirted with him. Teased him. They'd become fast friends. And she didn't seem to find him as dull as Gizelle did. She'd even called him "fascinating." Or had she meant "fascinatingly dull"?

He glanced at Lydia once more. She stood by the door, talking to Menno. Smiling at something he said. But her expression looked polite. Lending credibility to the statement she'd made about their being friends and nothing more.

He could hope. For that, and other things. Like that she would tell him what Judith had meant by the term "safe haven."

And for another kiss.

⌒

Lydia almost bounced the entire way back to the apartment. Even though she'd enjoyed the ice cream, she still wished she hadn't gone out at all. Especially with the scent of rain heavy in the air. The stifling humidity. She eyed the dark clouds overhead. Lightning flashed across the sky.

She shivered and quickened her pace. The cold wind whipped her dress around her knees. Thankfully, she would soon be indoors, and would not have to ride in a buggy for miles. But Caleb would have to. Unless he stayed with her until the storm had passed.

Hopefully, Caleb wouldn't bring up whatever he'd seen in the notebook. She couldn't talk about it. Not to him. Not yet. Maybe never.

"I didn't mean to make things awkward there at the end," Caleb said quietly. "I never should've asked Gizelle to be my girl. She never should've agreed."

Lydia frowned, unsure what he was referring to. Then she remembered Gizelle tossing a napkin at her, along with a glare. And how she had rather boldly grabbed Menno's arm as they'd left the ice cream shop. Had she and Caleb broken up? Must've.

"At least now you know."

Caleb edged a little closer to her on the sidewalk, as if he might want to hold her hand the way he had yesterday. But Lydia felt someone's glare boring into her back. Probably Gizelle. She seemed the type to resent a woman stepping in, even to claim a man she'd discarded. Even if she'd already latched on to another man. If Gizelle ever learned the reason Lydia had left home and kum here, Lydia's reputation would be shredded within a span of twenty-four hours.

She immediately regretted her unkind thoughts. *Lord Gott, please protect my reputation here. And if it's Your will, someday, I'd like to have a relationship with a man as wunderbaar as Caleb.*

Caleb unlocked the back door of the shop, then stepped aside so Lydia could enter. As she did, she took another glance at the sky. Thunder rumbled in the distance. She followed Caleb up the steps to the apartment.

"Glad we made it back before the storm." He inserted the key into the apartment door. "Do you really have an ice cream headache?"

Lydia sighed. "Would it be a sin to admit that I told a tiny lie? I just didn't feel like being with anyone else. Present company excluded." *Maybe.*

"It's a sin to lie, not to admit you lied." He shut the door, then walked over to the koffee table, picked up a notepad and pen, and wrote "KEYS" on a piece of paper. He tore out the note and handed it to Lydia. "Tape this to the inside of the door."

"I meant to do that very thing yesterday." Or was it the day before? She found a roll of Scotch tape in a desk drawer and followed Caleb's instructions. "Are you getting tired of being my hero?"

"Never. But I may not always be able to rescue you, Princess. How long did you sit outside yesterday?"

She shivered, remembering how cold she'd gotten. "I don't know. Too long."

"That's my point." Caleb smiled. "Do you want me to go?"

"Nein." She kicked off her shoes. Lined them up by the door. "I want you to stay."

He hitched an eyebrow and reached into his pocket. Pulled out the toy teeth and slipped them into his mouth. "Should plastic fangs be involved?"

She giggled.

"Do you want a hug?"

Lydia giggled again. "What, you're not going to ask for a kiss this time?"

He cringed. "Didn't mean to ask. Not for the kisses. Not for the hug."

"Are you saying that I make your brain take over your mouth?" she teased.

And stepped into his arms.

17

*L*ydia's comment was probably valid. Or was it that she made his mouth take over his brain? Nein, it was his heart—his emotions, his lust, his desire—that took over his mouth *and* his brain. Controlled his thoughts and his words, especially with her soft curves brushing up against him….

His breath hitched. His nerves shifted into high gear. His heart pounded. He closed his arms around Lydia and held her tight. Lydia, in his arms…ah, heaven. "Asking doesn't work so well. The last time I asked for a kiss, I ended up locked out. Without one."

"Aww, you poor thing." Lydia hugged him just as tightly. But when she started to release him, to pull back, he wasn't ready to let go.

Her citrusy scent teased his senses, and he couldn't resist burying his nose in her neck. Then his lips accidentally grazed her neck. His stomach clenched, and he pretended to be nibbling her with those stupid fangs. That didn't work very well. He wanted more. He wanted….

He yanked the toy teeth out of his mouth, tossed them somewhere over his shoulder, and nipped at Lydia's ear. Moved lower.

She leaned back and squealed.

He trailed kisses down her neck, feeling her pounding pulse beneath his lips. Moved across to the hollow at the base of her neck.

She twisted in his arms, laughing, and shoved his chest. "Caleb!"

He pulled back, not quite releasing her, and swallowed. "What?" His voice was husky. He couldn't keep his gaze from lowering to her lips.

She stilled. Her smile faded. Her laughter died.

"I've dreamed of this moment for five months," he whispered. "Ever since I saw you at Sam and Abigail's wedding, I've wanted to hold you in my arms. Kiss you."

Her eyes darkened, and she leaned toward him. A tiny, almost imperceptible movement, but it was there nonetheless. Her hands grasped his waist.

An invitation, if he ever saw one. He brushed his lips over hers. Pulled back and met her gaze. But the tiny kiss he'd gotten wasn't enough. With the smallest bit of encouragement, he was going in for another pass.

Her lips parted. Her gaze lowered.

Caleb tugged her against him. Lowered his head. And took control.

After a slight hesitation, she kissed him back. She raised her arms around his neck, her hands feathering through his hair, knocking his straw hat to the floor. She pressed against him and made a moaning sound deep in her throat that drove him wild.

She drove him wild.

Kissing Lydia was everything he'd dreamed of, and more. Lights flashed. Skyrockets boomed. And her kisses deepened to a level that rivaled his own passion. Her arms tightened around his neck.

Definitely heaven. He could get addicted to this.

"Lydia...." Her name came out as a groan. He pulled bobby pins out of her hair, careless of where they fell. Tossed her kapp aside. Her heavy braid tumbled, unhampered, into his hand. He grasped it tight against her neck, tilting her head for easier access.

More flashing lights and booming skyrockets.

He wanted more. Had to have more.

~~~~~~~~~

Lydia's knees had gone weak. Who knew kissing could be like this? *Wow, wow, wow.* Gizelle wasn't kidding when she called Caleb a great kisser. But Lydia didn't want to think about how Gizelle might have formed that opinion. Instead, she just kissed him back with everything she had.

She stiffened as his arms tightened around her, lowering her. The softness of the couch cushions met her bottom. At least it wouldn't matter if her knees gave out. She kept going down, sinking into the couch. Caleb's assault on her senses never ceased as his weight pressed upon her. She gasped, internal alarms going off. She tried to silence them, wanting to continue with this totally-beyond-wunderbaar activity, but the wails grew louder, fighting against nature to be heard.

Nature...the thunderstorm. She hated storms. Ever since Peter's tragic death, they had frightened her. She distracted herself once more with Caleb's kisses as they left her mouth and traveled across her face to her ear. Then lower. His hand slid down the length of her braid. She burrowed deeper into his embrace and let him help her forget—

A loud crack of thunder. She shuddered. Whimpered. And not because of Caleb.

He groaned. "Lydia. Ach, Lydia."

Something pinged against the windows. Hard. Steady. Hail?

"Caleb, nein." She pushed him back. "Nein."

He rolled off her and fell to his knees on the floor, breathing heavily.

She couldn't catch her breath, either. Wanted to tumble off the couch and back into his arms. But they weren't married. Would never be married. This was wrong.

The sirens faded, then suddenly increased. A flash of lightning revealed the greenish tint to the sky.

"Tornado." Lydia sat up. Had it been a storm like this one that had killed Peter? Gut thing Caleb had been inside with her, even if....

Nein. What she'd done—allowed—wasn't gut.

Caleb blinked at her. His gaze shot to the window. His eyes widened as they took in the electrical storm. Then he bolted to his feet. "Get downstairs. Does this building have a basement? Ach, my horse!"

❧

Caleb should've figured it would take an act of Gott to stop him from going too far if ever he got Lydia in his arms. And he'd tried so hard, for so long, to be gut. Had long ago stopped participating in the kissing games he used to play when he was fresh in his rumschpringe. Never again, he decided, until he met the woman he planned to marry.

And then...Lydia. Lydia of sunshine and fairy dust. Of glitter and sparkles. Of his every waking thought and nacht-time dream since he'd first seen her five months ago.

If only he could marry her in real life, not just his dreams.

Ach, Gott. Lydia.... Ach, Gott. It was a prayer, a confession, and an apology, all rolled into one.

She was amazing. *Amazing.* And, Lord help him, he still wanted her.

He ran out the back door of the shop. Ice-cold rain and pea-sized hail pelted him as he dashed across the street and down the road to the shop where he'd tied Blackberry. As he approached, he saw the horse stomp the ground and toss his head, then buck several times in succession.

"Sorry, Blackberry." Caleb rushed to untie the reins from the hitching post.

There was a two-car garage behind Judith's shop. Room enough for a horse and buggy, since Judith and Mark owned only one vehicle. But did Caleb dare go back inside the shop to be with Lydia? Or would it be safer to risk his life and head home? He could take shelter in a ditch if a tornado formed.

But his parents wouldn't expect him to return home in this weather. He was already in town. And he needed to make sure Lydia was safe.

"Kum on, Blackberry. Let's get you inside." He drove the buggy through the now-marble-sized hail to the garage, then jumped down and searched his ring of keys. Found one that opened the garage, and directed the horse inside. Then he closed the big door and let himself back into the shop.

He found Lydia in the cellar, where she sat with her knees to her chest on the floor against an interior wall. She'd taken the time to secure her hair and put her kapp back on. Wise.

He dropped down next to her, their shoulders touching.

She shifted aside, putting a Bible's width between them.

That hurt. He hadn't intended to ruin their friendship.

"I'm sorry. So sorry. I never meant to…." He frowned. He *had* meant to kiss her. "I never meant to let it get so far out of control."

18

*L*ydia opened her mouth to speak, but then she closed it again, unsure what she should say. She couldn't bear the thought of his shunning her after her confession. She needed to hold on to her tainted reputation back home for a little longer. Plenty of comments hovered on the tip of her tongue. Like how much she'd enjoyed his kisses, and how she wished she could marry someday, instead of being doomed to spinsterhood and having her life ruined by an already-married man. A man she didn't like and never had.

But when her fiancé had been struck by lightning, the plan of der Herr had been made clear. Nein escape through marriage for Lydia. The bishop back home had interpreted the entire situation from the perspective of Gott. Nein misunderstandings there. His words had pelted her like the hail falling outside, the sound echoing down the stairs and into the cellar where she huddled. *Fallen woman…ruining lives…Jezebel…never marry…kneel and confess.* And then the dreaded "S" word. *Shunned for six weeks following confession.*

She hadn't confessed, because she'd done nothing wrong. But it was her word against the married man who'd hit on her. The man who, when she'd refused his advances multiple times, retaliated by accusing her of trying to seduce him. And the bishop and preachers believed him. His frau, too.

The Bible story of Joseph and Potiphar's wife came to mind.

What if the bishop from back home notified the preachers here? Had Daed even considered that possibility when he'd made the arrangements with Aenti Judith? Lydia hadn't thought of it until now, though she'd expected the gossip to follow her. Eventually.

The punishment was too harsh to bear.

Caleb would find out. She would be shunned until she confessed, and for six more weeks after that.

And even then, her reputation was ruined. Irreparably.

A clap of thunder made her jump. Would nature's fury never cease? How she hated storms, especially since it had been a storm that snuffed out her dreams of escape. If only she'd been there, too, with Peter. Death was the only certain escape. Instead, she'd been here in Jamesport, at a wedding. The same wedding where Caleb had first seen her.

Wait.

Maybe Gott hadn't taken away her dreams of marriage, after all. Maybe Peter wasn't the ehemann He'd had in mind for her.

Could it possibly be that Caleb was the one Gott intended for her? Or had the bishop back home been right? If it was the latter, then pursuing Caleb would be leading him into sin.

And after what had just happened upstairs…. *Ach, Gott.* She was a Jezebel. Her stomach churned.

The lights flickered once, then went out. Lydia whimpered.

Caleb scooted nearer and wrapped an arm around her shoulders. "You're safe. I'm here."

If only. She stiffened, although she really wanted to relax in his arms. How could she begin to know the will of Gott for her, and whether Caleb was a part of it?

"I'm truly sorry, Lydia." Caleb sighed. "I never meant to disrespect you. Honest. Can we be friends still?"

Friends? *Friends?*

"You're kidding, ain't so?" Her heart broke a little. How could they be simply friends? Hopefully, he would still feel friendly toward her after the rumors arrived in town.

Silence for one beat. Two.

"Actually, nein, I wasn't kidding. I want—I *need*—to be your friend."

And I need to be your frau.

⁓

Caleb frowned as the quiet stretched on with nein answer from Lydia. She shivered in his embrace as a roar like a train sounded overhead. Something soft, furry, and warm sought solace on his lap. Rosie. Instead of her usual purring, though, she trembled, like Lydia, under his hand.

Gott protect us. Protect my family and friends, and anyone in the path of this storm....

He wasn't sure how long he prayed, or how long the storm raged, until silence finally fell.

Even then, they continued to sit, huddled together on the basement floor, unmoving. Lydia relaxed against him, her breathing becoming even. Rosie had stilled completely, except for the soft rise and fall of her chest as she inhaled and exhaled.

And Caleb sat, wide awake and listening, though he knew not what for. Maybe a still, small voice from Gott, answering his questions. Quieting his concerns. Making his pathway clear, according to the promise of Proverbs 3:5–6: "*Trust in the* LORD *with all thine heart; and lean not unto thine own understanding. In all thy ways acknowledge him, and he shall direct thy paths.*"

Caleb gently slid away from Lydia, stood up, and picked up Rosie in one arm. With his other hand, he flicked on his penlight and aimed it toward the stairs. He couldn't see much, but he was relieved, as he ascended, to see that the store was still standing. He went upstairs to Lydia's apartment. It, too, appeared undamaged, though they wouldn't be able to see much until daybreak.

He returned downstairs and decided to venture outside to check on Blackberry, expecting to hear him thrashing around in the garage. Hopefully, he hadn't damaged Mark's car.

Caleb took a few steps in the still-falling rain, then gasped and stumbled to a stop. Where was the garage? And where were Blackberry and the buggy?

All he could see was Mark's car, flattened by the tall tree that lay across it. Where had that kum from? It stretched across the back parking lot, and the street behind it, as best as Caleb could tell in the dim light.

Gut thing he hadn't gone home. His buggy would have been reduced to a pile of matchsticks. His horse likely killed. Of course, that could be the case now. But Caleb was alive. *Danki, Gott.* Hopefully, his family had survived, too. But he had nein way of contacting them.

Menno and Gizelle…they *had* headed home. Though Caleb hadn't actually seen them go. Were they safe, holed up in some farmer's barn or storm cellar?

He glanced around at the nearby businesses. Noted the now silent tornado siren that had saved him and Lydia, in more than one way.

Another round of thunder crashed in the distance, indicating the approach of a second storm. Rosie dug her claws into his shirt and clung. He carried her back inside and down to the cellar.

Lydia stirred as the beam of his pen light bounced off her. "Where'd you go?"

He sat down next to her. "Checked on the store. Still standing." That was all he could safely say without further study. He didn't want to worry her about the garage. Especially since the damage was already done. His stomach churned as he remembered his horse. Maybe Blackberry would've fared better outside at the ice cream shop rather than closed up in a garage.

How would Caleb reach Mark and Judith with the bad news in the morgen?

"Gut." Lydia leaned her shoulder against his. He shifted away long enough to free his arm, then reached it around her. She snuggled next to his side.

Gut. They were still friends. Or seemed to be. He would follow her lead.

"Are you in some sort of danger?" he asked, hoping not to offend by being so blunt. Nosy. He probably should've brought up the issue with Mamm or Daed first.

Lydia shifted away from him. "Nein. Why?" There was caution in her voice.

"Judith's notebook. I didn't read much—she has really cramped handwriting I'm not used to—but she mentioned something about this being a 'safe haven' for you."

"Mmm." A noncommittal reply. And…was that a sigh of relief?

So much for getting any of his questions answered.

"Well, I did lose my fiancé."

"I know." But that provided nein clarification as to why this was a safe haven. He would talk to Daed.

"What, you're not going to say you're sorry?" She nudged his side with her shoulder.

He shook his head. "Nein. Because if you hadn't, you wouldn't be here. With me."

Maybe he shouldn't have said that, either. But Rosie purred in his lap, and Lydia snuggled against him again.

⌒

"Hallo!"

Lydia was jarred awake by the shouts and pounding sounds coming from somewhere above her.

Caleb was hurrying toward the cellar stairs before she had gathered her wits about her enough to pull her skirts out of the way.

She struggled to her feet and followed him through the darkness. Still nein electricity. She wouldn't be able to open the store today. But in the wake of a tornado, if Aenti Judith and Onkel Mark were here and not away on a mission trip, they'd be out in the community, doing cleanup, helping with meals, distributing water bottles—whatever was needed.

How could Lydia help? Donate the quilts for sale in the shop? Would Aenti Judith count the loss of income worthy of this disaster?

Lydia was halfway up the basement stairs when Caleb flung open the door, ushering in a bright shaft of sunlight.

Caleb gasped. "Daed?"

A pause. A sob. Then, "You're alive. Praise Gott, you're alive."

Lydia blinked at the brightness, her eyes finally focusing on Preacher Zeke with his arms around Caleb, gently pounding his back with his fists. Tears ran unrestricted down his face.

Several other Amish men she didn't recognize stood with them. "When we found your buggy on the roof of the Weisses' barn, we feared the worst," one of the men said to Caleb.

"On the roof? Nein kidding." Caleb stepped away from his daed. "Any sign of Blackberry?" Tension filled his voice. "And what about Gizelle and Menno? They'd headed home last nacht, I think."

Lydia peered across the parking lot at the Englisch men with chainsaws working on a tree that'd fallen from nowhere and crushed her aenti and onkel's car. It had been parked in the garage—a garage that had been wiped off the map. Would Lydia need to deal with insurance claims? Or would that duty fall to Caleb, Aenti Judith's temporary accountant?

"Nein sign of Blackberry, nor Gizelle and Menno."

"Ach, I hope they're okay," Lydia said.

Preacher Zeke stepped back, his gaze moving to her.

He probably noticed every wrinkle in her dress, every loose strand of hair. If only she could've changed clothes and brushed her teeth. She supposed she could do that now. She glanced toward the stairs leading up to the apartment. "I'll start some koffee."

Except that there was nein electricity. Nein woodstove, either. Nein alternative method of cooking.

Well, nobody had acknowledged her comment, anyway.

She took the kitten from Caleb and went upstairs.

And about cried when she realized the door was locked. So much for her written reminder about the key.

Seconds later, Caleb climbed the steps. He leaned around her and unlocked the door, then brushed kisses across her cheek. "I'll be outside with my daed and brothers, helping." Then he turned and ran downstairs.

Lydia pushed the door open, stepped inside, and shut it behind her. Then surveyed the room.

Nothing had changed. Nein broken windows. Nein missing roof. And yet, at the same time, everything had changed.

She set Rosie down and stepped on a hairpin, her foot feeling a painful jab. She knelt and collected all she pins could find.

Remnants of last nacht's sin. Because even though they'd hadn't gone much further than kissing, they weren't married. And her bishop back home would accuse her of leading a young man astray.

Jezebel.

She found Caleb's toy fangs and put them on the koffee table.

And cried some more.

She took a quick shower—in lukewarm water—and had just put on a clean dress when someone knocked on the apartment door. Her hair was wet, wrapped in a towel. At least nobody could claim her head was uncovered.

She opened the door.

Preacher Zeke stood there. "Can I bother you for a glass of water?"

"I'm sorry for not making koffee. I couldn't, because—"

He held up his hand to silence her. "I know. Don't worry. Water is fine."

She nodded. "Please kum in." And turned to walk to the kitchen.

Caleb's vampire teeth snagged her attention. Would his daed notice them? Kum to a wrongful conclusion about what had happened here between them?

She stumbled but forced herself to keep going. Stopping to move the fangs out of sight would only draw attention to them.

"Are you doing okay?" Preacher Zeke asked as he followed her into the kitchen.

He'd been one of the two preachers who'd approached her to inform her of Peter's death. This wasn't the first time he'd seen her in shock.

He watched her take a glass out of a cabinet, walk over to the freezer, and push the lever to dispense ice and water.

Nothing came out.

She glanced at him. He didn't appear judgmental. Instead, he studied her with a look of apparent concern.

"I'm okay, jah." But her hand shook. Had Aenti Judith told him as well as Bethel? Was he judging her, even now? Caleb's toy teeth on the koffee table…him spending the nacht, albeit on the cold cement floor of a dark, spooky basement, while a tornado whirled overhead….

Lydia took several ice cubes from inside the freezer, dropped them into the glass, and then filled the glass with tap water before holding it out to the preacher.

"Danki." Preacher Zeke accepted the glass. "You know, if you ever need to talk, I've been told I'm a gut listener."

He knew. He must know.

Then again, Dolly had said her parents wanted Caleb to marry her. That wouldn't be the case if they had, in fact, heard the rumors.

That would kill all their matchmaking plans. Maybe Lydia should tell him.

Though she really didn't want Caleb to know. Ach, the shame. How had Joseph held his head high while suffering wrongfully in prison for the same thing?

You must have done something to lead him on.

If only she knew what it was that she'd done, she would never do it again.

Preacher Zeke drained his glass and set it on the counter. "The roof needs repair." He pointed toward the ceiling. "We'll take you home to stay with us for a few days, until the roof is fixed and the electricity is back on."

"Ach…uh, I'd hate to put you out. Maybe I could stay with Abigail, instead." It'd be nice to see her best friend. Talk over her latest problem with her.

Preacher Zeke's gaze was steady. "Newlyweds? Trust me, you shouldn't stay there. We have plenty of room. A whole empty dawdi-haus if you want some privacy. The girls have more than enough clothes to share, so you won't need to bring much."

"Just the cat?" Lydia forced the question past the lump in her throat.

"The cat, jah. And anything else you can't live without. Personal items." The preacher smiled. "We'll be glad to have you, Lydia. Bethel has wanted to kum out here with the girls and spend a day with you. This way, she can take care of that at home. It's important to her, you see, to…." He broke off his statement with a shake of his head.

But she knew what he was going to say. *Get to know the woman her sohn will marry.*

"I'm not going to marry Caleb."

There. Now the unspoken words were out there. Flat. Expressionless. Plain. A statement of fact.

"I was going to say, it's important she get to know you."

Ach. Her face warmed.

Preacher Zeke turned to go. "Pack what you think you'll need for a few days. We have plenty of cat food. And dresses. And people food." He glanced over his shoulder and winked. "And don't forget Caleb's vampire teeth. He might need them."

19

The men sawed the tree into pieces they then loaded into various vehicles. Because of the strong wind that still gusted, the Amishmen had removed their straw hats and stowed them inside their buggies or in the back room of the shop.

Caleb tossed the final log in the back of Daed's farm wagon. His brother Thomas covered the crushed car with a tarp to protect it from further water damage until the insurance adjuster could kum and assess whether it was salvageable or had been totaled. Thankfully, the insurance issues weren't Caleb's responsibility. Mark's brother, Anthony—also Mennonite—would take care of the claim. He was already there, snapping pictures with his smartphone of the crushed car.

Caleb's other brother, Isaac, had climbed to the shop roof to evaluate the extent of the damage. Shingles had been torn off and scattered all over town, not only from Judith's shop but also from various other local businesses. Someone else was on the roof of the ice cream shop, securing a tarp over an apparent breach.

Not seeing anything else he needed to do, Caleb went inside the store to check on the windows. They were in gut shape with nein visible cracks or breaks. He found a piece of paper and a bold marker, wrote a note explaining that the store was closed due to storm damage, and taped the note to the front door.

Daed came inside and looked around. "Everything okay in here?"

Caleb nodded. "Appears to be, jah."

"I saw your vampire teeth on the koffee table upstairs." Daed checked the safe, making sure it was locked. "Care to explain what's going on?"

"I...uh, I broke up with Gizelle."

Daed nodded. "And decided to act on your infatuation with Lydia?"

Caleb swallowed. Hard. Time for honesty. "Nein, not exactly. I am senseless, off in den kopf, where she's concerned. I want to be gut. I try, so hard, to resist the temptation she presents. I can't explain why she gets to me so much. I only know something about her intrigues me in a way I've never experienced with any other girl. It isn't all physical. I want to know—have to know—everything about her. And nothing but time spent with her will solve the mystery."

Daed sat on the stool behind the cash register. "I know you asked a lot of questions about Lydia before she came to Jamesport. You met her in December at Sam's wedding, ain't so?"

Caleb nodded, swallowing the bile that rose in his throat.

"Your mamm said she heard you followed Lydia around like a besotted pup, asking everyone about her."

Caleb hated the term "besotted pup." But it was a fairly accurate description. He'd stayed perfectly at heel with Lydia. "She doesn't remember me. Likely a gut thing." He would've scared her away, stalking her the way he had. He disliked the word "stalking," too.

Daed chuckled, but then he frowned. "You said she tempts you. How so? You also told me she was trouble. What has she done to give you these impressions?"

"Nothing, other than being her sweet self. I mean, she teases me sometimes...flirts...but I tease and flirt with her, too."

"'Nothing'? Just normal bu-maidal behavior?"

Normal? Caleb considered the question further. "I suppose. I mean…." He rubbed his chin. "Jah, some of the youngies act like that around each other. I haven't since before I joined the church." Hence his reputation for being a stick-in-the-mud.

Should he confess to Daed that he'd kissed her last nacht? Confess that he probably would've done so much more than that if a tornado hadn't ripped through town?

Nein. This conversation was uncomfortable enough.

"I've invited her to stay with us for a few days. Until the power in the apartment is restored and the roof has been fixed."

Caleb's stomach clenched. He glanced up, startled, anxious, and excited all at once. *Lydia, at the farm. In his home. For a few days.*

This could be bad. Very, very bad.

Mamm, Daed, and his sisters, all getting a bird's-eye view of how senseless he became around Lydia. Could he pretend she didn't affect him? Keep things friendly between them?

He had nein choice but to try.

⌒

Lydia packed a tote bag of items she considered essentials, then filled a plastic grocery bag with the bottle of white chocolate raspberry creamer and the partially consumed gallon of milk she'd bought. Onkel Mark's brother had told her not to worry about the rest of the food in the refrigerator; he was going to take it home with him for now. It belonged to Onkel Mark and Aenti Judith, anyway. Probably needed to be used. And until Lydia mastered the nein-longer-working electric appliances, it wouldn't be.

Someone knocked just outside the apartment. Lydia set the bags on the koffee table and went to open the door.

Caleb. His eyes didn't quite meet hers. "Ready?"

"I guess."

"Got your keys?"

Did he have to sound so brusque? He appeared just as horrified as he'd been when he walked into the shop on Monday and said, "You!" Like it was a bad thing. Like *she* was a bad thing.

Though maybe he didn't want her at his home any more than she wanted to be there. After all, he already regretted kissing her. He wanted to be just friends. And she…well, she must've tempted him, somehow.

She had. She'd kissed him on the cheek. Twice. And she'd given him a hug at his request. That had pushed him over the edge. His daed never would've invited her to his home if he knew she was such a Jezebel.

"Look, why don't I just stay here? I'd rather that, really. I know how to survive without electricity, and…."

He stepped past her. Snatched his toy teeth from the koffee table and shoved them into his pocket. Then walked to the hallway leading to the bathroom, the bedroom. Moments later, he reappeared with her keys dangling from his fingers, Aenti Judith's colorful notebook in his other hand. "You'll have time to read this." He tucked the notebook in a side pocket of her tote, then tucked her keys into the same pocket with the plastic teeth.

Read it? More like hide it from prying eyes. Worry about her secrets coming out. She'd only started to read it, then had cried herself to sleep in the closet. Was that just last nacht? She'd read enough to feel the condemnation afresh with the reminder of her accusation.

Going to stay with Caleb's family was a bad idea. Finding someone else to manage the shop, and leaving town while the getting was gut, was a better plan. For how could she stay here, acting as if everything was normal, when her world was falling apart at the seams, and the material was beyond mending?

Ach, Lord…help me.

But why expect Gott to help her when she didn't meet with His approval?

Caleb picked up her tote bag by the handles, then eyed the plastic bag holding the milk and koffee creamer. He frowned. "We have plenty of milk. And cream. We keep dairy cows, remember?"

"I know." Lydia nodded. "It's just…they might spoil while I'm gone."

Caleb sighed. Then took a final look around. "Guess we're ready to go, then. Get your shoes on. Where's Rosie?"

Lydia fought back the tears that burned her eyes. "Look, I don't like this situation any more than you do. I just haven't found a way to avoid it. I promise not to bother you. To stay out of your way as much as possible."

His answer was a dark, brooding look that contrasted starkly with the kiss on the cheek he'd given her when he'd unlocked the apartment for her only an hour or two ago. That morgen, she'd awakened in the cellar, snuggled in his arms. What had happened in the light of day to change his mind?

He carried her bags out the door.

Rosie appeared out of nowhere, gave Lydia a baleful glare, and ran after him, her tail high.

Wow. Even the cat despised her.

⁓

Caleb found Rosie's carrier in the back room of the shop, and put her inside. As he stepped out into the daylight, he glanced at the sky to make sure there wasn't another storm brewing. The memory of the tornado's sound, like a train hurtling down a track—so loud that it masked the screams of his horse—made him shudder.

He rearranged a few of the logs in the back of his wagon to make room for the cat carrier. Finally, he stashed Lydia's bags at the very bottom so they wouldn't blow off in the strong wind.

That left Lydia. And one very narrow seat for her to sit in, between Caleb and Daed.

Not that Caleb minded.

And therein lay the problem. How could he keep it "just friends" with Lydia when he wanted to be much more than just friends with her?

Maybe he should admit it. Accept it. To himself, to Daed, to Mamm, to his sisters. To the world at large. He loved her. Loved everything about her. And, jah, he wanted to marry her.

Except, he was still afraid of himself. Terrified of making the same mistakes he'd made before. Scared of the fairy dust surrounding Lydia, and everything it represented. Her curve appeal, and all *it* represented. Her beauty....

Though she'd already proved herself in other areas. She was smart, except when it came to math. He himself wasn't very skilled at dissecting Englisch words. Everyone had different gifts. She was caring. Helpful. Loving. Considerate. He could list complimentary adjectives all day long. Or adverbs. Whatever they were.

But she exited the store with the twinkle all gone. Her shoulders were slumped. "Preacher Zeke, I appreciate your offer, but I think—"

"I would worry too much if you were here alone, with a leaky roof and the possibility of more storms, of greater severity, coming in."

"More storms?" Alarm flickered in her eyes. But then she firmed her shoulders. "I'll be fine. Really."

Caleb swallowed. He wasn't sure whether he would rather she kum stay at his home, with him and his family, or remain here and remove his greatest source of temptation, at least for a few hours. Because he would make frequent trips into town to check on her.

"Nein, Lydia. Your daed would want to know you're taken care of. I'm going to have to insist."

She nodded. Tears beaded on her eyelashes. But she stiffened her shoulders even more. Raised her chin. Her demeanor screamed, *"I'm obeying because I have to, not because I want to."*

Caleb held out his hand to help her into the wagon, but she ignored him and clambered into the seat on her own. Then folded her arms across her chest, and bowed her head. Submissively.

Or maybe she was praying.

Daed's eyebrows shot up as he studied her. Then he glanced at Caleb, one eyebrow hiking even higher, if that were possible.

Caleb shrugged. There wasn't a lot he could say. She'd already voiced her objections. Was she afraid of him? Had her fear of the storm temporarily overcome her fear of his passion, and now, with the storm having passed, she was prepared to avoid him?

He'd apologize again if he had to. But he wasn't willing to just let go. Her touch had become as necessary as breathing.

He settled in next to her, noticing with some satisfaction that his thigh rested against hers.

She'd be forced to acknowledge him. Especially when Daed flicked the reins, and the buggy turned sharply onto the road. She fell sideways, against Caleb's chest.

He wanted to grab her and hold on tight.

But she righted herself.

"Bethel will really enjoy spending time with you," Daed said. "Getting to know you,"

Lydia nodded. But Caleb somehow sensed her withdrawing further.

He didn't know how to halt the process, other than to pray she'd return to being her happy, sunshiny self by the time they reached his home.

And to somehow get his hands on her aenti's colorful little notebook, and learn the secrets of Lydia concealed therein.

20

*L*ydia squeezed her shoulders inward, trying to keep from touching Caleb, and his daed. She didn't want either of them pointing fingers of accusation when they learned of her reason for coming here. Right now, everybody believed she'd kum to manage the gift shop in Aenti Judith's absence. While there was some truth to that, there was a lot more to the story.

She knew it did her nein gut to sit between these two upstanding men and sulk. She needed to get over herself. Preacher Zeke had been right when he said Daed would want to know she was being taken care of. Daed had sent her here for her own protection, and that was the reason she would remain here—for now. That was probably the rationale behind Daed and Mamm's prayers while they decided whether to stay in Ohio with her younger brothers and sisters or to move the family to Jamesport and be with her.

They might as well stay put. She missed them, to be sure, but it was just a matter of time before news reached Jamesport.

And then she would leave.

Caleb leaned a bit closer to her, as if he were so in tune with her emotions that he somehow sensed she needed comfort. If only she didn't.

The road, as well as the surrounding fields and even the trees, were littered with tufts of insulation, pieces of siding, and other miscellaneous building materials that had been splintered beyond recognition. She wondered how Menno and Gizelle had fared. And Caleb's horse.

At the sight of a pickup truck lodged in the branches of a tree, Lydia blinked to be sure she wasn't hallucinating. How would anyone even begin to get that truck down without wrecking it? Despite the truck's precarious location, it appeared mostly undamaged by the twister. And what about Caleb's buggy, sitting safe and sound on the roof of a barn?

The voice in her head was quiet yet insistent: *We are hard-pressed on every side, yet not crushed; we are perplexed, but not in despair; persecuted, but not forsaken; struck down, but not destroyed.*

Lydia shivered, not accustomed to having Bible verses kum to mind with nein warning.

Daed had quoted 2 Corinthians 4:8–9 to her before she'd left home. Whispered it in her ear again mere moments before she boarded the bus. Whenever he wrote her a letter, he would probably include it. Or ask Mamm to remind her.

A wave of homesickness washed over her. She would give anything to have her mother's arms around her right now, to see her father's kind smile and feel him kiss her forehead as he quoted the verse yet again. *We are hard-pressed on every side....*

She fingered the strings of her kapp. There was nothing to stop her from praying now, but she didn't know how or even what to pray. Would it be selfish to ask that although she felt as helpless as that pickup truck stuck in a treetop, Gott would somehow uphold the promises of the Scripture passage Daed had quoted so often? That she would be hard-pressed but not crushed. Perplexed, but not in despair. Persecuted, but not forsaken. Struck down, but not destroyed.

Ach, Lord, if it be Your will, please, let it be so.

Trust Me.

Again, the answer came out of nowhere. But peace eluded her. Staying with the preacher and his family—Caleb, in particular—would mean trouble. She was bound to do something wrong. Or the gossip from home would make its entrance. Or something.

She turned to Preacher Zeke with a forced smile. "Danki for taking me in. I look forward to spending time with your family, too."

Preacher Zeke glanced at her. Raised one eyebrow, as if questioning whether she really meant it.

Well, she had gotten into the wagon in a sulky mood, as if they were dragging her away against her will. Nein wonder he suspected her shift in attitude.

She did mean it. Sort of. She loved Caleb's family already. It was just that she feared her past catching up with her. Feared the inevitability of Caleb and his sweet family discovering she had been accused of trying to seduce someone else's ehemann.

Her breath caught, and she nearly choked on air. Her eyes watered as she coughed violently, multiple times, trying to resume her normal breathing.

Caleb rubbed her upper back, which helped a little.

When Bethel had stopped over on Lydia's first evening in town, she'd said, "Judith told me everything."

Did "everything" mean, well, *everything?*

If so, then both Bethel and Preacher Zeke knew about the rumors and the lies, and they were welcoming her into their home, anyway.

Of course, the strong possibility remained that Bethel didn't know what she thought she knew. And if that was the case, then Lydia still needed to watch her step. She would keep a lookout just to be safe. The fruit of the spirit was too deeply engrained. *Love, joy, peace, longsuffering, kindness, goodness, faithfulness, gentleness, and self-control.* Well, most of them. Peace had gone on an extended vacation.

Gott, help me.

Caleb's arm settled around her shoulders in a loose hug.

If Preacher Zeke had responded to her comment, she hadn't heard him, lost in thought as she'd been. But he didn't seem to mind her failure to reply. A small smile played upon his lips as he drove the wagon. A smile not unlike the one on Caleb's mouth. Both men were very similar in their mannerisms.

As the buggy entered the circular drive at the Bontragers' haus, Lydia squared her shoulders.

Both men glanced at her. "It'll be fine," they said in unison.

She giggled.

If only she could share moments like this with Caleb's family forever, by his side.

⌒

Caleb hadn't quite worked out the logistics of Lydia's stay when they arrived back home. Should he treat Lydia as a friend to avoid the uncomfortable teasing? Or should he act toward her as he would a future frau, so his family would *know?* The latter option might help him get used to the idea, and to bury the past, once and for all.

Would burying the past include confessing to Lydia and his parents all the horrors he'd been involved in during his rumschpringe? Or could he leave the past in the past, dead and buried?

Was he overthinking all this again?

Probably so.

"Whoa." Daed pulled back on the reins with both hands, directing the horse, Shooter, to stop in front of the woodpile. The horse tossed his head the same way Blackberry often did. Caleb's heart ached at the reminder of his missing steed.

The door opened, and Mamm stepped out of the haus, her left hand wearing an oven mitt, her right hand clutching a wooden. "Caleb! Praise Gott. Are you okay? And—ach, Lydia!" She rushed down the porch steps and across the yard toward the buggy.

"I'm fine," Caleb assured her as he helped Lydia down. "So is Lydia. I stayed in town last nacht with her."

Daed jumped out of the buggy. "Judith's shop lost electricity and needs a new roof, so Lydia will be with us for a few days. I knew that would be alright with you." He moved around to the front to unhitch Shooter. "I figure the dawdi-haus would suit well. Close enough for her to be a part of the family, yet with the option of privacy."

"Perfect." Mamm gathered Lydia in a tight hug. "I'm so happy you're here."

"Wow. At least I know how I rank," Caleb teased.

Mamm stepped back from Lydia and smacked his hand with the spoon. "You hush. You know better."

Caleb grinned. "I'll put Lydia's things in the dawdi-haus." He went around to the back of the wagon and reached for Rosie's carrier. "Cat in the haus or the barn?"

"Barn," Daed said.

"Haus," Mamm replied simultaneously.

Caleb chuckled.

"She's used to being inside." Mamm glanced at Daed.

He shrugged. "Listen to your mamm."

Lydia eyed the wagonload of wood. "How can I help?"

"Kum on inside. We're getting dinner ready. You can clean the asparagus. First of the year."

Caleb's stomach rumbled. He loved asparagus.

"Today's the birthday of Birdie Hilty, our married dochter. But she and Aaron won't be here for dinner, since they live in Indiana, where Aaron's from. We always celebrate, though, with or without her." Mamm smiled. "Of course, we're also celebrating Caleb's survival of the tornado, your visit with us, and all the firewood Gott provided. Lots of reasons to celebrate today."

Caleb unearthed Lydia's two bags from the back of the buggy, balanced them in his other hand, then started toward the dawdi-haus. "Open the door for me, Lydia, please?"

Lydia nodded, but Mamm said, "I've got it." They both trailed Caleb to the small attached haus, and Mamm opened the door.

"Where do you want these?" He nodded at the carrier, the plastic grocery bag, and the tote bag.

"Put them in her bedroom, of course." Mamm shut the door, then turned to Lydia. "If I'd known you were coming, I would've readied this place for you. It's clean, but it needs new curtains, and fresh linens and a quilt on the bed."

"Ach, it's fine as it is," Lydia said.

Caleb glanced at his mamm. "Upstairs or down?"

"The one downstairs isn't really a bedroom." Mamm smiled at Lydia. "It's more of an enclosed porch with a pull-out couch. We used it the final years of Daedi's life, when he couldn't climb stairs anymore." She looked at Caleb again. "Put her upstairs, in the big, sunny front room."

He nodded, then went upstairs to the rooms Lydia had declined to see on her tour of the dawdi-haus, all because she thought he would share them with Gizelle. *Danki, Gott, for sparing me that.*

"Yellow curtains," he called down from the landing.

"Yellow?" Mamm's voice carried up the stairs. "Who says it's your decision?"

"Anything is fine, really," Lydia assured her.

Caleb put the tote bag on the bare mattress, then set the cat carrier on the bedroom floor. He didn't let Rosie out. Unless Mamm rethought the whole indoor-cat thing, he would have to go back to town and retrieve Rosie's litterbox from the apartment.

He headed downstairs. "She said she wanted yellow curtains. The evening I showed her the dawdi-haus, she talked about yellow curtains. And jonquils in a vase on the kitchen table. And sunflower throw pillows in the living room, with yellow curtains to match." He smiled at Lydia. "She didn't mention how she would decorate the bedroom, though."

Lydia's face flamed an alarming shade of red.

Mamm stared at him as if he'd grown a set of horns.

He merely shrugged. "At least I was listening, ain't so? And if this is going to be her home—"

"Temporarily." Lydia twisted the fabric of her apron in her hands.

"—she should have what she likes." Caleb strode into the kitchen, daring to dream of seeing what a twirling Lydia had envisioned the other nacht kum to life. He'd liked her ideas, too. Nein need to mention to Mamm that if Lydia truly became his frau, the changes would be made. Mamm knew it. And he knew, beyond a shadow of a doubt, Mamm's ultimate goal. She'd made it more than clear. Daed had, too, though he tended toward caution when voicing his opinions, and took time to listen to Caleb's worries.

"Then yellow it is," Mamm said. "I think I have a sunflower quilt already made. Throw pillows, too. I was going to take them to the mud sale, but you have an immediate need of them."

Caleb grinned as he went outside and headed over to the farm wagon to help Daed unload the logs they'd collected. As Caleb hefted one that would need to be split into fourths so that the wood could fit into the stove, he glanced at Daed. "We didn't bring a litterbox for Rosie."

Daed nodded. "Guess the cat will end up in the barn, then, at least until the next time we go to town. We do have a couple of litterboxes we use for training the kittens, though. I suppose we could clean one out for Rosie to use."

"I'll take care of it after dinner." Caleb put the big log on one side of the pile, then went back for another.

"What's your mamm up to?"

"Mentally redecorating the dawdi-haus. Expect it to be finished by tomorrow."

Daed laughed. "What's the plan?"

"Lots of yellow."

"Guess that settles the color of the mums she plans to plant." Daed grabbed another log.

Caleb rubbed his chin. "Mums?"

"For your wedding."

"My wedding?" He looked up.

Daed winked. "She believes in planning ahead."

"Is that where I get it from? The desire to have everything planned out, lined up in neat columns, ready to go?"

"From your mamm? Probably in part, but I suspect you got it more from me. My side of the family. Your großeltern. You kum by it honestly." Daed tossed the log on the pile. "Just remember, love should be like a rubber band that stretches and gives. You can't insist on following a blueprint. Love can't be explained in mathematical terms." Daed smirked the way he had the other nacht. "Lydia is...what some might call 'flighty,'" Daed said. "Spontaneous."

Caleb nodded. Not to mention forgetful, spur-of-the-moment, yet surrounded by glitter and fairy dust.

And that reminded him.... "Judith mentioned something about this being a safe haven for Lydia. Do you know anything about that?"

⌒

Lydia couldn't keep from smiling as she followed Bethel through the door connecting the tiny kitchen of the dawdi-haus to the big kitchen in the main haus. The darling little abode would be hers for a few days.

In the Bontragers' kitchen, Dolly was carrying a stack of stoneware plates to the table. "Lydia! You're back!" She let the plates fall with a clatter on the tabletop. "Nothing broke!" she pointed out with an apologetic grin at her mamm.

Lydia returned the girl's embrace. "I'm back for a few days, jah."

"Gut! You can listen in to the kitties' bedtime story to-nacht."

Lydia smiled. "I'll bring Rosie. She's probably missed that."

Caleb's sister Bethlehem rolled her eyes as she worked on slicing a pie. Such an interesting name. She must've been named after her mamm, or maybe she had a Christmas birthday. Vi stood at the sink, peeling hard-boiled eggs, while Dottie cut a chicken apart. Potatoes simmered on the stove.

Bethel turned to Lydia. "Do you know how to clean asparagus? I was planning to pan-fry it, but since we're grilling the chicken, it makes more sense to grill the asparagus, too. If you don't know how, you can finish preparing the pies. My Birdie doesn't like cake. She always requested molasses pie for her birthday. So I am making a few."

"That's an understatement," Bethlehem muttered. "Five pie crusts. Hope you like molasses pie, Lydia."

"I was mixing up the filling when you arrived." Bethel held up the wooden spoon, then handed it to Bethlehem. "You take over mixing the batter, and then ladle it into the piecrusts. I'll check the grill."

As the door closed behind Bethel, Vi turned to Lydia. "You didn't answer. *Do* you know how to clean asparagus? I know some people don't eat it."

"I know how." Lydia gathered up the stalks and carried them over to the sink. "I've never had it grilled, though. Mamm always boils it."

"Ach, grilled is my favorite way to eat it." Vi put the table knife down and ran water over the eggs and rinsed them, then picked up the knife and started cutting them in half, as if preparing to make deviled eggs. "Why are they putting you in the dawdi-haus? I'm surprised you aren't sharing a room with us. We have an empty bunk."

"Your daed said something about privacy." Lydia began rinsing the asparagus.

"Jah, so Caleb can court her instead of Gizelle," Dolly put in.

Lydia's face heated, especially when the other three sisters turned to look at her. Appraising her. Likely wondering how she would fit into their family.

"Caleb and I aren't courting." She ducked her head, focusing on the asparagus, not Caleb's gossipy sisters. If these girls were anything like her own sisters, they would be relentless in their teasing. She'd make sure to thank Gott—and Preacher Zeke—for the privacy of the dawdi-haus. She'd likely need it, staying here. In fact, she would like to retreat there right now.

"Nein, but he's in serious like with you." Vi wiped her hands on her apron, then touched Lydia's arm. "We've known it since December. Mamm says Caleb's infatuated."

Infatuated. That was a fitting label for the way she felt about him.

"Girls." Preacher Zeke's voice boomed from behind Lydia. "Your brother and Lydia are just friends. I don't appreciate your gossiping about their relationship. Right now, we need to focus on making Lydia feel welkum in our home."

"Jah." The four sisters nodded.

Lydia glanced over her shoulder, hoping to communicate a silent "danki" to Preacher Zeke. But it was Caleb's gaze her eyes met.

He winked.

She looked away, her stomach filled with flutters.

21

*F*inally, Caleb would get some answers. His heart pounded as he followed Daed into the living room. Daed paused by the small round end table beside his favorite chair and removed a trifold paper from the big German Bible, the one they kept at home and in which they recorded births, marriages, baptisms, and deaths.

Caleb didn't see the point of keeping a Bible that wasn't used for church or Bible study. He used his personal Bible at least twice on a daily basis. Some days, more often. Though he supposed if he ever needed to track his family tree, the big keepsake Bible would be a gut place to start. And it might eliminate the need to consult the elusive *list* everyone referred to that kept track of who was related to whom, and how. Someone who didn't know the identities of his cousins, or second and third cousins, would find it useful.

Caleb knew who his cousins were. He'd grown up alongside his extended family, on both sides of the tree. And neither Lydia nor Gizelle was related to him.

Daed unfolded the page. His eyes moved from right to left as he read. Then, without a word, he handed the note to Caleb.

A thrill of excitement worked through Caleb. Now he would discover Lydia's secrets. He'd find out why it was that she needed a safe haven. He inhaled a shuddery breath.

To whom it may concern:

I have asked my sister, Judith, to take in my dochter, Lydia, for a time. Judith has agreed to employ Lydia as a shopkeeper while she is away on a mission trip. Lydia needs a safe place to stay, though she has done nothing wrong. She recently lost her fiancé, who was tragically killed, and our bishop came down pretty harshly on her as a result, making some outrageous claims.

Caleb frowned. Maybe the bishop of Lydia's home district had been acting under the influence of an undiagnosed brain tumor, as the former local bishop had done for a while.

We thought it would be gut for her to visit with her best friend, Abigail Stutzman Miller, in addition to helping at the gift shop. This setup may end up being permanent, if our family should choose to move to Jamesport.

I appreciate your understanding in this matter, and humbly ask that you do all that you can to make Lydia feel welkum in Jamesport.

Sincerely,
Edward Hershberger

"It doesn't tell us anything." Caleb's hopes deflated. His pulse calmed. It'd be wunderbaar if Lydia could stay here permanently. Except.... "What were the 'outrageous claims' the bishop made?"

Daed looked pensive. "This is the letter Judith presented when she approached us, the preachers, about Lydia. At that time, we were going through a lot as a community—destruction in the wake of an ice storm, the passing of the bishop...." He took the note back from Caleb, opened the Bible, and thumbed through it, stopping in the book of Psalms. He flipped a few more pages.

Nein. Caleb's heart skidded to a stop. Maybe it was mere coincidence Daed had opened the Gut Book to Psalm 51.

"We discussed it. Decided to extend grace and let her kum here, for a time. The inquiries I've made have revealed nothing but gut things about Lydia, as you likely were aware." Daed tucked the letter back inside the Bible. "But I haven't been able to reach her home bishop. Yet."

Caleb nodded. He'd made similar inquiries about Lydia, albeit probably not as discreetly. Had gathered that she was kind. Considerate. Loving. Merciful. And that was just the beginning of a long line of complimentary adjectives. Or adverbs. Whatever they were. He figured he couldn't fault her lack of math skills when he himself struggled with something as simple as parts of speech. He wouldn't know a superlative if one were to join him in the clockmaking shop.

"But Mamm said that Judith told her 'everything.'" Caleb glanced toward the kitchen, making sure none of his nosy sisters was eavesdropping. Or, worse, that Lydia wasn't standing right behind him.

"Ach, you know how women gossip. They probably discussed how the poor bu died, the details of his funeral—such as who attended and who didn't—how deeply Lydia mourned, and how they wanted to find her an ehemann while she was here. I think you can guess their top choice." He gave a small grin. "Though I don't hear you objecting too loudly."

He didn't object at all. Well, except for his past mistakes, and how they tended to blind him, to predispose him toward poor decisions. He sighed. That was a pretty big objection.

But the idea of being married to his sunshiny girl, with her glittery fairy dust…. The sparkles, the twinkles, the magic of getting lost in her arms and making love to her….

He sucked in air, shut his eyes, and lowered his head. Hopefully, Daed didn't notice the desire—the lust—that probably appeared in full bloom in his expression.

Daed closed the Bible with a thud. The Bible. *The Psalms....*
"If you need to talk, Sohn, I'll be in the barn."

Caleb cleared his throat, hoping his voice would sound
normal. That it wouldn't be obvious he was disconcerted by the
way Daed had deliberately gone looking for a particular chapter
in Psalms as a home for the letter from Lydia's daed. "Should we
ask Lydia why she needs a safe haven?"

"Ach, I'm sure the topic will kum up." Daed's hand closed on
Caleb's shoulder, squeezed gently, then released it with a slight
pat. "On her timetable, not ours. When she's ready, the conversation will happen." Another pat. "I'll be in the barn."

Why did Caleb get the sense they weren't talking about
Lydia anymore?

Caleb raised his head and looked to see if Daed had left. He
had. Caleb opened the Bible to the book of Psalms. Daed had
aligned the top edge of the letter just beneath the chapter heading. *Psalm 51.*

Caleb swallowed the fear that rose in his throat, threatening
to spoil his appetite.

It was a fluke. It had to be a fluke. There was nein way....

But somehow, Daed knew.

⁓

As she stood at the sink cleaning asparagus, Lydia felt a
gentle touch to her upper arm. She glanced over her shoulder.
Preacher Zeke smiled at her. "If you ever need someone to listen,
I'm available."

Her breath lodged in her throat.

Then the preacher turned and strode outside. She watched
through the window as he headed for the barn.

Should she...? Was he implying...?

Nein.

Fear engulfed her.

And she was stuck here until the roof of Judith's Gift Shop was replaced. Until the electricity came back on.

Did Preacher Zeke know? Or did he just want her to think he knew?

The contents of her stomach rose to meet her breath. Combined, they did a wunderbaar job of cutting off oxygen.

Vi leaned closer. "What was that about?"

Lydia glanced at her. She couldn't answer—not with her life hanging in the balance somewhere between choking and smothering.

Caleb was next to enter the kitchen. He gave her a wide-eyed look, and his skin had paled. Did he know, too? Was his delayed judgment about to begin? Without a word, he went outside and followed his daed to the barn.

Lydia turned off the water and stared at the dripping-wet asparagus. Should she continue helping prepare for a birthday dinner that might not be a happy one? Should she follow Caleb outside for the inevitable discussion with Preacher Zeke? Or should she feign a headache and hide out in the dawdi-haus?

Breathe. Breathe. Breathe.

⌒

Caleb found Daed not in the barn but in the clockmaking shop. He'd picked up the cuckoo clock Caleb hadn't finished and now concentrated on stringing the weights through the hole at the bottom of the base.

"I meant to do that the other day." Caleb pulled out the drawer where the hour hands were stored, selected one, and then did the same with the drawer of minute hands. Then he sat on a stool and eyed the clock Dottie had painted with a pattern of royal blue flowers sometime yesterday.

Daed worked in silence. Nein doubt a technique he'd picked up from one of the police officers who'd kum out to investigate all the crimes that had occurred in the community over the past year. *Wait until the guilty party confessed.*

Memories collided in Caleb's mind. That night in the apartment…a candle burning in the smoky dark…the agony of fighting temptation until he had nein fight left…. He had resisted her for as long as he could, but in the end, nature proved too strong. Or his faith proved too weak. Or maybe God was too demanding.

Anger boiled up within him. The words tumbled out, an avalanche of confessions he half heard. Tears burned his eyes. Tracked down his cheeks. Dropped off his chin.

Struggling to compose himself, he pushed off the stool and strode to the window.

"It was never supposed to happen. She wanted a listening ear. She left the Amish, left me, and married him. He gave her diamonds. Gold. I'd planned to marry her, you know. We courted. But I couldn't offer any of that. She was sparkly and happy. Glittery and sunny. Like Lydia."

Daed kept his eyes on his work. "Mmmm."

Thankfully, he didn't remind Caleb that he'd been only eighteen when he'd courted Molly Graber. Not yet old enough to know his own mind.

"Two years later, her ehemann was deployed, so he sent her home to be near her family. But she was virtually shunned. Alone. Her family was ashamed she'd married an Englischer, a soldier, and that she'd left the faith. She turned to me, for someone to talk to. We used to be friends, ain't so? I…I only wanted to be a friend. I told her so. I didn't want anyone to get the wrong idea. She assured me nobody would. But…a hug has the power of starting a man down a slippery slope. And the next thing I knew, I woke up in her arms. In her bed."

Hadn't Daed warned him about Molly's flightiness? The illusion of light that drew him in as a moth to flame?

Not unlike Lydia. Did Daed see the similarities as clearly as Caleb?

Guilt riddled Caleb like so many bullets. He was a paper target, worthless against the power of his own hunting rifle.

"I'm so sorry, Daed. I've tried to be gut enough since then. I gave up all the kissing games at the frolics. I stopped courting. Only occasionally do I take a girl home from singings, if she doesn't have another ride. I've turned into a 'stick-in-the-mud,' to quote Gizelle."

"Gott isn't too demanding, Sohn. You're human. You sinned. And He offers grace and forgiveness. Freely."

Caleb shook his head. "But Satan's tempting me again, with Lydia. He knows I'm not strong enough. He knows I'm attracted to her. He knows she's a lot like Molly. That's why I asked Gizelle to be my girl. Because she's nothing like Molly. Nothing like Lydia." He raked his fingers through his hair, knocking his hat off center. "Nothing like what I want."

"And you think Gott wants you to be unhappy because of your past?" Daed grunted. "I've said this before, Sohn: What if the life you want, and the future Gott has for you, is hiding in your biggest problem, your worst failure, your greatest fear?"

Caleb sighed. "I joined the church, Daed. I've tried to live right. I'm still not gut enough."

"Nein. And you never will be, on your own. But only through Jesus. For Gott so loved the world—including you—that He sent His only begotten Sohn. He knows what you've done, and He's ready to forgive you. To accept you, in Jesus's name. I know what you've done, and I forgive you for not living the way I raised you. I still love you. I still accept you."

Caleb gazed out the window, across the yard at the haus. His shoulders shook with shame. With longing.

"What if Gott is waiting for you to stop trying to be gut enough, to confess your sins, and to accept His grace…His forgiveness…His mercy? In Ephesians, it says, '*For by grace you have been saved through faith, and that not of yourselves; it is the gift of God, not of works, lest anyone should boast.*' We aren't saved by being 'gut enough,' Caleb. Nor by joining the church. Only by grace."

More tears followed those that had already coursed down Caleb's cheeks. He turned away from the window.

He remembered when Daed had started attending a series of verboden meetings. Prayer gatherings. Bible studies. And then he came home one nacht with a smile and a statement: "Everything has changed." If only Caleb had listened to him then. *If only.*

He staggered across the room and fell on his knees at his father's feet. "Daed, I want to believe. Help my unbelief."

22

*L*ydia was still suffering from stress-induced lack of oxygen when Bethel came inside with a platter of grilled chicken and set it on the table, then went back outside to grill the asparagus. All for a feast in honor of a dearly loved—and dearly missed—member of the family.

Would Lydia's parents celebrate her birthday, even in her absence? Maybe Mamm would make a pizza with all her favorite toppings, a side of tossed salad, and cherry cheesecake for dessert. Lydia's stomach rumbled loudly.

Vi giggled. She must've heard it.

"Pardon me," Lydia muttered, her face heating.

"I'm hungry, too." Vi grinned. "Want to go to the barn and tell Caleb and Daed that dinner's ready? We'll finish up the preparations."

Lydia nodded. She slipped her shoes on and stepped outside. The air was muggy, and the leaves hung upside down on the trees—an indication of imminent rain. A strong wind blew, lifting Lydia's skirts probably high enough to reveal her knees to anybody who might be looking. With her forearms, she pressed the material against her legs to keep it from billowing immodestly.

When she entered the stifling barn, a horse's whinny breached the silence. Somewhere among the stacks of straw, a cat meowed. Lydia paused in the dim, dusty entrance and peered past the buggy that was parked nearby. Nein movement. "Preacher Zeke? Caleb?"

A scratching sound came from somewhere. A bleat. Another whinny. And then a dark form flew past her ear.

She squealed and jumped back. Was that a bat? She stared up into the darkness where it had disappeared.

Nein use. Whatever it was, it had vanished.

"Preacher Zeke?" she shouted. "Caleb?"

Still nothing, except for the noises of the livestock. And a *scritch, scritch* coming from the loft above. Another bat? Or maybe a mouse?

Perhaps Preacher Zeke and Caleb had gone to the workshop. Lydia exited the barn, hurried across the gravel driveway to the outbuilding, and, with the help of a gust of wind, opened the door. It banged against the exterior wall before she could stop it. The lamp in the room illuminated both men as they knelt by the workbench. At her noisy entrance, they turned to look at her.

"Sorry." She smiled sheepishly. "I didn't mean to let the door slam."

"Quite all right." Preacher Zeke nodded. "Pretty windy out there."

That was an understatement.

Caleb's eyes were bloodshot, as if he'd been rubbing them. Or crying.

Was he upset over the breakup with Gizelle? He'd seemed to take it well, but maybe he'd just put up a front for Lydia. Of course, it probably hadn't helped that she'd turned around and tempted him beyond what he could bear.

"May we help you?" Preacher Zeke raised his eyebrows expectantly.

She sucked in a breath, her own eyes burning. "Ach, dinner's ready." She fled without waiting for a response. Raced across the driveway to the dawdi-haus, up the porch steps, and through the unlocked door. Collapsed in a heap on the kitchen floor and tried to focus on breathing.

Privacy. Jah, she needed it.

But Lydia couldn't give in to her longing to hide out, have a gut cry, and punch a pillow a time or two. Later would have to do. She was expected at the dinner table. Expected to smile, speak, and otherwise interact with her hosts.

She pulled in a shuddery breath. *Gott, I need help. I…I need You. I suppose it'd be better to confess now and not wait for the gossip to catch up with me, but I don't want Caleb and his wunderbaar family to know the truth.*

Not right now, at least. Later. Ruining a birthday celebration, even if the guest of honor wasn't present, didn't seem like a gut idea.

Besides, how could she *confess* anything, really? She'd be going in on the defensive. It hadn't worked when she'd tried to explain everything to the bishop back home. She'd hoped for protection. Instead, she'd gotten accusation, judgment, and curses.

She got up from the floor, straightened her skirts, and washed her face. When she returned to the kitchen of the main haus, she saw candles glowing in Mason jars at either end of the table. A bouquet of dandelions graced a vase in the center. Lydia smiled. The flowers reminded her of home, and of her youngest sister, Phoebe, who often collected the centerpiece flowers for Mamm. A wave of homesickness welled up within her. She would write another letter to her family to-nacht. Mamm and Daed would worry when they heard about the tornado.

And they would hear. The Amish hotline crossed state lines quicker than a high-speed train.

Dottie carried glasses of ice water to the table, while Vi set a koffee mug at both Preacher Zeke and Caleb's places. She looked at Lydia. "Will you want koffee with the meal?"

Lydia shook her head, not wanting to explain her addiction to fancy koffee. She'd rather go without. Well, unless she ended up with a headache from caffeine withdrawal…. "Water's fine, danki."

Lydia surveyed the bounty adorning the table. In addition to the grilled chicken and asparagus, there was a plate of deviled eggs, a bowl of mashed potatoes topped with melting pats of butter, a bowl of grilled corn cobs, a basket of crescent rolls, and assorted crocks filled with home-churned butter, jams, jellies, pickled eggs and beets, and chow-chow.

"Did you tell them dinner was ready?" Bethel asked.

Lydia looked at her. "Jah, I did."

"Did they say they were coming?"

"I…I don't know. I guess I didn't wait for a reply. But I'm sure they heard me."

"Want me to go call them?" Dolly asked.

The door opened then, and both men entered. They took off their shoes and lined them up by the door, then took their seats. "We washed at the outside pump," Preacher Zeke explained. "Shall we pray?"

The women all scurried to the table and settled in their seats. Lydia ended up on the bench beside Caleb again.

She bowed her head.

Gott, get me through—

Caleb's warm, callused hand closed around hers on the bench, erasing all coherent thought.

⌒

That evening, after a heavy rain had cooled the temperature by ten degrees or so, Caleb approached the dawdi-haus with his hand full of pebbles to toss at Lydia's bedroom window. But he saw a lantern light glowing in the kitchen, so he dropped the small rocks on the porch and tapped on the door.

A moment later, the door opened. Lydia tilted her head at him. "Caleb?"

He glanced past her, at the tablet of paper and pen on the kitchen table. "Writing a letter?"

"Jah, to my parents. I want to let them know I'm alright. They'll worry when they hear about the tornado."

Caleb reached into his pocket for his cell phone. "Why not just call them?" He extended the device to her.

Lydia shook her head and giggled. "I'm too dumb for smartphones."

Caleb chuckled. "Me, too. This isn't a smartphone. But I can enter the number and hit 'send,' if you'd like. May I kum in?"

A look of discomfort crossed her face. "Won't your parents mind?"

He cringed. She was probably thinking of how he'd taken advantage of her the previous nacht. "I doubt it. With nein curtains or shades, they can see right in. Not to mention, there isn't a lock on the adjoining door." He nodded that direction. "Not as bad as being alone in your apartment." He averted his eyes and shuffled his feet. Alone in another apartment where a hug had started him down another slippery slope.

"Ach, okay." She opened the door wider. "Kum in."

He shook his head. "Never mind. I came to ask if you wanted to go for a walk. But you should call your family first, so they won't worry. I'm ready when you are."

"It's for the phone in our barn," Lydia said, and then she recited the number.

Caleb typed in the numbers, then hit "send." When the ringing started, he handed the phone to her. "I'll wait outside."

She nodded. Her pink tongue peeked out, moistening her lips. Against his will, his gaze dropped, and a surge of longing raced through him. He shut his eyes.

"Daed?" Her voice caught on a sob. "It's Lydia."

Caleb shut the door and sat down on the top porch step.

A few minutes later, the door to the main haus opened. The porch floorboards creaked beneath the weight of the booted person who approached.

Daed sat down beside Caleb. "Everything okay?"

"Jah. Just waiting while Lydia uses my cell phone to call her parents. Didn't want them to worry that she'd been injured or killed by the tornado."

"That was gut of you."

"I...uh...asked her to go for a walk. Just a walk." It was important to him that Daed know his intentions.

"I trust you." Daed patted his back, then stood.

That was the thing, though—he shouldn't be trusted. He couldn't trust himself.

"I'll pray for you, but you'll be fine. And I'll be in the workshop, if you want to talk when you get back."

Caleb nodded. But he didn't have anything more to confess, beyond last nacht with Lydia. And Gott had stopped him in time. He'd apologized, both to Gott and to Lydia.

Daed strode off across the yard. Moments later, Dolly burst out the door. "Hi, Caleb. I'm going to tell the kitties their bedtime story. You can kum listen, if you want. Bring Lydia."

"She's on the phone right now."

"That's okay. I'll wait a few minutes." Dolly dashed across the drive and disappeared into the barn.

Caleb wasn't sure how much time had passed when the door to the dawdi-haus opened. He stood, intending to turn, but Lydia came alongside him and stood on the top step. Tears ran down her face as she held out the phone to him.

"Is everything okay?" Caleb took the phone and slid it into his pocket. He wanted to reach for her, take her in his arms and kiss all her tears away, but he somehow forced his hands to stay still.

She wiped her eyes, but the tears kept coming. "I didn't know how much I missed them. I thought it was nein big deal, that'd it be gut to get away. That...." She gulped.

And then she stepped forward and wrapped her arms around him.

⌒

Lydia tucked her fingers around the straps of Caleb's suspenders and held on tight as tears coursed freely down her cheeks. She knew she shouldn't have kum outside. Should've stayed inside until she'd regained composure. But the appeal of finding comfort in Caleb's arms had been too great.

Caleb stiffened for a moment, then awkwardly patted her back once, twice. And then, blessed relief, he flattened his hand on her lower back and pulled her tightly against himself. Warmth flowed through her. She seemed to absorb his strength, his comfort. She molded herself to his body as his other hand came around her, and he held her close with a gentle sway, the way a mamm would rock her crying boppli.

Her grip on him tightened as she cried on his shoulder.

He brushed kisses across the top of her head.

After a while, the dampness under her cheek caught her attention. She released Caleb long enough to wipe her face once more. "Sorry." She reached up, planted a quick kiss on his prickly jaw, and patted the wet spot on his chest before stepping back. She teetered a moment on the edge of the porch.

Caleb looked over her shoulder and made a strangled-sounding noise.

Fear rippled up her spine. Had *he* followed her here from Ohio?

Something bumped against her back. Then another something. She gasped. Lost her precarious balance on the edge of the top step, and fell backward.

Caleb grabbed her by the arms, stopping her from falling.

She looked up and saw the tossing head of a horse.

The horse whinnied. Bared its teeth. Dipped its head.

Was it going to bite her? In the face? She screamed.

Her vision swam.

And then the world went black.

23

Caleb lifted a limp Lydia in his arms to carry her inside. He turned around, surprised to see Mamm standing on the porch.

Mamm stepped forward. "I'll hold her." She sat in the bench swing and held out her arms.

Caleb laid Lydia next to Mamm, with her head on her lap, and swallowed his shallow argument that Lydia was *his* responsibility. That he wanted to take care of her.

She wasn't his girl.

With Mamm handling his top priority, Caleb summoned a smile and went to his horse, still standing at the base of the porch steps. "Blackberry! Where'd you kum from?" He wrapped his arms around the animal's neck in a hug. Not quite as satisfying as hugging Lydia, but it would have to do for now. Besides, his horse had returned. Alive. Hopefully unharmed.

That was the next thing to do—check for injuries.

"Get me a damp washcloth, please," Mamm said to someone.

The screen door slammed.

Caleb turned and saw the entire family gathered on the porch. They must've kum running when they heard Lydia scream. His sisters were in their nacht-gowns and robes, their long hair woven into braids that hung over their shoulders.

"What'd you do to her, Caleb?" Dolly sounded indignant, as if she really believed Caleb had hurt her.

Caleb patted Blackberry's nose. "I guess she was startled by the horse."

"That wasn't a startled scream." Dolly planted one fist on her hip. "Don't lie to me, Caleb."

"Dolly, that's enough," Mamm said. "Her iron is probably low. Some girls deal with that at certain times of the month."

Caleb's face heated. He returned his attention to the horse.

Blackberry's harness must have kum off in the tornado. Either that, or someone had taken it off him. Caleb checked his pockets for a treat he could offer, such as a sugar cube. His fingertips grazed a piece of horehound candy. He wasn't sure whether horses could eat hard candy, but they would probably be tempted by it enough to be led into a barn.

"Caleb, wait." The screen slammed shut again. He turned, and Bethlehem handed him a slightly shriveled Jonathon apple. Then she gave Mamm a damp washcloth.

Lydia stirred.

"Shh," Mamm whispered, pressing the cloth gently to Lydia's forehead.

Caleb forced himself to turn away. A walk wouldn't happen. Not to-nacht. But maybe he could sit with her in the dawdi-haus and talk after he'd taken care of Blackberry. If not, there was always tomorrow.

Daed followed him to the barn, and into Blackberry's stall. Caleb patted the horse and rewarded him with the apple, and then he and Daed made quick work of checking Blackberry for injuries.

"He threw a shoe." Daed lowered the horse's left hind leg. "But I don't see anything else amiss."

"Me, neither." Caleb wiped his hands on his pant legs. "I'll get him some food and water. What a blessing he's unharmed."

Daed nodded. "God is gut."

Caleb smiled at the expected response, but he didn't chime in with the refrain "All the time." Instead, he left Daed in the stall to groom Blackberry while he went to retrieve some food and to fill the water trough.

Then he hurried to the haus. And Lydia.

⌒

Lydia lifted her head from Bethel's lap, sat up, and glanced around at the gawking faces of all the female members of the Bontrager haus-hold. Dottie handed her a glass of ice-cold lemonade.

"Are you feeling better?" Bethel asked, offering her the cool, damp washcloth.

Lydia nodded, even though her head still swam. She wiped her face, feeling slightly revived.

"My Birdie always needed more iron at certain times of the month. I'll plan an iron-rich meal for tomorrow. Maybe liver and onions, with spinach."

Lydia's face burned. She couldn't believe Bethel spoke openly of women's issues. At least there were nein men within earshot. She'd blamed her loss of consciousness on the sight of a horse baring its teeth at her when she had nein way of escape. Some horses did bite. One of Daed's snapped at her every time she went near him. He'd even bitten her arm once. It'd hurt. And this horse had gone straight for her face.

Should she correct Bethel's assumption? Maybe not, or she might end up admitting her fear of a stalker. And that would broach a topic she wasn't at all ready to discuss.

She hadn't noticed any blood on the washcloth. She wiped her face again, just to be sure. Relief filled her when the cloth remained clean. She took a sip of lemonade.

"Go on to bed, girls. Lydia's fine." Bethel shooed her dochters inside. She glanced at Lydia. "Do you need help getting ready for bed?"

Lydia stared at her, wide-eyed. Then she cleared her throat. "Uh, nein, but danki. I should be able to manage."

Bethel picked up the washcloth and stood. "I'll leave you alone, then." She glanced toward the barn, and Lydia followed her gaze. Caleb came out of the big doors and headed toward the haus. "Tell Caleb he can do his courting right here on the porch swing," Bethel added. "It's nice and cool, and you probably shouldn't go for any walks to-nacht."

Lydia glanced at the windows of the main haus. All of them wide open. That explained how Bethel had known he'd asked her to go for a walk. Lydia tried to remember if he'd said anything embarrassing, but she couldn't. "We aren't courting."

Bethel waved her hand dismissively. "Ach, you will be, as soon as he comes to his senses."

"Mamm. Please." Caleb stopped at the bottom of the steps and gave a nervous chuckle. "My senses are just fine."

Bethel rolled her eyes. "Jah, and that's why you asked Gizelle to be your girl." She disappeared inside, muttering to herself.

"You okay?" Caleb approached Lydia but stopped about a foot away from her.

She nodded. The wooziness had subsided almost completely.

He glanced at the open window. Grimaced.

Lydia stood. "I feel better."

"Gut. Do you want to walk down to the pond?"

She nodded. Then shook her head. She really shouldn't tempt him. She hadn't meant to in the first place, but….

She shouldn't have cried in his arms earlier. She wiped her hands on her apron, opened her mouth to apologize, then glanced at the open window. Bethel was probably listening in.

"Your mamm suggested you stay on the front porch." It was safer there. They would refrain from hugging and kissing. She wouldn't be able to tempt him too far.

He chuckled again. "Jah, but she knows I won't. I don't need Mamm telling me what I should've done differently." He hesitated. Frowned.

"You haven't done anything wrong." The out-of-control kissing had been her fault. She'd tempted him. And yet he was the one who'd apologized. Taken the blame.

He shrugged. "If you feel like walking, the pond isn't too far. Probably a half mile, tops."

She tested her balance by taking a couple of cautious steps. Then she quickened her pace. She felt fairly steady. "Jah. Jah, I do. I think."

"The grass'll be wet. How about I grab an old horse blanket from the barn for us to sit on? We'll need to be careful, though. The bank will be muddy, the rocks slick."

Maybe they should go inside the dawdi-haus, then. Lydia glanced in that direction. As she did, her eye caught the movement of curtains being dropped over a window of the main haus.

Bethel was definitely spying.

Probably Preacher Zeke, too, since he'd never kum in from the barn.

If they'd heard even a part of the rumor that she'd seduced a married man, they probably wanted to keep a close eye on her.

But then, she'd been alone with Caleb on multiple occasions. With their apparent approval.

Lydia was utterly confused.

She should try to find out what they knew—if anything—so she could decide how to proceed.

Caleb started down the steps.

Lydia shrugged. Then hurried to catch up with him.

⌒

Caleb strode into the barn and grabbed an old blanket from the back of Mamm's buggy.

On his way back out, he passed Daed standing near the door, stroking the fur of the mama cat, who purred in his arms. "Don't stay out too late, Sohn."

"We won't. I'm taking her to the pond beside the school. We'll be in plain sight. Plenty of other youngies hang out there." He tucked the blanket under one arm and carried it outside.

He wasn't sure if his words had been intended to earn Daed's trust or to voice a silent plea for help in staying on the right path. Maybe both.

Lydia stood in the middle of the driveway, playing with the hem of her apron.

He wanted to reach for her hand but didn't want to hear the comments Mamm would surely make about it. He knew she was watching, just as surely as Daed had been doing.

Even though the pond was close by, it was far enough away to make it difficult for Mamm and Daed to spy on them. The area was in plain sight of the road, but nobody else was around, either at the pond or on the volleyball court at the school. Probably because everything was still fairly damp.

Caleb spread the blanket on the grass, then sat down and held out his hand to help Lydia. She grasped his hand and lowered herself gracefully, keeping to the other side of the blanket. He could still hold her hand…if he stretched his arm as far as it would go.

Not gut enough. He scooted closer to her, then lay back, his arms folded behind his head, and stared up at the sky. Too overcast for stargazing, but the clouds made interesting shapes as they drifted in front of the not-quite-full moon.

Lydia sat stiffly. As if afraid he would attack her if she dared loosen up.

He sighed. "I am sorry, Lydia. Can you forgive me?"

Her head lowered. "It wasn't your fault. I'm the one who hugged you. And…and I did it again, today."

"Hugged?" His breath lodged in his throat. Surely, Daed hadn't told her what he'd said—that a hug could start a man down a slippery slope. That was Caleb's story to confess to her. Someday. When the time came for them to be honest about such things, because they were getting serious.

Okay, he was serious now.

But he wasn't quite ready to confess everything to her.

She gave a slight nod, dipped her head further, and resumed fiddling with her apron hem. "I tempted you. Even the innocent kisses on your cheek were wrong. I'm sorry for misleading you. I'm not looking for a relationship. I don't want one. All we can be is friends, and friends don't go around hugging and kissing."

Ach. Relief that Daed hadn't told her warred with anguish that she wanted to keep things friendly. But she had told him as much before. Warned him that she didn't plan on staying here. Except that her daed's letter had mentioned the possibility of the family's moving here. Didn't Lydia know about that? He sighed, trying to keep the pain at bay. "Holding out for someone back home, huh?" He held his breath, dreading her answer.

There was a slight gasp. Then silence.

His heart broke.

24

*L*ydia opened her mouth, ready to correct Caleb. But she shut it again without answering when movement across the pond caught her attention.

A man. And a woman. Amish, given the shape of their clothes. But all she could see were dark figures.

They didn't appear to have noticed Caleb and her. In fact, they must have assumed nobody was watching, for the man reached for the woman, and the two figures merged into one.

Lydia glanced down at her lap and sighed. How she wanted to be part of a couple someday. Before Peter died, she'd had the impossible, unrealistic dream of starting over with her true love—not that Peter hadn't been her true love—in Jamesport, near her best friend. She really needed to visit Abigail soon.

"Is there anything I can do to help you forget him?" Caleb's voice was low. Broken. Filled with pain. "To convince you to pick me instead?"

Lydia blinked. "Huh?" She turned to face Caleb, but he was gazing skyward, so all she could see was the silhouette of his clenched jaw. "Forget whom? Pick you for what?"

He hesitated one beat. Another. "You mean, you're *not* holding out for a man in Ohio?"

"Nein! What gave you that idea?"

"Why won't you even consider being in a relationship with me? Do you find me boring? Like Gizelle does?" He shifted to a sitting position.

Lydia reached for his hand, intending to clasp it. When he entwined his fingers with hers, it made her heart race.

"Nein, Caleb. You aren't boring at all. You fascinate me. You're wunderbaar. But...." She swallowed. She didn't know how to tell him about what had happened at home.

Just spill it.

Easier said than done. What if he condemned her? He would condemn her, nein doubt, if he remembered their tryst in Aenti Judith's apartment. She said it again, with another sigh: "I tempted you."

"Tempted? Jah. Jah, you did. But only because I...I.... Ich liebe dich." His face reddened. "I realize it's too soon to say it, but it's true. It's been true ever since I first saw you, at the wedding in December. My heart stood up and took notice. It shouted, 'There she is! She's the one.' I know you don't remember me. It's fine. You'd gotten bad news and were in shock, but I followed you around the whole evening. Listened to your every word. Quizzed your aenti Judith and your best friend, Abigail, to learn as much about you as I could."

He couldn't be serious. His whole speech sounded rather... unbelievable. Unreal. Inconceivable. Lydia frowned. "Then why'd you ask Gizelle to be your girl?"

"Because I didn't think I was worthy of a beautiful, sparkly princess like you. Besides, if I married a girl sprinkled with fairy dust, I'd probably get glitter in my beard. Not sure how that'd look."

Lydia giggled, but disappointment quickly took root in her heart. He wasn't serious, then. "I'd love to see you sprinkled in glitter." If only what he'd said were true. That he loved her.

Wanted to marry her. It'd be possible only if his parents didn't know the lies being spread about her, and if they approved.

She needed to find out the extent of the "everything" Aenti Judith had shared with Bethel.

"Does that mean you'd marry me?" His voice still had a light-hearted, teasing tone, as if he weren't serious.

She tried to see his face to confirm her impression, but it was too dark.

Lydia glanced across the pond for another glimpse of the lip-locked couple, but they were gone. She hadn't seen them leave. Maybe they'd spotted her and Caleb sitting here, talking, and had gone someplace more private. Or maybe they'd simply become invisible in the gathering darkness.

Lydia leaned toward Caleb and, with her most playful tone of voice, whispered, "I'd marry you in a heartbeat."

And she would, if she could.

Unfortunately, she couldn't.

Besides, he wasn't serious.

Not to mention, reality would cause their dreams to crash and burn.

Caleb scooted nearer to her, wrapped his arms around her shoulders, and hugged her close. He brushed a series of kisses across her cheek, down to the corner of her mouth. He lifted his hand and gently turned her face toward him. Then he cradled the back of her head as he took full advantage of her parted lips, wiping away all her unspoken objections. He claimed her mouth with confidence rather than the unsure, tentative exploration he'd kissed her with the first time—well, at least at the beginning. Now, his kisses were as hot and passionate as the final ones in Aenti Judith's apartment. Kisses that ignited a hunger deep inside her.

She wrapped her arms around his neck and pressed her body against his. She would never get enough of this. Never. He tasted of koffee, licorice, and desire. A muffled sound rose in her throat, born of need. Want. Every thought faded until all that remained was Caleb, and the fire he'd lit.

Caleb moaned. Shifted. "I want you." He lowered her down, down, down. Their bodies tangled on the blanket as his hands began a slow exploration of her waist, her ribs.

Her fingertips roved over the planes of his back. Feeling the strength, the muscles. She tugged at his shirt, needing to touch skin.

Someone giggled.

Caleb froze, his hands falling away from her body. He rolled off her with a grunt.

Lydia's face flamed as she stared up at Menno, his face illuminated by the flashlight in his hands, and a girl she didn't recognize. Seemed he was active in the dating scene, seeing more than one girl at a time. Lydia felt a smidgen of pity for Gizelle.

Menno gave the girl's hand a tug. "Kum on, let's leave them alone. We've gotta go." He shrugged apologetically at Caleb and Lydia.

At least Menno wouldn't ask her out again. Or, if he did, he would surely understand when she told him nein. But it was a gut thing he'd interrupted them, because even though Lydia hadn't meant to, she'd tempted Caleb to participate in yet another make-out session. She checked to make sure her prayer kapp was still in place. Where was her self-control? She closed her eyes in shame. *Gott, forgive me!*

"Menno!"

That voice, Lydia recognized. *Gizelle.* She opened her eyes. Glanced over her shoulder.

Gizelle was running toward them, her kapp waving in her hand, her flashlight's beam bouncing.

Menno groaned. The girl with him remained silent, but she tugged her hand free from his and dropped down onto the blanket beside Lydia. "Hallo. I'm Amanda."

Lydia wasn't in the mood to make pleasantries with the people who'd caught her in a compromised position with Caleb. She folded her legs in front of her and hugged her knees against her chest. She hunted for a smile. "Hey. I'm Lydia."

She probably shouldn't have given her name, just in case. Then again, this girl was likely the female half of the lip-locked couple across the pond earlier. In that case, she was just as guilty, ain't so?

"Nice to meet you, Lydia." Amanda scooted closer.

Menno lowered himself onto the blanket next to her.

"Let the games begin," Caleb muttered as he sat.

"I thought I'd never catch up with you." Gizelle sounded breathless when she reached them, as if she'd run the whole way. She looked around at everyone. "What's going on?"

Menno shrugged. "We were gonna play volleyball. Didn't expect it to be so muddy. So, we're hanging out."

Lydia grinned. Menno was quick at thinking on his feet. Part of her was grateful to him for covering up for her and Caleb. Yet she felt a simultaneous twinge when she suspected he was covering up his own indiscretions, as well.

Caleb crossed his legs. "You're welkum to join us."

"Danki." Gizelle sat down between Caleb and Menno. "Lydia, I didn't know you played volleyball. You didn't seem interested your first nacht here."

"Meow," Menno muttered.

"Oh, I play; it's just that the teams were equal that nacht, and I didn't want to upset the balance."

"Well then, why wasn't I invited this time around? Why wasn't my brother, William? Or my cousins who live right across the street? Would've made for bigger teams." There was a note of annoyance, or maybe even suspicion, in her voice.

Neither Menno nor Caleb answered, other than to give a slight shrug.

Caleb met Lydia's gaze. Even from this distance, his eyes smoldered.

Lydia shivered. And the flame from earlier flared back to life.

⌒

It was gut that Gott had sent another interruption to cut short a make-out session, though a tornado was almost preferable to another couple's showing up. Caleb hated not having control of himself, but it seemed that even the most innocent physical contact with Lydia reignited an ever burning fire. Marrying her—sooner rather than later—seemed wise.

It finally registered with Caleb that this was the first time he'd seen Menno and Gizelle since the tornado. He glanced at Menno. "Where were you when the tornado struck? Were you able to take cover?"

Menno leaned forward. "Preacher David Lapp's barn. They have a storm cellar beneath it, and we hid down there with the family. You?"

"We were down in the basement beneath Lydia's aenti's store. My horse and buggy didn't fare as well, though. I'd stashed them in the garage, which was destroyed by the twister. Blackberry came home just today, but my buggy is still on the Weisses' barn roof."

Menno chuckled. "Crazy weather, for sure. My Englisch neighbor would've been out in it. He was a storm chaser."

"Was?" Lydia frowned.

"Jah, was. Past tense. He's the man who died in that motorcycle accident the other day." His voice wavered. He cleared his throat.

Caleb winced at the reminder of the carnage from the accident. At the way death could kum in a moment, without warning. *Danki, Gott, that I'm right with You again.*

"Heard Timothy Weiss was treated at the hospital and released." Menno's voice was somber. He cleared his throat again. "Any word on when they're going to get your buggy off the roof?"

"Daed said tomorrow, weather permitting." Something wet plopped on Caleb's nose. He glanced at the dark sky. Clouds obscured all the stars. He picked up his straw hat and put it on his head as a drop of water hit him on the arm. Then another big raindrop splattered on his hand. They needed to start home before they got drenched.

"How was the woman…what was her name? Irene?" Lydia wiped at her own arm.

"Ilene. She's my cousin. They gave her something to stop the labor. Heard her ehemann might have to put their buggy horse down. He was too scared after the accident to be taken out in traffic. Completely ruined him," Caleb said, shaking his head.

"We need a horse whisperer in these parts," Amanda said.

"That's what my daed does, in addition to farming." Lydia glanced at Amanda. "He works with buggy horses that've been traumatized, abused, or otherwise hurt. He's thinking of moving here. Maybe." She wiped away another drop of water from her arm. "Of course, whether my family moves or not depends on Gott's leading—and on me."

So, she was aware of the possibility of their coming here. Why hadn't she mentioned it to Caleb?

"Ach, I hope your family moves here." Amanda wiped at a drop that had splattered on her hand.

Caleb stood. "Think we'd best get home, before it really starts raining." He held out his hand to help Lydia up.

"Aw, it's hardly sprinkling," Menno said, but he got to his feet. "And since when is 'home' the same place for you two?"

Caleb's face heated. He supposed an explanation was in order. "Ach, Lydia's staying with us until the electricity is restored to her aenti's apartment, and the roof is repaired."

Menno winked at him. "Well, give me a call if they're going to get the buggy down tomorrow. If I'm free, I'll try to help."

Caleb nodded. "Danki."

Twenty minutes later, Caleb snuck into the haus and tiptoed up the stairs, avoiding the creaky step. A soft snoring sounded inside Mamm and Daed's bedroom as he passed by. He eased open his own bedroom door, lit the lantern, and gasped.

Daed was sitting at the desk.

Caleb shut the door with a quiet click. "You startled me."

"You were out later than I expected."

"Sorry. We met up with Menno and Amanda and Gizelle at the pond, and talked awhile." Almost the whole truth. "Since you're here, I might as well tell you...I need to marry Lydia."

Daed blinked. "Need to, or want to?"

"Need to."

"Why do you say that?" Daed didn't smile. Instead, his expression sobered. Pierced.

"I...uh...I want to kiss her. Actually, I did kiss her."

"You kissed her?" Daed hitched one eyebrow. His lips twitched. "And a kiss equals a *need* to marry?"

A blush warmed Caleb's face. "Okay, okay. I *want* to marry her. I want to have the right to do what I want to do but can't. Gott has stopped us. Every time."

"The right...? Gott...every time?" Daed's eyebrow rose even higher.

"You know what? Never mind." Coming on the heels of his confession about Molly, this sounded bad. Caleb rubbed his jaw and willed himself to stop rambling. "Did you want something?"

"Jah." Daed frowned. "Well, nein. Gott woke me up and told me to pray for you. I guess now I know why. I'll have a talk with Lydia to see if she's open to the idea of marrying you."

"Danki, Daed."

"Are you thinking this coming fall, as your Mamm predicts?"

Caleb nodded, but then he swallowed. Shook his head. "Really, next week would be much better."

⌒

The next morgen, Lydia tied a bandana over her braid before hurrying to the main-haus to help with breakfast. She opened the connecting door and stopped. Too late. Bethlehem was stacking dirty dishes beside the sink, and Vi had begun filling the sink with water. On the kitchen table, a plate of waffles and bacon, a small bowl of fruit, and a glass of juice waited at the place Lydia had occupied at dinner the nacht before.

"Gut morgen!" Bethlehem greeted her. "Have a seat and eat your breakfast. Mamm, Dottie, and Dolly are working on laundry, and Daed and Caleb went to the Weisses' to attempt to get Caleb's buggy down from the barn roof."

"Why didn't someone wake me?"

"Daed said you came in late last nacht, and that we should let you sleep." Vi squirted some dish soap into the water.

Jah, she'd been out late, but nein later than Caleb. She didn't want the Bontrager family to think she was lazy. She ate her breakfast quickly, then carried her dishes to the sink. "What can I do to help?"

Vi peeked out the window. "Looks like they're about finished hanging the laundry. How about you start some bread? We need to bake cookies, too."

Bethlehem handed Lydia a jar of starter dough. "Mixing bowls are in the bottom cupboard." She pointed in that direction. "If you need the recipe, it's is taped inside the upper cabinet door."

Lydia opened the cabinet and skimmed the directions. "Looks similar to the recipe Mamm follows."

It felt gut to be useful. Hopefully, by helping out, she would redeem herself for having slept in.

Later on, when the bread was rising on the counter and the cookies had just kum out of the oven, the door opened, and Caleb and Preacher Zeke came inside. They both paused long enough to take off their boots. Then Preacher Zeke poured two mugs of koffee and headed for the table.

"How'd you get the buggy down?" Bethlehem wanted to know.

Caleb grinned. "Two very tall ladders, six men, and lots of prayer."

Preacher Zeke nodded. "We tied rappel ropes to it. Two men held the ropes, and four of us carried the buggy down the ladders." He sat in his chair and laid an envelope on the table.

"Sounds dangerous." Bethlehem set the sugar bowl and pitcher of cream on the table. "Would you like some cookies?"

"What kind did you make?" Caleb stirred some cream into his koffee, then added a spoonful of sugar.

"Oatmeal raisin. Fresh out of the oven." Lydia filled a plate with the still-warm cookies cooling on a rack. As she set the cookies on the table near the two men, she glanced at the envelope. It was folded and crumpled, as if it'd been carried around in someone's back pocket for several days.

But the bold, black masculine handwriting in the upper left-hand corner read "Thomas Glick." The bishop back home.

Her heart skipped a couple of beats. Her hands turned clammy.

Preacher Zeke reached for a cookie. "Danki, Lydia. As soon as I've finished my koffee, I'd like for you to take a walk with me."

25

*C*aleb sipped his koffee, testing the taste and temperature. Perfect. He picked up a cookie. The table shook as Lydia gripped it and sank into a chair, the way Grossmammi had often done when she'd gotten older, and all the strength had left her legs. The color had washed out of Lydia's face, and she wore a haunted expression. The light had gone out of her eyes.

Caleb lowered his cookie without taking a bite. "Are you okay?"

She opened her mouth as if about to speak, then pressed her lips shut again, jumped out of the chair, and dashed to the bathroom. The door slammed shut. Muffled retching sounds followed.

Daed calmly took another sip of koffee, as if nothing were wrong. Of course, nothing was wrong, if his request to walk with Lydia was made with the intent of talking to her about marrying his sohn. What was wrong was Lydia's reaction.

Both Vi and Bethlehem stopped what they were doing and stared down the hall in the direction of the bathroom. The door remained closed, but Caleb heard water running. Was the idea of Daed's talking to her about marrying Caleb so sickening? Last nacht, she'd said she would marry him in a heartbeat. Well, she probably hadn't expected him to ask his daed to talk to her so quickly.

Or did her sudden illness have something to do with the letter Timothy Weiss had handed to Daed that morgen? Caleb strained to read the return address on the envelope. Ohio. Was it bad news about her family? Caleb was ignorant as to the contents of the letter, but after reading it, Daed had gone off to discuss something with the other preachers.

Lydia emerged from the bathroom as Daed drained his mug. Caleb had lost interest in his own koffee and went to dump it in the sink.

Even though Lydia had clearly scrubbed her face till it was red, fresh tears beaded on her eyelashes. She sighed and glanced at Daed. "Let's get this over with."

"It's okay." Caleb meant to encourage her. The worst thing she could say was that she didn't want to marry him, despite her words to the contrary last nacht. He'd be disappointed, for sure, but it'd be better to know now.

She glanced once more at the letter as Daed picked it up and headed for the door. He paused to put on his boots, then looked over his shoulder. "You might want to kum, too, Sohn."

"Me?" Caleb frowned. "But—"

Daed shook his head.

Ach. So it had nothing to do with his desire to marry Lydia, and everything to do with the contents of the envelope. Something bad regarding his Lydia? Inconceivable. Did this have anything to do with her reason for needing a safe haven?

Caleb's stomach roiled. He slipped his feet into his boots and followed Daed and Lydia out the door.

The three walked in silence around the barn and out into the recently planted fields. Lydia's shoulders were squared, her back ram-rod straight, her fists clenched at her sides. Tears glistened on her cheeks.

Caleb resisted the overwhelming urge to put his arm around her and shelter her from this imminent storm.

⌒

Lydia stopped walking and turned to Caleb and his daed. "Just. Say. It."

Preacher Zeke nodded once, then pulled the letter out of his pocket and handed it to her. "Timothy Weiss was on his way to deliver this to me when he was involved in that motorcycle accident."

She knew what the note said without having to open it. She willed her hands not to shake as she pulled the paper out of the envelope, unfolded it, and quickly scanned the brief missive. It was dated the day before she'd left Ohio.

To whom it may concern:

Lydia Hershberger has been shunned and is no longer in gut standing with the church until she has knelt and confessed her sin of seducing a married man.

Bishop Thomas Glick

Lydia swallowed hard. She stuffed the letter back inside the envelope, which she then returned to Preacher Zeke. He passed it to Caleb, who read it in silence before handing it back to his daed. She could see the question marks in his eyes. The disappointment. The hurt. The air became heavy with tension. Or maybe it was her own shame making it hard to breathe, hard to function, hard to face these two upstanding men.

Not to mention hard to see her hopes for a fresh start die, officially and completely, right before her eyes. At least she'd gotten a gut, long sleep the previous evening. Who knew where she would be to-nacht?

"Lydia?" Caleb's voice was low. Raw. Filled with pain.

Preacher Zeke surveyed her. Silent.

What could she say, other than to blurt out the truth? *I didn't do it.* But that would sound too defensive a protestation to warrant belief.

The silence stretched on. Caleb opened his mouth again but quickly shut it when his daed shook his head. And they continued to wait. For what? For Lydia to confess? Or for her to nod, walk away, and begin her lifelong sentence, because she wouldn't confess to something she hadn't done?

She tried to control her breaths to avoid hyperventilating. Instead, her throat constricted to the point that she couldn't breathe, let alone talk.

After what seemed an endless amount of time, Preacher Zeke nodded. "I know what you are accused of. I know what I've been told by your daed and your aent, as well as what I've observed. Now, why don't you tell us your side of the story?"

Lydia finally managed a deep breath, then let out a lengthy exhalation, along with a rush of words she had nein control over, nein hope of editing. "He came to our roadside stand to buy vegetables. His frau was in a wheelchair, injured in a buggy accident, and they had all these kinner. I used to give them a special discount, and I'd always have little treats for his kinner, and flowers or a book for his frau to help cheer her up."

Preacher Zeke nodded.

"After a while, he started coming alone. One time, he kissed me on my cheek and thanked me for my kindness." Like she'd kissed Caleb, several times. She cringed. "I hugged him back. Once. I'll admit it. But I did so out of pity. And then it got worse. Whenever he saw me, he'd try to catch me alone and steal a kiss. He started to have this…this unsettling gleam in his eyes when he looked at me that made it feel like he was undressing me."

Caleb made an indistinct sound and clenched his fists.

"I wasn't safe anywhere. Sometimes, I'd find him lurking in the shadows of the barn, waiting for me to kum outside to do my chores. I always called for Daed to kum talk to him."

Preacher Zeke tugged at his beard.

"He even threw pebbles at my window at nacht. I made the foolish mistake of going out one time to tell him to leave me alone. I was dressed in my nacht-gown, but a thick robe covered it, and my hair was braided, as it is now, and covered with a bandana. That much is true."

The preacher nodded once more.

Caleb's brown eyes had hardened into dark, angry orbs.

"I told Mamm and Daed what was going on, and Daed went to the preachers and the bishop. But the man only accused me of trying to seduce him, to draw him away from his frau. Nobody believed me but my own parents, because they *heard* the conversation between us on the front porch. They heard me tell him to leave me alone. Heard the scuffle that followed when he grabbed me and tried to force me to go with him, before Daed came to my rescue. If I need to confess to hugging a married man, and for the little gifts of kindness, I will. I didn't mean to tempt him. But that won't be gut enough. They'll expect me to confess that I deliberately tempted him. Tried to seduce him."

Another nod from Preacher Zeke.

Lydia took another deep breath. "But I didn't try to seduce him. Not intentionally. Nor did I intend to tempt Caleb. But I did hug him and kiss his cheek. And both times…both times…." Her voice broke. "Both times, I lured him into sin, but Gott stopped us. I am a Jezebel, and cursed, just like Bishop Thomas said. And that's why I'll never marry." She glanced at Caleb, silently begging him to forgive her. Hopefully, he believed her account.

"That the man pursued you, and not the other way around, is exactly what we were told by your aent. And it's what I reminded the other preachers of this very morgen." Preacher Zeke's voice was calm. Quiet. "I believe you, Lydia, and I see nein reason for you to kneel and confess for acts of kindness and mercy."

She wasn't going to be condemned! At least not by Preacher Zeke. She was afraid to look at Caleb. What if he disagreed with his daed?

"Unfortunately, word of the shunning will get out. And while the other preachers and I won't enforce it, the acting bishop from the other community will announce it in church, so you will be shunned nonetheless."

Lydia swallowed a fresh round of nausea. "My reputation will be ruined." Even though they believed her, the shunning would follow her. She would need to move on to a new place. And then another. And another.

Or confess.

She bowed her head.

"Daed…." Caleb's voice broke. "Is there nothing we can do?"

"I'll pray about it some more, and discuss it with the other preachers. And we'll see how Gott leads." Preacher Zeke patted Lydia's shoulder. "Go in peace." He started to walk off, then stopped and turned around to meet Caleb's gaze.

Lydia couldn't decipher the nonverbal communication that passed between Caleb and his daed. Their hand motions were completely foreign. The only thing she recognized was the unmistakable look of longing in Caleb's eyes.

Caleb could not believe the accusations that had been lodged against Lydia. Nein wonder she needed a safe haven! If only he could give her his name and protect her that way. He held his hands out, palms facing up, in a silent petition for Daed to please ask Lydia if she could ever consider marrying him. One last, begging effort—conveyed via sign language, which the family had mastered when Grossmammi had gone deaf. But Daed stood firm. *Nein. Not now. Wait.*

Still, Caleb begged. Wouldn't marriage solve Lydia's problems? Maybe not all her problems, but some, at least.

After a seemingly endless moment, Daed shook his head. *Wait.* Then he walked off, leaving Caleb and Lydia alone.

Wait? Until Lydia's situation was resolved? Until Caleb confessed his sins—so much worse than hers—to Lydia? Would he need to confess his sins to the church and face shunning, too? He'd need to ask Daed.

But now they stood together in awkward silence. She blatantly avoided his eyes, while he overtly stared at her, wishing he could take her in his arms and tell her everything would be okay.

"*We are hard-pressed on every side, yet not crushed; we are perplexed, but not in despair; persecuted, but not forsaken; struck down, but not destroyed,*" she whispered.

"Amen." He smiled and held out his hand to her. "Somehow, someway, it will all be okay."

She put her hand in his. "I'm trying to believe."

He wanted to stay there and gaze into her eyes all day long. Declare his undying love. Tell her he'd meant every word when he'd talked of marriage. Instead, he touched a kiss to her forehead. Allowed his fingers to trace her jawbone.

But until her shunning was over, until he confessed his secrets, marriage was out of the question.

And that meant he needed to keep himself under tight control.

26

*L*ydia wanted to mourn the loss of her dreams, her reputation, and her time here in Jamesport. Even though Preacher Zeke had said that he wouldn't shun her, what about the rest of his family, when their acting bishop announced it? Her best friend, Abigail? Others in the community?

She would have nein choice but to leave. Only she didn't know where to go, or even how she'd get there. Holing up in Aenti Judith's apartment seemed to be the most viable option—but that wouldn't be possible until the roof was repaired, the electricity restored.

Dear, sweet Caleb accompanied her on her hasty retreat to the dawdi-haus. He reached for her a time or two, but when she shied away, he let his arm fall to his side without a word of protest.

She could imagine the questions swirling in his mind. The puzzle pieces fitting together, connecting her wanton behavior with her reputation for being a seductress. What if he believed she wasn't as innocent as Aenti Judith and her daed had claimed? After all, they were family. Willing to do anything to defend her—maybe even lie.

Ach, Gott.

A tear ran down her cheek.

She increased her speed. She couldn't—wouldn't—break down in public. She had to reach the privacy of the dawdi-haus. She'd be alone there.

"Slow down, Lydia." Caleb reached for her again, this time succeeding in catching her arm as they reached the door to the dawdi-haus.

"Leave me alone." She jerked away from him, yanked the knob, and rushed inside as a waterfall of tears erupted. She slammed the door behind her.

Three sets of eyes stared at her. Bethel. Dolly. And Dottie.

So much for being alone.

Through the blur of her tears, Lydia studied the yellow gingham curtains freshly hung over the kitchen window. The pedal sewing machine had been set up in the entryway between the living room and the kitchen, and Dottie occupied the chair behind it, feeding another curtain panel across the throat plate.

The sunflower pillows lay on the couch, along with a matching, folded quilt. It looked exactly the way Lydia had imagined. Only now it seemed more like a nacht-mare than a dream kum true. This place, even prettier than it'd been just that morgen, would soon be ripped away from her.

Her breath lodged in her throat, then came back in a series of gasps as she fought to control her emotions, both from the recent conversation with Preacher Zeke and from the sudden burst of joy at seeing all the yellow.

The door clicked open. "Lydia!"

Didn't Caleb know how to knock?

"Lydia, what's wrong?" Dolly planted her fists on her hips. "Did Caleb hurt you again?"

Caleb came inside. "What do you mean, 'again'? I'd never intentionally hurt Lydia."

"You all are so gut to me," Lydia sniffled. "Danki."

"So, those are happy tears?" Dolly asked.

If only.

Lydia swallowed. Swiped a hand over her eyes. Then she looked at Bethel. "How can I help?" Maybe work would take her mind off her impending shame.

Bethel's eyes, dark brown like Caleb's, were filled with sympathy. Had Preacher Zeke stopped in to share the contents of the letter with her before going into the main haus?

"How about you take the quilt up to your room and spread it on the bed?" Bethel nodded toward the couch. "Caleb, she's fine. You can go help your daed. I'll send someone to get you both in a bit."

Lydia gathered the soft quilted fabric in her arms, and hugged it to her chest as she headed toward the stairs. As she passed the end table, she noticed Aenti Judith's notebook sitting there. She snatched that up, too. Even if word of her shunning would get out, she didn't want people reading about it. Assuming that Aenti Judith had written about her shame.

She walked up the stairs and down the hall to the bedroom, set the notebook on the bedside table, then spread the quilt over the mattress. The patter was beautiful—solid white, with long green stems and leaves leading up to a circle of golden sunflowers.

She smoothed out a wrinkle, then sat on the quilt. She needed to pull herself together. This family was so wunderbaar, so sweet, and she didn't want to subject them to all her drama.

If only she could ask Preacher Zeke to reconsider his offer for her to stay here.

But that would seem rude, especially after Bethel and her dochters had gone to such extremes to make her comfortable. To make her feel loved and cared for.

The colorful dolphins on the cover of the fat little notebook beckoned. She swiped her fingertip under her eyes once more, chasing away the tears, then reached for the notebook. Flipped it open.

Lydia...

She skimmed past the pages she'd read earlier.

…So I will start by saying that I'm glad to offer my home as a safe haven for you…Gott's providence. Your daed…went to the bishop about the married man….

She found where she'd left off, and began to read.

You have been so heavy on my heart ever since your daed called me. I'm sorry your bus tickets were delayed so that we won't be able to spend time together before I have to leave. I long to hold you close, pray over you, and tell you that God has a plan. We might not know what it is on this side of heaven, but the Bible is full of assurances that He has good plans for us, that He will direct our paths if we follow Him, that He loves and cares for us.

I told Bethel everything….

So Bethel really did know everything? And still wanted to make her welkum? A strain of joy filled Lydia.

…and she wants you to feel comfortable going to her, knowing you are accepted and loved without judgment. Her husband, Zeke, was more concerned by the rumors, and wisely followed up by calling to talk to your daed, along with a few others in Ohio, to get a sense of your character. I think he was satisfied with what he learned.

So, Preacher Zeke had known everything all along, too? The details hadn't kum as a surprise to either him or Bethel? And they'd still accepted her? But they wouldn't have done so if they'd known she had tempted Caleb and succumbed to his kisses. And she'd even mentioned it to Preacher Zeke. He was probably questioning Caleb right now. Demanding answers. And then he would be quick to kick her out.

Lydia's stomach churned again.

Then again, he'd told her he believed her.

She returned her attention to Aenti Judith's note.

I love you, Lydia, and even as I'm serving God overseas, I'll keep you in my heart and prayers.

Don't be afraid to open your heart to love. I know you're wounded after losing Peter, and after the harsh words your bishop spoke in your hearing—none of which is true. You are worthy of love. Even if that man misread your intent to comfort and show mercy, it doesn't mean you are evil. You had good intentions. Continue to let God guide your heart and your actions. Trust Him to take care of you.

It was such a relief to realize Aenti Judith had recognized her gut intentions. She tried to believe Gott would take care of her. He had done so thus far. But trusting Him completely was hard. Hopefully, as Gott continued to meet her needs, her faith, and her capacity to trust Him, would continue to grow.

I know there's a certain young man in Jamesport who is very interested in you. He spent hours asking about you, question after question. I didn't tell him you were coming, specifically, only that my niece was going to manage the store in my absence. I'm rather curious to hear how he reacted when he learned it was you. I'm sure he was shocked, to say the least. He doesn't handle surprises well. He likes everything planned out in advance, and he puts a lot of thought into everything he does. Seeing you turned his world upside down.

Caleb. Warmth filled her. But then, she thought back to the day he'd learned she was Judith's niece. His facial expression had been one of horror. Or had she misread it?

All that is to say, don't be afraid. Be open to romance. God's love is readily available. You are accepted in the beloved. Trust God. Trust Zeke and Bethel. And trust that young man, as soon as he's brave enough to tell you how he feels. Because you can be certain that if he says it, he means it.

He'd said it. He'd specifically told her he loved her. But he hadn't sounded very serious. They'd been teasing, ain't so? Or maybe he'd meant it, after all, and he just hadn't wanted to risk getting hurt if she didn't return his feelings, so he'd kept his tone light.

She read on.

You are not a Jezebel. You are not cursed. You are loved.

Loved.

In Jeremiah 31:3, God says to you, "I have loved you with an everlasting love; therefore with lovingkindness I have drawn you."

If only Lydia could understand. The Gott of these people, this family, wasn't the Gott of the Amish in her home district. That Gott was a harsh judge. Angry. Quick to punish and reject.

That didn't sound like a Gott who loved with an everlasting love. Lydia's heart longed for a Gott who really loved. She hoped and prayed Aenti Judith was right.

What made that Gott different? Maybe Aenti Judith would explain. Or Preacher Zeke, or maybe even Caleb.

Lydia returned her attention to the note.

You're accepted in the beloved. Remember that.

Talk to the Amish preachers in Jamesport. I think you will find that they are all men of God. And if you read on, I will tell you more about the love of God. I've learned a lot since I married your onkel and became Mennonite.

Footsteps sounded outside Lydia's room. She closed the notebook, set it back on the bedside table, and glanced toward the open door.

Bethel peeked in. "Are you okay?"

"Jah, I...."

Caleb's mamm entered the room, sat down beside Lydia, and put an arm around her shoulders. "You poor dear. I'm so glad Zeke brought you here. You don't need to be alone right now."

A fresh round of tears welled up in Lydia's eyes. "I hate to drag your family into my problems. People are going to judge you for not shunning me." Her voice cracked.

Bethel shrugged. "Some might. But I've found that the ones who matter will offer grace. To all of us."

Lydia wiped her eyes. She leaned away from Bethel. "May I help with the sewing?"

"Nein, danki. Dottie and I have the project well in hand. I think it'd be a gut idea for you to visit your friend Abigail today. Sammy stopped by while you were walking with Caleb and Zeke, and he said Abigail is anxious to see you. I told him I would send you over. If you feel like a visit, ask Caleb to drive you over there."

It'd be preferable to visit Abigail before her shunning became common knowledge. Lydia smoothed her hand over the quilt again. "But I hate for you to go to all the trouble of making curtains and pillowcases for me with nein contribution on my part."

Bethel waved her hand dismissively. "It's a pleasure, Lydia. Don't rob us of the blessing of doing this for you." She stood. "Now, go find Caleb, and tell him his mamm said to take you to Abigail."

Lydia smiled weakly. "Danki."

Bethel wrapped her in a quick hug, then stood. "I'm going to measure the windows in here. Would you send Dolly up to hold the other end of the tape?"

Lydia glanced at the fat little notebook. She wanted to slide it under the mattress or tuck it beneath her pillow so nobody would be tempted to snoop inside, but hiding it now would be too obvious. Besides, Bethel already knew everything. Aenti Judith had probably even shown her the letters she'd received from Daed. But Dolly...did she know?

Lydia squared her shoulders and hurried downstairs. Dottie was trimming the threads that dangled from the curtain panel, while Dolly twirled around the room with Rosie, singing a made-up song, Rosie chiming in with her own plaintive chorus of meows as she dug her claws into Dolly's green dress.

"Dolly? Your mamm asked me to send you upstairs to help."

"Okay." She sang that word, too, then darted up the stairs, Rosie attempting to climb to her shoulder.

"That poor cat is going to be so traumatized," Dottie muttered. "I think all the kittens are glad when they leave here, and finally get to escape Dolly's undivided attention."

Lydia laughed. "Danki for all your work on the curtains. They look amazing."

Dottie grinned. "Nein wonder Caleb calls you his sunshine. This place will be so bright." She added a wink.

Lydia's face heated. He'd said that? Really? Too sweet. But he probably wasn't thinking sunshiny thoughts about her right now. Her current forecast was dark and gloomy rain clouds. With a parting glance in Dottie's direction, Lydia stepped outside.

She found Caleb cleaning the cow barn. He dumped a shovelful of manure into the already- piled-high wheelbarrow, then glanced up as she walked in. "Hey."

"Hallo, Caleb. If you aren't too busy, I'd appreciate the opportunity to talk with Abigail before…well, before…." Lydia fingered the strings of her kapp. "Please."

"I'll always have time for you." Caleb laid the shovel across the top of the wheelbarrow. "Just let me empty this and clean up, and we'll go."

⌒

Even though Caleb had five sisters, he'd never realized how loud a woman could squeal. Abigail had run out of her residence, a former hunting cabin, screaming and crying, before

Caleb had even set the brake on the buggy. It hadn't taken long for Lydia to start crying, as well. Now, the two women clutched each other while squealing, sobbing, and jumping up and down. Simultaneously.

Incredible.

Abigail's ehemann, Sam, stared at them, likely just as flabbergasted as Caleb.

"Didn't they just see each other five months ago?" Sam adjusted the boppli he held against his shoulder—his adopted sohn, Peter James—better known as Peanut. "I don't remember their doing this at the wedding."

Peanut scrunched his face, turned red, stiffened, and then wailed louder than both women were squealing.

The women didn't pay him any mind.

"There, now you've gone and done it." Sam grinned at his frau and Lydia, not that they noticed. "Kum on inside, Caleb. We can have koffee and some of the cake Abby baked this morgen. They'll come in soon enough, ain't so?"

Caleb stepped around the women, shaking his head. Wouldn't they need to stop for a breath at some point? After another long, fascinated look at the two squealing, bouncing friends, he followed Sam inside, took a seat at the kitchen table, and waited, with one eye on the window and the ongoing commotion outside.

It was gut to know Lydia had other friends in this community who cared about her and would prayerfully support her in the days to kum.

Sam put Peanut in a wooden highchair, handed him a bottle of water and half a graham cracker square, then poured two mugs of koffee. He glanced out the window and shook his head. "Amazing. Simply amazing. I didn't know they could do that."

"Me, neither." Caleb tore his attention away from the women to look at Sam.

Peanut silenced, apparently fascinated by his new "toys." It didn't take him long to hammer the graham cracker into crumbs with the bottom of his bottle. Or to notice that water squirted out of the rubber nipple with every thump he gave it on the high-chair tray.

Caleb cringed at the mess the bu was making. It seemed life was never as structured and orderly as he would prefer. Messes happened.

Sam cut two thick slices of chocolate cake with white icing, plated them, and handed one to Caleb, along with a fork. "Cream cheese frosting. I can't wait to taste it. So, what's going on with you? Did you get the buggy down without incident? I wanted to be there to help, but I had to work my shift on the ambulance. Not every day you get to rescue a buggy from a barn roof. Kind of disappointed to have missed it."

Outside, the squealing quieted. Finally.

"Jah, the buggy is in gut shape, remarkably. A few scratches, maybe, but otherwise none the worse for wear." Caleb shifted in his chair. Should he bring up the issue that his family—and the whole community—would need to deal with now? Or would it be a violation of Lydia's privacy to talk about it before the news became public knowledge?

Sam sat across from him. He stirred a spoonful of sugar into his koffee. "Glad to hear it. How's it going doing the bookkeeping for that Mennonite gift shop?"

"Haven't really done that much, so far, beyond recording sales and making deposits. But Judith said something about quarterly taxes being due in a couple of months, so I'll have to assemble some information together for her tax preparer. And I'll need to pay her vendors. Thankfully, there weren't any losses to her merchandise from the tornado." Just an overly rambunctious kitten.

"And Lydia…how is she adjusting?" Sam leaned back in his chair, his cake untouched, cradling his koffee mug in both hands.

The women started squealing again. Caleb glanced out the window. They'd resumed jumping and hugging, too. *Wow.*

Sam grinned. "I'm guessing she shared our news. Abigail's going to have a boppli this fall."

Caleb yanked his attention away from the women. "Congratulations."

"What, you're not going to squeal and jump up and down?"

Caleb chuckle. "Nein, sorry."

"Anyway, how *is* Lydia adjusting?"

Caleb shrugged. "I'm not sure how to answer that. I mean… well, Sunday, the acting bishop is going to…well…." Ugh. He hated that his words were so scrambled. "She's going to be shunned."

Sam's eyebrows shot up. "Whatever for? Lydia's about the sweetest thing next to honey. The nicest, too. She couldn't have possibly done anything that bad."

"She didn't. Seems some married man back home misinterpreted her gifts of mercy, and when she refused to give in to his demands, he claimed that she tried to seduce him."

"That's nonsense." Sam thumped his half-empty mug on the table.

"Jah." Caleb nodded. "Her bishop back home says she's shunned until she kneels and confesses. And so it will be announced here on Sunday. I won't be in church. Doubt Lydia will be, either. But Daed says that he and the rest of the preachers won't enforce it."

"They'll have to, or face quieting." Sam raked his fingers through his short beard.

Caleb frowned. Quieting? Did that mean it was a possibility the temporary bishop from the other community would revoke Daed's calling as a preacher, and silence him? Not only Daed, but also Preacher Samuel and Preacher David?

Sam looked concerned. "But Daed hasn't said anything to me about it."

"My daed found out just today." Caleb picked up his fork and stabbed it into the slice of cake.

Sam leaned forward. "I admit that I'm not exactly as nonconfrontational as I should be. Daed says I need to take time to pray before I rush in where angels fear to tread. When Abigail's stepdaed denied her existence, I called him and demanded answers. Didn't work so well. I often wonder if it would've been better to go talk to him in person. Then again, he might've greeted me with the working end of a pitchfork."

"The working end of a pitchf—" Caleb blinked. "That's it!" He shot to his feet, letting his fork clatter to the table. He barely caught his chair before it hit the floor. Then he rushed across the room and threw open the door. "Lydia, we've got to go—now!"

❦

Lydia and Abigail had been strolling arm in arm toward the newly built barn behind the log cabin dwelling. It was so gut to see her best friend and to begin catching up after five months apart. And it was so jarring when Caleb interrupted them with his declaration that it was time to go.

"But you just got here." Abigail released Lydia.

"I need to talk to my daed." Caleb reached for Lydia's hand.

"Then go talk to him, and let Lydia stay here. Sammy will drive her home later." Abigail firmed her jaw. "We've hardly had a chance to visit."

"But…." Caleb took a deep breath and glanced behind him at Sammy, who'd kum out of the cabin and now approached, Peanut in his arms.

Sammy looked as confused as Lydia felt.

"Abby, let's just reschedule the visit. Caleb isn't impulsive or capricious in his decisions. If he says they need to go, then they do."

Lydia allowed Caleb to grasp her hand. Sadness engulfed her. "I'd like to say we can get together again soon, but, honestly, we probably won't. I'll be shunned on Sunday. Well, actually, I'm already shunned. But Sunday is when it'll be announced in church."

Abigail gasped. "Shunned? That's ridiculous. What'd you do? Wait—does this have anything to do with that man back home who kept trying to get you alone?"

Lydia nodded. "The bishop believes I tried to seduce him."

Abigail rolled her eyes. "He obviously doesn't know you at all. What are you going to do? You can't confess to it, can you?"

"She's not going to." Caleb pulled Lydia against his side. "That's why we need to go. Sam gave me an idea that I need to talk about with Daed, Mamm, and Lydia, right away."

Abigail glanced at Sammy, one of her eyebrows hitched.

Sammy shrugged. "Don't ask me. All I know is, it involves pitchforks."

"And maybe going to Ohio," Caleb added. "If Daed agrees."

27

*B*ack home, Englisch and Amish vehicles clogged the driveway. As Caleb maneuvered his rig around them, he recognized Viktor Petersheim's pickup truck, Preacher Samuel's horse, and Josh Yoder's buggy, from the birdhouse that hung off the back.

Caleb drove his own buggy into the shed and parked it next to Daed's, then pastured Blackberry.

Lydia trailed close behind him, her tension almost palpable, as he hiked past the sea of black vehicles between the shed and the barn, the low hum of male voices growing louder as they approached. But there was nothing Caleb could tell her just yet. All he had were vague ideas, with nein clue as to how they would play out. He needed time to think. To plan. To pray.

She wanted answers. Now.

"I *won't* go to Ohio," she said again. She'd made her intentions clear at least five times during the drive home from the Millers'.

Caleb sighed. "I know, Princess. I don't blame you for not wanting to." *But sometimes you have to do what you don't want to do.* He didn't need to waste his breath reminding her.

"It would be nice to see my family, though."

His lips twitched. If she kept this up, she'd talk herself into going without any encouragement from him.

He strode through the barn to the space Daed had dubbed the "conference room." Mamm liked to say that the tack room was where most of the "meetings of the male minds" happened when men stopped by to discuss something with Daed.

Caleb peeked in the open door. It did appear to be a meeting of the minds, which explained all the buggies parked outside. Preachers Samuel and David, Josh Yoder, Reuben Petersheim, and his gross-sohn, Viktor—though he'd left the Amish and became Mennonite. Odd he'd been included. All of them seated on bales of hay arranged in a circle.

Was this the reason Mamm had wanted Caleb to take Lydia to see Sam and Abigail? So that she—they—wouldn't be around during this meeting? Or had this gathering been spontaneous?

Caleb started to back away, but Daed looked up and met his gaze. "Kum on in, Sohn."

Caleb opened the door wide enough to slip inside. He hesitated just inside the doorway, unsure whether he should shut it behind him. What about Lydia?

"You can kum in, too, Lydia." Daed settled the issue. "We just finished a prayer meeting, and now we're discussing you, in addition to some other church business."

Church business? Caleb blinked. Viktor wasn't a member of the church. Neither Reuben nor Josh was a preacher.

Daed didn't offer an explanation. Instead, he motioned toward an empty hay bale.

Preacher Samuel glanced at Caleb. "We're hoping the temporary bishop will be agreeable to the idea of our drawing lots this Sunday for a new bishop. It's time to make an official appointment. Bishop Joe passed away five months ago. We've dragged our feet with an interim bishop long enough. We also need to draw lots from among our married men for a new preacher, to replace the current preacher who ends up being selected as bishop."

Caleb nodded, unsure how else to respond, since it was none of his business. As a single man, he was ineligible to serve as a preacher.

Lydia sat next to him on the hay bale, a lost expression on her face. Her eyes were wide with apparent fright.

Preacher David looked at Caleb. "We're hoping that if we do appoint our own bishop, the temporary bishop will permit us to handle our own church business, and then we will be able to decide for ourselves how to address the charges against Lydia. Otherwise, the interim bishop will have the power to enforce the shunning ordered by Lydia's home bishop…and I believe he would do so, since he doesn't know Lydia and likely wouldn't be interested in doing the footwork necessary to gather testimonies on her behalf."

Lydia glanced at Caleb, her breathing shallow.

Caleb swallowed. If only he could comfort her somehow. "I was just visiting Sam Miller, and he mentioned a time he phoned someone in Ohio in order to call him out for his treatment of Sam's wife, Abigail." He glanced at Preacher Samuel. "He said he suspected he would've gotten better results if he'd gone to Ohio in person, but that he was afraid he'd be greeted with the business end of a pitchfork."

Preacher Samuel quirked his lips and then nodded.

"I think…." Caleb squirmed on the hay bale. His hip bumped against Lydia's, and he stilled. "I think that maybe he had a gut idea—"

"Bethel!" A man's voice shouted outside.

Daed stood up. "Hold the thought, Caleb." He strode to the door and disappeared into the main part of the barn.

"Caleb, please," Lydia whispered urgently. "Nein."

Caleb grimaced. The preachers were likely to veto his idea, anyway, but he felt compelled to present it, anyway. Guilt filled him, as if he were betraying Lydia by trying to solve the problem.

He'd make sure to share her objections. But her unjust shunning wasn't going to disappear unless something was done.

"Lydia!" Daed appeared in the doorway. "Bethel needs your help."

Lydia cast Caleb one final look of desperation, then stood and left the room.

When Lydia exited the barn, she found Bethel seated, as a passenger, in a buggy. The driver was a man Lydia didn't recognize. A muscle ticked in his jaw, and he gave her an angry look as she approached.

"Lydia, this is Luke King." Bethel nodded in his direction. "His frau is my niece Ilene, and he says she's in labor. Their midwife is attending another birth, so he came to get me." She hoisted a black bag for Lydia to see. "But I'm a doula, not a midwife. And I seem to remember Caleb mentioning you had experience with midwifery. We need your help."

"I'm an EMT, but I should be able to help until her midwife arrives, or the professionals show up." While Lydia was glad to have escaped the men's meeting, she wasn't sure her assistance would be welcomed by a stranger.

Bethel smiled. "Climb on in, dear."

Lydia nodded, and then, with a cautious glance at the stern-looking man, crawled into the buggy and settled herself on the narrow backseat.

Luke barely waited for her to get situated before he flicked the reins and clicked his tongue, prompting the horse to take off.

"She's early." Luke glanced over his shoulder at Lydia. "After the accident with the motorcycle, the doctors gave her something to stop the labor, but they said she was carrying twins, and the boppli would likely kum earlier than usual. We didn't tell the midwife, because she insists on a hospital setting for multiples."

"You'll need to call for an ambulance," Lydia told him. "Twins that are born too early usually need immediate professional attention. Besides, the doctors at the hospital might be able to give Ilene something else to stop her labor. The longer those boppli remain in the womb, the better."

Lydia also didn't want this angry man blaming her for anything that might go wrong that would be out of her control.

Luke grunted. "What gut are you, then?" he muttered.

Bethel swatted his arm. "You stop it, Luke King. You want Ilene to have the best care possible, don't you?"

He nodded begrudgingly as he urged the horse into a gallop. "I'll call for an ambulance as soon as I get home."

"You do that," Bethel said.

~

Caleb fidgeted as the other men talked quietly among themselves, all of them waiting for Daed to return to the room. After a few moments, Preacher Samuel slowly rose from the hay bale he was seated on, and limped across the room to Caleb.

"How's it going?" With a slight grunt, Preacher Samuel lowered himself onto the hay next to Caleb. "Just ignore my moans and groans. I sprained a muscle in my leg."

Caleb frowned with concern. "That must be painful."

"I'm managing." Preacher Samuel chuckled. "My frau would tell me it's my own fault for going across the street to play volleyball with the youngies in the schoolyard the other nacht. Sometimes, we of the middle-aged generation have trouble remembering we're on the downward slope of the hill and can't do certain things anymore."

Gut thing the preacher hadn't decided to play volleyball last nacht, when Caleb had been at the court with Lydia.

"Been trying to go over there more often when I see youngies about," Preacher Samuel added. "Figure they'll be less likely to get into trouble if there's a chance a preacher might show up at any time."

Caleb nodded. He certainly wouldn't have started kissing Lydia if he'd thought the preacher might wander across the road.

"So, about Sam and the pitchfork...I think I know what you're proposing. I'll discuss it with Zeke and David, and we'll pray about it. But my initial impression is, why not? It'd settle the issue one way or another, and right quick, ain't so?"

Caleb sighed. "Lydia doesn't want to go back." He ran his fingertips over the rough hay. "She does miss her family, though."

"Can't blame her any. Can you?"

Caleb shook his head. "If she won't go, we can't do anything."

Preacher Samuel patted Caleb on the back, just below his left shoulder. "Let's pray, and see how Gott leads."

"Jah." Caleb bowed his head and stared at his knees. "Sometimes, I wish Gott would provide detailed, handwritten directions for these situations. But He doesn't. Just gives us a vague promise that He'll direct our paths." He glanced up at Preacher Samuel. "How do you know Gott is the one directing them, and not your own wants and desires?"

"Hard to tell sometimes, isn't it? But you left off some important parts of the passage you were alluding to. The entire passage says, '*Trust in the* LORD *with all your heart, and lean not on your own understanding; in all your ways acknowledge Him, and He shall direct your paths.*'"

⟿

Lydia braced herself as the buggy careened into a driveway, and Luke pulled on the reins, bringing the vehicle to a skidding stop. "She's...she was pacing the floor in the living areas. Bedroom's upstairs. I'm going to the phone shanty to make the call."

Lydia scrambled out of the buggy and dashed toward the haus. "Medical personnel!" she shouted, on instinct. Though it wasn't a rule among Amish, when she'd worked on an ambulance crew back home, they were required to announce their arrival in those terms.

Bethel trailed her at a slower pace. "Don't think I can move like that anymore."

They found Ilene in the kitchen, doubled over, a puddle of amniotic fluid around her feet. Definitely too late to stop her labor now. But they could hope that the ambulance crew would arrive in time to administer something that would slow down her contractions for at least the amount of time it took them to transport her to the hospital.

Lydia ran to the sink, turned on the hot water, and grabbed a bar of lye soap. It felt gut to be somewhat in control of a situation that had been out of control prior to her arrival. To focus on something other than her own private issues, and serve someone else for a change. "How far apart are the pains?" she asked Ilene.

"Almost." Inhalation. Exhalation. "Constant." Inhalation. Exhalation.

"Try not to pant so heavily," Bethel counseled her. "Find a focal point, and try to regulate your breathing."

Lydia tore off several squares from the roll of paper towels, and dried her hands and arms. "Do you have any rubber gloves in that bag?" she asked Bethel.

"Jah, a whole box. Medium. Hope those work."

Still clutching a paper towel, Lydia opened the black bag and yanked two latex gloves out of the box. As she stretched one over her fingers, she peered inside the bag once more. "Wow. You have a whole doctor's kit in there, ain't so?" It was a relief to have the needed supplies at hand.

Bethel chuckled. "Probably more than the average doctor's kit. I even have a fisherman's scale for weighing a boppli."

Ilene groaned, and Lydia turned to her. "Your ehemann has gone to call for an ambulance—"

"Nein." Several pants. "Have." Pant. "Them." Pant. "At." Pant. "Home."

"There might be some issues, with the boppli being born premature," Lydia explained calmly. "It would be best to give them professional care. But let's get you out of that puddle, for now." She helped Ilene over to a kitchen chair.

"Not…going…anywhere," Ilene panted. "Need…to…push."

Bethel grabbed a mop from the closet and glanced at Lydia, wide-eyed.

"Okay." Lydia knelt down in front of Ilene and adjusted the mother's skirt. "Push."

Outside, a vehicle squealed into the driveway. A door slammed. Seconds later, an Englisch man burst into the room. "First responder. Ambulance is en route. What do we have here?"

Ilene inhaled a deep breath, then released it with a grunt.

A slippery, blotchy, pink-faced infant slid into Lydia's hands. "A girl."

28

The paramedics had decided not to wait for the second boppli, even though there was a gut chance they would end up delivering the other boppli en route. Once the ambulance carrying Ilene and one newborn boppli had left for the hospital, siren wailing, Lydia and Bethel got to work. As Bethel took down the clean laundry and folded it, Lydia scrubbed the kitchen floor, then washed the few dishes from breakfast.

She was drying a plate when the kitchen door burst open. Luke King's frame filled the doorway. He gave a desperate look around the room before his eyes fell on Lydia. "Where is she?"

"On her way to the hospital by ambulance. She—"

"You let them take her?" he growled, fists clenched.

"You have a dochter," Lydia said quietly. Why was he acting so angry? Was it an overflow of crippling concern for his wife? For the two boppli?

"Please step aside, Luke." Bethel came up behind him with a laundry basket full of folded clothes. "Your newborn dochter needed to go to the hospital. She was having difficulty breathing, since her lungs aren't fully developed. You would've made the same choice. All there is to do now is pray for the health of the other boppli."

"Jah, but who gave *her* the right to make the decision?" Luke snarled. "Isn't she the one everyone's been whispering about? The

228

one who seduced a married man in Sugarcreek, Ohio? Think of me and my reputation, being alone with her in my haus with my frau gone."

Lydia wrung the dish towel in her fists. A dizzy spell washed over her.

"That's enough from you, Luke King." Bethel put the basket on the floor beside the door. "First of all, I'm standing right here, so you aren't alone with Lydia at all. Second, why do you assume it was Lydia who made the decision?"

Luke shook his head. "Gizelle says that she tried to seduce Menno Schwartz, and even your sohn, Aenti Bethel." Luke swiveled to face Lydia. "And that—"

"I don't know where Gizelle is getting her information, but it's nothing more than vicious lies." Bethel huffed. "Who are you going to believe now? The preacher's frau, or a youngie who's jealous because the new girl's getting all the men's attention?"

Luke scratched his beard. "But—"

"Not to mention, Gizelle has been caught in a lie many times, usually trying to ruin other girls' reputations. Her own sister, for one."

Luke scratched his beard again and cast an apologetic glance at Lydia. "Put that way...."

"Wise choice." Bethel nudged the basket out of the way of the door. "Haus is clean, laundry is folded, your bed is made up with fresh sheets, and as soon as word gets around, meals will start being delivered. If I were you, I'd find a ride to the hospital and check on your frau and your dochter—your dochter Lydia delivered. That'd be far better than spreading lies about a newcomer who's been nothing but kind and gracious to you."

"Sorry. Didn't mean any offense. Guess I should've made sure I knew the real story." Luke nodded at Lydia. "Danki for your help." Then he disappeared out the door.

Lydia's knees buckled. She fell backward against the counter but caught herself and remained upright. "It's started."

Bethel shot her a firm look. "And we're going to end it. One person at a time, if we need to. Or maybe in front of the whole church on Sunday, when we announce that we won't honor a shunning that's based on lies." Bethel gathered Lydia in her arms. "Breathe."

"It'll be best if I leave."

Bethel's embrace tightened. "Nein, it'll be best if you hold your head high and don't let them see you sweat. They don't know anything, and if you run now, it'll only make you look guilty."

"But how'd Gizelle find out?"

"Who knows? Maybe Timothy Weiss told her. The letter was delivered to his home, since his daed was the former bishop, Joe. He died around the time of Sam and Abigail's wedding. Or maybe someone else learned of it in a personal note or a chain letter. It doesn't matter. It's untrue."

Lydia's vision blurred. "Caleb wants me to go back to Ohio."

Bethel released her and held her at arm's length. "If he does, it's on a temporary basis, and only because he thinks it might do some gut. Listen to him."

Lydia shut her eyes and swayed.

"He has a gut head on his shoulder, Lyd…. Ach, nein."

Arms closed around her again. Supporting her.

"Breathe. Just breathe."

~

After all the men had left, Caleb put his straw hat on again and heaved a sigh of relief. He wasn't used to being included in Daed's Bible study and prayer group. Even though he'd grown up knowing most of the men who were involved, spending time with them in that context had taken him well beyond his comfort zone. Especially when he remembered Mamm's brother—his onkel Joe, the former Bishop—berating the activity and preaching against it.

But then, there was a lot that'd gone wrong under the leadership of Onkel Joe. It was nice that all the current preachers made a practice of turning to Gott first and acting second.

Still, something about seeing and hearing the men pray together had tugged on Caleb's spirit and drawn him closer to Gott. He wanted to be a better man as a result.

With nein chores to do until evening, Caleb wasn't sure how to spend the rest of his afternoon. Lydia and Mamm still weren't home from wherever it was they'd gone, and Daed had caught a ride into town with Viktor to check on the progress at Judith's Gift Shop. On the one side, Caleb hoped the electricity had been restored and the roof repaired so that his home life would get back to normal—and he could spend quiet evenings *alone* with Lydia after tallying the gift shop's daily deposits. On the other side, having built-in chaperones, while frustrating, was also helpful.

Caleb went to the clock workshop to install weights on the cuckoo clock that was nearly finished, and to get started on the next project.

What would Lydia think if he made a clock for her, and his sisters painted it with sunflowers? Or would that be overkill, after Mamm had gone all out preparing the dawdi-haus according to what she perceived to be Lydia's tastes? But then, Caleb was the one who'd told Mamm about the things Lydia had envisioned aloud when he'd showed her the dawdi-haus the first time she'd visited.

He handled a smooth piece of wood, the beginnings of the next cuckoo clock, his fingertips sliding over the shape.

It would make a nice gift. And her birthday was coming soon. He glanced at the calendar. Three weeks.

It'd be nice to present her with a clock for her birthday. Along with a clean reputation. And his protection.

But nobody had said one thing about Caleb's idea, pro or con. Only that they didn't blame Lydia for not wanting to go to Ohio, and that they would pray about it.

Well, Viktor had spoken up, reminding everyone that he'd taken on the bishop before, done what he wanted, and won.

Sort of. He did end up leaving the Amish.

The workshop door opened, and Daed came in. "The electricity is back on, but the roof had sustained more extensive damage than originally thought. So, Lydia will be here a few more days, at least."

Caleb nodded, groaning internally at the delay. Maybe he could manage to get Lydia alone for a walk to-nacht.

"Have Mamm and Lydia returned from the Kings' yet?" Daed asked. "Heard the ambulance go by before I left for town."

Caleb shook his head. "I haven't seen them. But I really haven't looked for them, either." Though, he had been thinking about one of them. How long had he been working in the workshop? Funny that he always seemed to lose track of time while surrounded by clocks.

"I'll check in the dawdi-haus. I didn't see them in the kitchen when I peeked in." Daed started for the door, then stopped and turned back. "Regarding the question you asked Preacher Samuel about discerning the will of der Herr...I've always figured the simple answer is, what Gott has given you a passion for, He's given you permission for. In your case, He's given you a passion and a love for Lydia. But He's going to expect you to honor Him in your relationship with her, and not to spend every moment alone with her involved in actions that should be reserved for marriage."

Caleb's face heated, and he averted his eyes from Daed's. So, Daed knew about those times, too. But that didn't necessarily mean Menno or Amanda had reported them after finding them by the pond. Lydia had revealed a lot to Daed when she'd explained what had happened in Ohio. And if Preacher Samuel had seen them, he would've put a stop to it right quick, rather than letting it go and simply waiting to report it to Daed.

"I'm still praying about what you suggested in the meeting. I'll inform you and Lydia of the final decision either later today or early tomorrow morgen. If the answer is jah, we'll have to act quickly. Make a phone call to her parents, purchase tickets for the next available bus, and whisper down the grapevine, so the word gets out."

Caleb snickered. "Danki, Daed. Will I be allowed to go along?"

"Oh, I'm sure Lydia's daed wouldn't mind letting you muck stalls. Always gut for a bu to do hard labor for the father of the maidal he's courting, ain't so?" Daed's lips twitched. Then he walked out, chuckling.

Lydia continued to battle waves of dizziness when she returned to the Bontragers' farm. Bethel had hushed up Luke King, but what about everyone else? The word had gotten out. Somehow.

Lydia stepped inside the blessedly deserted dawdi-haus. The yellow gingham curtains over the open windows fluttered in the breeze. Dottie had even made a tablecloth, table runner, and set of placemats with a sunflower theme. Yet the sunny atmosphere failed to cheer Lydia.

To Lydia's surprise, Rosie didn't kum to greet her, even when she noisily poured some kitty treats into the plastic Cool Whip container she was using as a food bowl. Either Rosie was hiding after too much attention from Dolly, or the little girl had taken the kitten along with her somewhere.

After filling Rosie's other dish with fresh water, Lydia carried her purse upstairs to the bedroom, hung it on a hook, then went back downstairs and into the main haus to help fix dinner.

A pleasing aroma of tomatoes and spices greeted her when she walked into the big kitchen. Dottie stood at the stove, where spaghetti noodles boiled in a big stockpot, and red sauce simmered in a smaller saucepan. Vi was slicing a loaf of bread, evidently preparing to spread it with butter and sprinkle it with garlic powder, from the looks of the ingredients on the countertop.

"It smells wunderbaar in here," Lydia said. "Is there anything I can do to help?"

"You can toss together a salad." Dottie moved away from the stove, got out a big glass bowl, and handed it to Lydia. "Use whatever you can find in the refrigerator. There's lettuce, mushrooms, cucumbers, green peppers, carrots, tomatoes, celery, cheese...."

Lydia set the bowl on the counter next to the refrigerator, then opened the door, began collected an assortment of vegetables, and rinsed them in the sink. "Where's Bethel?"

"Weeding the garden with Bethlehem and Dolly," Dottie said. "Dolly took your cat with them."

"My aenti's cat," Lydia corrected her. "Where would I find a vegetable peeler?"

Dottie pointed to a drawer. "Knives are in there, too."

Vi approached Lydia and wrapped her in a hug. Lydia stiffened for a second, not accustomed to displays of affection, but then she hugged her back. It was gut to be loved. The knowledge soothed a parched place in her heart.

"Mamm told us what happened at Luke's. Rumors are awful, but we'll all stand behind you. And I know Daed and the other preachers will do something about the false accusations. Caleb says he wants to prove beyond a shadow of a doubt they're untrue."

"I don't want to go back to Ohio." How many times had she said that today? She pulled away from Vi and reached for the knife drawer. "I'm considering moving on. Didn't my aenti talk to a local girl about managing her shop?"

Vi nodded. "Suzanna. But if you run, everyone will think you're guilty. Like the rowdy buwe who scurry into hiding when the preachers or the police kum around, because they don't want to get caught drinking in the back fields. Or doing whatever else it is they're doing. Best to hold your head high and let Gott handle it. That's what Daed always says."

Lydia managed a smile. "I like the preachers here, so far. The ones back home would be more likely to say, 'There's some truth in every rumor.'" She started peeling a carrot over an old newspaper someone had spread out on the counter.

Dottie shrugged. "Maybe there is, and maybe there isn't. Who are we to judge? Just last church Sunday, one of the preachers quoted a Bible verse that said something like, 'Judge not, lest you be judged.' It's in Matthew, I think."

"Matthew seven, verse one," Preacher Zeke said as he strode in through the door.

Lydia glanced over her shoulder. Caleb and Preacher Samuel entered next.

Preacher Zeke eyed her. "Lydia, we've reached a decision. We leave for Ohio at first light."

29

*C*aleb studied Lydia's expression. Her eyes widened as she stared at the preachers. Then she swallowed, and pursed her lips in a show of disapproval…or was it dismay? The color faded from her face, robbing her of the healthy glow she usually wore, and leaving a pasty-white pallor in its place. *Nein*. Her mouth formed the word, but nein sound emerged.

Her gaze met Caleb's. Another gulp.

"Um…what about church Sunday tomorrow?" Lydia asked, sounding desperate. Grasping. "You were going to draw lots for a new bishop." It was a flimsy excuse, but a glimmer of hope flashed in her eyes as she glanced at Daed.

Caleb knew that nothing would change. They were going. Tomorrow. Besides, if he were honest, he wanted to take a road trip with Lydia. Have a chance to cuddle with her in the backseat of a bus.

But then, Daed would be along as chaperone. Cuddling wouldn't happen. And Caleb would face *her* daed at the end of the trip. Jah, he would be on his best behavior.

"Nein hurry on calling a new bishop." Preacher Samuel pulled his hat off and hung it from a hook on the wall. "The temporary bishop is unable to make it tomorrow, and he's busy next church Sunday, as well. That gives us a few more weeks to pray. Preacher David won't mention anything about you, and neither will I. I'll just deliver another carefully worded sermon based on the verse Dottie just mentioned. Matthew seven, verse one. The reminder would be gut, ain't so?"

Nobody answered him. At least, not verbally. Caleb nodded, never taking his eyes off Lydia.

"I'll go with you to Ohio," Daed said.

Of course, he would. Caleb had known that. But maybe Daed had said it for Lydia's benefit.

Lydia swiped the back of her hand across her cheek.

"And I'll be there," Caleb added. In case she didn't know. "Along with the singular intent to muck the stalls, and do whatever else I can to help your daed." Whatever it took to earn the man's approval, so that he would give Caleb his blessing and let him marry his dochter.

Lydia didn't smile at his attempt at a joke. Maybe she realized he'd said it in jest. Knew that his sole intent was to support her, and expose the man who would have her shunned.

Caleb wouldn't think about the ways in which the plan might backfire. On second thought, maybe he ought to examine the weak angles. Now that he had Daed's support, they needed a watertight plan.

Caleb's fingers twitched, wanting to feel the firmness of a pen. The smoothness of a paper under the nib as he began recording his thoughts as they formed.

"Isn't she a flight risk?" Vi wiped her hands on a towel. "She said she wouldn't go, and that she was considering—"

Lydia cleared her throat loudly, silencing her. Caleb noticed a flash of emotion in Lydia's eyes, but it disappeared before he had a chance to identify it.

Daed chuckled. "Flight risk? Really, Vi? Lydia's brave. She can handle this."

Lydia gave the tiniest shake of her head, as if to deny his words.

Hmm. Judging by that reaction, Caleb would need to spend the nacht in front of the dawdi-haus door. If she hadn't been considering fleeing already, she definitely was now.

"I already called your parents," Daed told her. "Your daed is going to spread the word of your imminent return. I must say, he's looking forward to having you home for a time."

"I miss them." Her voice broke.

"He mentioned they're still considering putting their farm up for sale, and he asked me to keep an eye open for something in this district. Can't say I know of anything offhand, though." Daed patted her shoulder on his way to the table. "Don't worry, Lydia. We will settle this. Whatever it takes. Nothing is too hard for der Herr."

She sighed. "Whatever it takes? You mean, even if I have to kneel and confess something I didn't do?"

"We'll do our best to avoid that. Keep in mind, though, Christ suffered punishment for sins He didn't commit. The sins of the world. I'm thinking you could probably think of something to confess. Hugging him, or kissing him on the cheek, as you mentioned having done."

Lydia nodded. Her gaze darkened as it met Caleb's. She stared into his eyes for a long moment, then looked down at his mouth with an expression of regret, or maybe shame. Was she thinking she'd done more things here, with him, to warrant confessing than at home?

His heart rate increased. He wanted to—*had to*—answer the lure and cross the room. Gather her in his arms. Kiss her until he was senseless.

She dipped her head, breaking the spell.

He forced himself to stay put rather than move toward her. But, ach, he wanted…needed…had to….

Later. Not in front of his family.

Vi filled three mugs with koffee and carried them to the table, while Dottie piled a plate full of cookies—sugar, oatmeal raisin, and chocolate-chocolate chip.

"Will it bother you if we continue with the meal preparations?" Vi asked the men. She frowned at her sister, a silent reminder that it *was* suppertime, even if the men would appreciate dessert first.

Dottie got out the cream pitcher. "Are you staying for dinner, Preacher Samuel?"

"Nein, can't, but danki. Sam and Abigail are supposed to visit us this evening. Apparently they have some news to share."

A soft smile flitted across Lydia's mouth as she resumed chopping vegetables.

Caleb grinned to himself. Sam had shared the news with him, too. A boppli, due sometime in autumn. He kept his mouth shut but figured Preacher Samuel suspected as much.

A chill rippled through him. Lydia had nodded in agreement with Daed, indicating there was something she could confess. She'd immediately taken a shame-filled glance at Caleb's mouth. Then, there was the comment she'd made earlier, one that closely mirrored Caleb's own confession about a hug starting him down a slippery slope.

And the harsh word she'd added as a whisper. *Jezebel.*

Did it mean she would confess to deliberately leading him on? Him, the married man. Him, Caleb. Both of them.

Because…she hadn't. It'd been mutual. They'd been falling in love. Deeper in love. Well, at least Caleb had.

Maybe the other man had felt the same way. Maybe he'd imagined himself in love with the glittery, vibrant Lydia. A woman who embodied life, while his frau needed help with even the most basic self-care.

But Caleb had believed Lydia felt the same way about him as he did about her. That she was falling in love with him.

After all, she'd allowed him to....

Caleb shut his eyes and shuddered.

She'd allowed him, but she'd also warned him that there was absolutely nein chance of a happily-ever-after.

Not for him. Not with the one he'd dreamed of for five months. Loved for five months. Not with the one he wanted.

Not with *her*.

◦

Lydia's stomach churned as she crawled into her bed early that nacht. Yet sleep eluded her. After tossing and turning for what seemed like hours, she finally slipped out of bed, her stomach still in knots. The bus would leave the station at three a.m. Meaning they'd have to leave the haus around two. Why had she bothered going to bed in the first place?

Maybe now that she was awake, she should figure out a way to escape. Such as hiking into town and returning to Aenti Judith's apartment. It didn't matter there wasn't any electricity. But that would be the first place they'd look. And Caleb had a key.

Maybe she could hide out in the spooky basement under the shop. But, nein. They'd likely look there, too. The best hiding place—Daed always said—was in plain sight. Except that she wasn't sure where that would be.

What about the cellar beneath the big farm haus? After Caleb and Preacher Zeke left for town in search of her, she could move to a better hiding place.

Would Abigail let her stay at her haus until she made a plan and hired a driver?

The better question was, could she remember how to get to Abigail's haus?

They would probably look for her there, too.

She'd figure out the details later. Right now, she had to hide. Somewhere. Anywhere. Not taking the time to dress, she reached for her robe and pulled it over her nacht-gown, knotted the belt, and slid her feet into the fuzzy purple slippers she'd discovered on a shelf in the closet. They must've belonged to Caleb's grossmammi. They were warm and comfortable and made her toes want to sing.

Lydia tiptoed downstairs and opened the door to the porch. Caleb fell in backward, his eyes opening just when his head was about to hit the floor.

He caught himself on his elbows and looked up at her. "Going someplace?" His voice was groggy with sleep.

She couldn't keep a sob from escaping her throat. Though, judging by the way he grinned, it must've sounded more like a giggle.

"Guess not." She forced a smile.

"Gut choice." He rose to his feet and turned to face her. His dark eyes met hers and held her gaze, mesmerizing her, pulling her in. Wow, she loved this man. Wanted to spend the rest of her life getting to know him. Taking care of him. Loving him.

But she couldn't. Not until the situation with the man back home was dealt with.

But facing *him*? She couldn't. The fear was too great.

Something flared in Caleb's eyes as his gaze skimmed her robe. Her hair hanging loose.

She fingered a lock, twirling it around. "Sorry. I didn't know you'd be right outside."

"You're so beautiful." He stepped forward, one arm swinging backward to push the door shut. Then she was in his arms, his fingers tangling in her hair, his lips on hers.

Passion flared.

Wow. Just…wow. She hadn't known how heady it felt to have a man rake his fingers through her hair. Sensations she hadn't known existed sprang to life. She wrapped her arms around Caleb's neck as he deepened the kiss.

He walked her backward until she stood against the far wall, his body pressed to hers. Every nerve ending tingled. She moaned, and he made an answering sound deep in his throat. Then he froze, raised his hands, and stepped away.

An apology shone in his eyes. He shook his head, backing further away. "I—"

"Don't. It's okay." Did her voice betray her despair? She was the guilty party here. Not dear, sweet Caleb. She was the Jezebel.

"Nein, it's not okay. We're not married. And Daed warned me against taking liberties I shouldn't be allowed before marriage."

"I'm sorry for tempting you," she said, trying to resign herself to her fate.

"Lydia…." He reached for her. Cupped her cheek with his hand. His thumb trailed over her lips. "You did nothing wrong. Ich liebe dich."

Her heart melted. She leaned into his touch, but with a small shake of his head, he stepped away once more. "I'll be right outside the door. All nacht. If you want to talk, you should get dressed"—his gaze lowered to her robe, then jerked upward again—"and join me on the swing. Otherwise, go back to bed. Because there's nein way I'm going to let you exercise the flight option. You're going to stay and fight."

Fight? Fight for what? Her dignity? Her reputation? Her gut name? Her future with Caleb? The possibility of what might lie on the other side of a trip to Ohio was overshadowed by the ripple of fear *he* would show up and try to steal more from her when he heard she was coming home.

Didn't Caleb realize she was woefully inadequate for the challenge?

And scared?

Terrified was more like it.

The door opened behind Caleb, but this time, he braced himself to keep from falling inside. Lydia stepped out beside him, barefoot, verboden hot-pink polish on her toenails. Her hair was still loose, but she'd put on a royal blue dress.

He wouldn't point out the absence of her kapp. He loved the sight of her sun-streaked hair. Loved knowing he might have the opportunity to run his fingers through the silky strands. Again.

In all likelihood, he would play with her hair. And kiss her. She was like oxygen. He couldn't get enough.

He stood, took Lydia's hand, and led her to the porch swing. They'd have to be quiet, because Mamm and Daed's bedroom window was right above the porch, and it was open wide to let in the cool breezes. Mamm liked the room as cold as it could get, even during the winter. She said it helped her to hibernate. She didn't sleep well during the hot, sticky, muggy summer nachts.

Lydia settled beside him, and he wrapped his arm around her shoulders, pulling her close.

"I can feel your heartbeat," she murmured.

Then she could probably tell that it was pounding. Caleb took a deep breath, willing himself to calm down. He straightened slightly, putting some space between himself and Lydia.

"I'm scared." Lydia sniffed. "As much as I want to see Mamm and Daed and the rest of my family, I don't want to see *him*. Especially after last time, when he tried to abduct me. How am I supposed to go home, knowing I might have to see him?"

That was the plan. Caleb wanted him to look for Lydia. Ideally, at a time when there would be witnesses. Still, he hated to think what the man would've done to Lydia if he had managed to get her away from her home, her family. If he came for her, and Caleb wasn't there to protect her with a pitchfork. But.... "The future is scary and uncertain. Maybe we're supposed to cling to Gott for today, and let Him worry about tomorrow."

"But sometimes my faith falters, and I worry that Gott might not hear me. Sometimes, it feels as though I'm waiting…waiting for answers that will never kum."

"Caleb shook his head. "Remember the passage you quoted the day of the tornado? '*We are hard-pressed on every side, yet not crushed; we are perplexed, but not in despair; persecuted, but not forsaken; struck down, but not destroyed.*' Don't let them destroy you, Lydia. Gott didn't abandon you. He is still here. He says, '*I will never leave you nor forsake you.*'"

She huffed.

"If Gott is in control, then what we know about Gott is more important than what we know about our circumstances."

She sighed and leaned against him once more. "I need to trust that He has this, I just don't see how."

"I know. And that's what it means to have faith." There were things he had a hard time trusting Gott with, too. Like Lydia. *Gott, I love her so much.* And how to tell her about his past. With hers being so similar—the difference being that he'd taken those awful, extra steps—he didn't know how she would react. He didn't want to know. If only he didn't have to tell her. But, at some point, he would have to.

Maybe…maybe he should pray. For this trip. For Lydia. For…everything. He bowed his head. Closed his eyes. *Lord Gott, please go before us to Ohio. Prepare the way for us to clear Lydia's name and to reveal the truth to the bishop there. Protect us. And, most of all, help Lydia—help us both—to trust You, to rest on Your promises.*

She needs to hear it.

Um…. Caleb didn't know what to think about that. Praying out loud? Didn't the Bible talk about the importance of praying in secret rather than in public places?

Not the same thing.

Okay, then. Caleb cleared his throat. He would take this first step of faith. "Lord Gott, please be with us as we travel to Ohio. Go ahead of us and make our paths straight. Help us to internalize those verses from Second Corinthians. Let us never forget that though we may be pressed on every side, we are not crushed. We may be perplexed, but we should not despair. People may persecute us, but You, O Gott, will never abandon us. We may be struck down, but You will not allow us to be destroyed. And help us to rest in Your promise never to leave us or forsake us. Amen."

Lydia turned and peered up at him, a small smile on her face.

He dropped a quick kiss on her lips.

And help me to be able to tell her the truth about what I've done. Help her to forgive me.

She snuggled closer, her face still turned toward his, and parted her lips.

Ah, jah. Maybe another kiss wouldn't hurt.

He threaded his fingers through her hair. Lowered his head.

Passion sprang to life anew.

An unknown amount of time passed as they alternated between talking, sitting in silence while praying or worrying, and kissing. At some point, they both must've dozed off, because the next thing Caleb knew, a flash of light jarred him awake.

He stretched and yawned as the bright beam of Daed's lantern flashlight shifted away from his face. Beside him, Lydia made a soft sound, then pushed away from his shoulder, against which she'd been sleeping. Wrapped in his arms.

Lydia's hair still hung loose, tangled from the innumerable times Caleb had run his fingers through it. Kissing or not, he hadn't been able to get enough of the silky texture of those strands. Or to stop imagining how it would look, spread out on a pillow on their wedding nacht.

Ach, Lord. Let it be so.

Daed shifted the flashlight again, directing the beam toward the porch. "Were you out here all nacht?"

"Is it morgen already?" Caleb winced. "Jah, we've been out here talking and praying." *And kissing.* Caleb averted his eyes, an action Daed would likely notice and later call him out on.

"The driver will be here soon. Lydia, get ready to go, and kum join us for breakfast. Dolly will care for the kitten while you're away." Preacher Zeke's gaze fell briefly on her unbound, uncovered hair. Then he went back inside the haus, where Caleb could hear dishes clattering in the kitchen.

An aroma of sweet cinnamon and tangy yeast drifted out the open window.

Caleb's mouth watered. Mamm didn't make cinnamon rolls often. They were a rare treat. He leapt off the swing, sending it swaying wildly. Then he stopped, turned around, and gripped one of the chains it hung from, to still it. He held out his other hand to Lydia.

She took his hand and stood. "It'd be nice if Gott could still our fears by just putting a hand on them, like you just did with that chain."

Caleb frowned. "He can. Remember when Jesus calmed the sea? All He did was stand, hold out His hand, and say, 'Peace, be still,' and it was so. Maybe all we have to do is be still and wait on Him. In the book of Psalms, He says, '*Be still, and know that I am God.*'"

"But waiting on Him would mean not having to go to Ohio, ain't so?" She flashed a cocky grin.

Caleb chuckled. "Nice try. But Daed said you were brave, and I know that to be true. You've traveled across the country all alone, twice: for Sam and Abigail's wedding, and to kum manage your aenti's gift shop. The question is, will you trust Gott because of who He is, or do you need a promise of a happy ending?"

30

*L*ydia wanted a guaranteed happy ending. But would it be wrong to admit that to Caleb? Conceding it to herself was almost the same as admitting it to Gott, since He knew her every thought.

She mulled over the question for most of the trip to Ohio. Even prayed that Gott would give her grace to accept it if He said nein to a happy ending, instead of breaking down in tears or throwing a private temper tantrum, as she was likelier to do.

Dawn painted the sky red, orange, yellow, and pink as the bus rolled farther into Ohio. Beside Lydia, Caleb slept, his head lolling back against the headrest in his partly reclined seat, his hand still clasping hers. Preacher Zeke sat on his other side, his seat also reclined, his eyes shut. Soft snores emerged from his mouth.

Der Herr *could* promise a happy ending. If He chose to. But trusting Him only if He were to make such a guarantee?

Knots tightened in Lydia's stomach. Pulled.

How could she trust a Gott who might allow this trip to have been made in vain? If whatever it was that Caleb and Preacher Zeke had planned—and she knew there was a plan, though they hadn't shared any details of it with her—didn't work out the way they hoped, then she would be shunned.

But she was already shunned.

Lydia shifted. Worst case, she would confess to sins she hadn't committed. Or hadn't *knowingly* committed. Best case, she would somehow have her name cleared. Maybe even receive an apology for having had her name dragged through the mud. But that might be asking too much.

Even though she despised the accusations he'd made, she didn't want anything bad to happen to him as a result. He had his disabled frau and their kinner to care for, and if the Amish community shunned him, his frau would suffer, as well. Though she likely already suffered, simply knowing her ehemann had been unfaithful.

Or maybe she believed her ehemann when he'd alleged that Lydia had tried to seduce him.

What about the next girl *he* went after? Surely, he wouldn't have stopped with Lydia.

Lydia's stomach churned.

She probably shouldn't think about it.

But how could she not?

Lord, what am I walking into?

They whizzed past a green road sign. *Sugarcreek. Eighteen miles.*

I'm so scared. She dug the fingernails of her free hand into her palm. She must've done the same with her other hand, for Caleb jerked his hand away. But his eyes didn't open. His breathing remained regular. How could he sleep at a time like this?

Lord Gott….

We are hard-pressed on every side, yet not crushed; we are perplexed, but not in despair; persecuted, but not forsaken; struck down, but not destroyed.

Lord, let it be so. Please. I don't want to be crushed, left in despair, forsaken, or destroyed. But give me the courage to face whatever lies ahead.

The courage didn't kum. Fear still gnawed at her. The contents of her stomach threatened to erupt—and probably would have, if the partial cinnamon roll she'd choked down at two thirty that morgen hadn't already vacated the premises.

Instead, her gut grumbled loudly. She pressed her hand against it, as if to quiet the rumbling, but they wouldn't be silenced. Thankfully, the sound didn't seem to disturb Caleb, Preacher Zeke, or the other passengers dozing on the bus.

The bus exited off the highway, going down another street before it growled to a stop in front of the bus station.

Lydia peered out, scanning the shadows for any familiar faces. Would her family kum to greet her, now that she was shunned? Would they send a driver? Or would she and Caleb and his daed be completely on their own, left to find their own way to her home? *Former* home.

What had she returned to?

Time to face the unknown. It felt a lot like descending into the dark, dank cellar beneath her aenti's store, clueless as to what might jump out at her.

She sniffed, coughed, and nudged Caleb.

Caleb stretched, grabbed his hat, and stood, almost colliding with another passenger as he stepped into the aisle. He stopped and motioned for Lydia to exit the bus ahead of him.

She would rather have gone after him, flanked from behind by Preacher Zeke. Protected on all angles.

Was it too late to change her mind?

⁓

It was a chilly morgen in Sugarcreek. Caleb resisted the urge to shiver as he followed Lydia down the narrow steps of the bus. She moved as if descending into a lion's pit.

Daed exited the bus two people behind Caleb, carrying his small travel bag and a plastic sack filled with the remainder of the cinnamon rolls, which Mamm had sent along—probably enough to share with Lydia's family, if they sliced them into halves.

"Lydia!" A form emerged from the crowd, and Lydia had no sooner gotten both feet on solid ground than she was wrapped in someone's arms. A young man's.

Caleb stiffened, hating the surge of emotion that rolled through him with the force of an electrical storm. Then he forced himself to take a final, big step off the bus. Who was this man? Not the one Lydia feared, or she would be fighting to escape his embrace. But what gave him the right—

"Sure you don't want a cinnamon roll?" Caleb heard Daed say.

"Would love one, thanks," the bus driver answered. "Smelled them the whole way here. Would've taken one earlier, but I'm not allowed to eat while driving."

"Understood." The plastic bag rustled.

"Move along, sohn. You're blocking traffic." A hand pressed firmly on the back of Caleb's shoulder.

Caleb stumbled onto the ground, then stepped aside, still observing the reunion of Lydia and whoever this was.

The man released her, then took her by the arm and led her toward the side of the building. Daed, apparently having parted with the entire sack of cinnamon rolls, didn't hesitate to follow them. Caleb trailed him.

"…my brother Kenan." The first part of her sentence had gotten lost in the loud conversations all around them. But Caleb had heard enough. The jealousy receded.

"Nice to meet you," Kenan said to Daed. "Looking forward to putting this all behind us. My daed stopped at the hardware store where the codgers gather to shoot the breeze. He'll spread the news of Lydia's return. Mamm told her quilting group yesterday, so the gossips are well aware, and hopefully *he* will get the news."

Lydia pressed her hand against her stomach. "So that's the plan? For me to see him? And to...what? Treat him cordially? You must've forgotten, his brother's the bishop. He'll likely honor the shunning and stay far away from me."

"We hope he doesn't. We pray he doesn't. Calm down, Sis. We need to face this giant," Kenan said firmly.

"With more than a few stones and a slingshot," Daed put in. "But she needs to go to the battle with the name of the Lord on her side. Too often, our prayer is for Gott to keep things from happening. Maybe that's why Gott is sometimes silent—because we aren't praying for His will but rather for ours. Maybe we should pray for courage to fight this giant, as Kenan said, instead of asking for help with running and hiding. Jah, we might fail, but at least we tried, ain't so?"

"Aenti Judith wrote something very similar in the notebook she left for me." Lydia cast a sidelong glance at Caleb. "I read it just last nacht. She said Gott has a reason for allowing things to happen. We may never understand His wisdom, but we have to trust His will."

Caleb nodded. "Except, bad things that happen are often the result of a fallen world, and not necessarily part of Gott's plan." He stepped up beside Lydia—closer than he should be, but he wanted her brother to know how he felt about her—and extended his hand to Kenan. "Caleb Bontrager. I'm anxious to get this settled."

Kenan eyed them both, then grinned, as if he understood and accepted this extra reason for forcing a showdown to clear Lydia's name.

"We are, too." Kenan shook Caleb's hand. "Nice meeting you. I'm Kenan Hershberger. Mamm said she'd have breakfast waiting when we got back to the farm. Need to pick up Daed on our way past the store. Got everything? Buggy's that way." He pointed with a tilt of his head, then started walking.

Daed shifted his duffel bag. "Will the bishop kum by to visit with us, do you think?"

"Jah." Kenan nodded. "He said he'd stop by after dinner to-nacht to have a talk with you."

Lydia still looked a little pale. Caleb reached for her hand. Never mind what Daed or her brother might think about his public display of affection. She needed reassuring.

Kenan cast another measuring glance at Caleb, as if speculating about his intentions toward his little sister. There would probably be a conversation between them in the barn later on.

For now, Caleb ignored him, anxious to get the mission of this trip over and done with. If things happened the way Lydia had described them happening in the past, the man would be quick to respond—unless he somehow found out that others would be standing nearby to serve as witnesses.

Hmm. Caleb probably shouldn't be seen walking hand in hand with Lydia in public. It should appear that she had returned home alone.

Well, if Plan A failed, they'd have to kum up with Plan B.

But Caleb hoped Plan A would work, because he didn't have the vaguest idea where else to go from there.

❧

The buggy felt cramped with four adults inside. It would be even more crowded when Daed climbed in, likely in the backseat beside Lydia, since Preacher Zeke was seated up front next to Kenan. And Lydia was already pressed against Caleb as it was.

As they neared the hardware store, Caleb pulled her against his side and wrapped his arm around her shoulders. She welcomed the gesture of support. Then she caught Kenan's backward glance at them, his raised eyebrows. What would Daed think? Preacher Zeke didn't look askance at them, but then, he'd already caught Lydia asleep in Caleb's arms that very morgen—though it had been on the porch swing, not in a bed. Besides, she'd told Preacher Zeke outright—albeit accidentally—that she and Caleb had kissed. Proving to him that she was a Jezebel.

And yet, he'd been accepting toward her. Forgiving.

Amazing.

She yearned to comprehend his clement reaction. Caleb's, too. Both men had forgiven her, had taken her word as true, and had not condemned her.

Belief. Trust. Those weren't things one took for granted. Did those qualities have something to do with the men's shared view of Gott? They certainly seemed to have an easier time placing confidence in Gott's will.

Kenan brought the buggy to a stop along the sidewalk in front of the hardware store.

Daed waved gut-bye to his friends, who all gathered around the buggy as he climbed into the backseat next to Lydia.

"Welkum back, Lydia!" they greeted her in unison. Evidently, they had collectively chosen to ignore her shunning.

Daed wrapped her in a hug as Caleb released her. "Glad you're back. So glad. Remember, Gott has this. He has you." He pulled away and peered at Caleb with a wry grin. "And you must be Caleb. The one my frau is all in a tizzy about."

Caleb chuckled. "Jah, I'm Caleb, but there's nein need for a tizzy."

"Your mamm wrote my frau about the blooming romance. I think my frau has already bought some material for a wedding dress. I saw blue fabric near the sewing machine. But don't quote me on that."

"A wedding dress?" Lydia's breath caught in her throat. Hope flared, but she snuffed it out. Until this whole ugly mess was cleared up, it wasn't possible. "But…we're hardly…I'm not…."

"Nice to meet you." Caleb leaned forward with a smile. "And, jah, we have discussed marriage."

Lydia turned her head toward him. "We have?"

"We have. And you agreed." Caleb winked.

Lydia tried to think back to the conversation he was referring to, but she drew a blank. She shook her head.

"You told me you'd marry me in a heartbeat."

Lydia frowned. "I did?"

"At the pond." Caleb's voice lowered to a more intimate tone. "Remember?"

Her face heated as the memory flashed in her mind—along with a remembrance of their shared passion. His kisses, his touch…. She inhaled deeply. "But…you were just teasing. You said something about having to wear glitter in your beard."

His smile was slow to appear. "I was so *not* kidding."

Aenti Judith had mentioned something in the notebook about Lydia's ability to trust that if a certain young man said something, he meant it. That he truly had meant it seemed too wunderbaar to believe.

Preacher Zeke chuckled and glanced over his shoulder. "Sounds like we'll have a wedding to plan after this is over."

Daed nodded with a smile. "I'm anxious to get to know my future sohn-in-law."

Lydia's heart flooded with joy. Caleb really did love her and wanted to marry her.

That was an incentive to fight the man who had given her reason to doubt.

But at the reminder of the imminent fight, and its uncertain outcome, Lydia's stomach settled in a hard knot. They had nein promise of a happy ending. Not yet.

31

While Caleb remained in the barn to help Daed sharpen axes and saw blades, Lydia hurried toward the roadside produce stand carrying a crate of vegetables from their garden. Green tomatoes, green beans, onions, and baby potatoes. Plus a handful of plastic bags, to replenish the supply.

A couple of buggies and an Englisch van were parked along the road in front of the stand, and Lydia slowed when she recognized *his* horse. Uzzah Graber's mare had unique markings on her right hind leg, as though she'd stepped in a bucket of white paint.

Lydia swallowed her fear, squared her shoulders, and marched into the stand via the back door. She glanced around at the crowd of customers gathered around the counter, and noticed *him* standing there with his smallest sohn, who appeared to be about three or four years old. Still too young to be able to speak Englisch. Uzzah's gaze was fixed on her sister Mariah's chest, and he leaned over the counter toward her.

Nein. Lydia wouldn't let him go after her sister. "Green tomatoes here!" Lydia announced, a little more loudly than was necessary.

It worked. Uzzah's assessing gaze turned into a leer as he ogled Lydia's curves. Lydia resisted the urge to grimace as she unloaded her crate onto the nearest table. *Danki, Lord, that Caleb and Preacher Zeke are here, and that they have a plan—whatever it is. Help me to trust them, to trust You, and to know how to behave.*

They'd told her to "act normal." With a quick exhalation, she began filling green produce quarts with potatoes, onions, beans, and green tomatoes. Her legs shook all the while. Hopefully, her face appeared calm. Happy.

She carried several containers over to a display table, then smiled down at Uzzah's sohn. "Hallo, Joseph. Nice to see you today. Would you like a piece of candy?" She reached into her pocket for a wrapped butterscotch, then glanced at Uzzah as she held up the candy piece, level with her chest. *Oops.* She lowered the candy toward the bu.

The bu looked at his daed for approval.

Uzzah nodded.

Lydia handed the treat to Joseph, then stepped back. Her gaze shifted to the elderly Amish couple standing nearby. Theirs used to be one of the largest vegetable gardens in the district, until their sohn and his frau had taken over. The frau preferred flowers to vegetables, and she was a successful Amish florist.

Gut thing there were other customers to wait on. She'd run out of the ability to act normal around Uzzah. "Hallo, Darius and Winnie." Lydia grinned at them. "How are you today?"

"So gut to see you back home, Lydia." Winnie patted her hand. "We've missed your smiling face and twinkling eyes around here. I was hoping for some yellow squash, but Mariah told me that you've run out."

"We had only a few small yellow squash, but I'll make sure to set several aside for you next time." Lydia glanced at Mariah, who nodded back at her. Nearby, an Englisch lady reached for a quart of potatoes and began sifting through them.

"Lydia has a rare sparkle about her," Uzzah spoke up, using Pennsylvania Deitsch. "I'm sure many young men are glad she's back."

Lydia forced a smile that hopefully appeared real. "Danki, Uzzah. That was kind of you to say. Is your frau doing any better?"

Hopefully, the reminder that he was married would discourage him from eyeing the maidals.

"She's been trying some of those essential oils, hoping to restore some mobility to her legs." He spoke in Englisch now. "Not sure they're doing any gut, though. A waste of money, if you ask me. But our neighbor insists they work."

"Oh, they do!" the Englisch lady chimed in as she picked up a quart of green beans. "They've made a huge difference in my allergies. I've never tried them for arthritis, though."

Uzzah grunted, but he didn't correct the woman's mistaken assumption and explain that his frau's problem was partial paralysis caused by a buggy accident that had broken her back.

"I'll take these"—the lady held out the beans—"and those potatoes. Do you have any jam? I heard that one of these roadside stands sells jellies and jams."

Lydia gave the woman verbal directions to the stand in question, then bagged her produce purchases and processed the sale. As she handed the woman her change, she glanced in Uzzah's direction. He was still gawking at her chest.

She resisted the urge to cross her arms over her bodice.

Her youngest sister, Phoebe, touched her arm. "I have to go to the bathroom, but I'll be back," she whispered, giving a subtle nod toward the leering man.

"Do you have peaches?" Uzzah asked Lydia. "The ones you sold last year were almost as sweet as you."

"My brother brought some back from Arkansas." Lydia pointed to one quart box on the other side of the counter. There was a whole big boxful beneath the table. "They'll need to be eaten immediately, though, since they're already ripe."

"Please carry whatever you have out to my buggy for me. My frau can make peach butter from the fruit we don't eat."

Lydia tried to stop the shudder that worked its way down her spine. So, that was his plan? While she loaded the peaches, he'd lift his sohn into the buggy, and then, under the guise of helping her with the peaches, he'd try to pinch her backside? Or, at the very least, pat it.

With a resigned glance at Mariah, she proceeded to fulfill his request.

❧

"He's here!"

Caleb looked up as Lydia's littlest sister came running into the barn, shouting frantically.

"Who's here?" Edward asked, but the glance he gave Caleb told him he knew.

Caleb stiffened and resisted the urge to run outside to the produce stand.

"That man. He's staring at her. Just…staring, and making comments about how her eyes twinkle and how sweet she is." Phoebe tugged at her daed's hand. "Kum, now!"

"We'll wait a bit." Edward nodded. "He knows she's here. This is a gut thing."

"But who will protect Lydia?" Phoebe sounded close to tears.

"Mariah is out there. And other customers, as well. She'll be fine."

Jah, she would be. But Caleb still wanted to run out there with the blade in his hand, and drive the other man away. Stake his claim.

A claim he had no right to make until…. He sighed.

Hopefully, Edward would approve of his request to marry his dochter, someday.

"Caleb and I will protect her." Edward ran his finger over the blade of an ax.

Was there a significance to Edward's having named Caleb first? Was he entrusting the care of Lydia, in large part, into his hands?

Lord, make me worthy of his trust.

The little girl hugged Caleb's waist tightly, catching him by surprise. "I'm glad Lydia has you. You'll go see, ain't so?"

"I'll take a peek and make sure everything's okay," Caleb assured her.

Hand in hand with the sweet little girl, Caleb left the barn and walked around to the front of the haus.

At the end of the long drive, he saw Lydia lifting a box into the back of a buggy in which a small bu was seated. An older, bearded man came up behind her, a bag in one hand. The fingers of his free hand were spread wide, and he was aiming for Lydia's backside.

When he made contact, Lydia jumped and scooted away. The man said something to her, then climbed into the buggy.

Caleb was too far away to be of any assistance, but red-hot rage coursed through him.

Two days later, Caleb spread fresh hay for the horses and filled the troughs. Darkness had fallen, and most Amish folk were already in bed. He and Daed had spent the past three days visiting, talking, eating, and getting to know Lydia's family. In the evenings, the men had discussed various methods of getting the bishop to be there when *he* came. *If* he came.

At this point, it was becoming an unlikely scenario. After all, Phoebe had reported his presence once—and Caleb witnessed his grabbing Lydia's backside. Mariah had verified that he'd stared at her the whole time.

Even so, Edward cautiously optimistic that today was the day. Rather, that to-nacht would be the nacht the creep showed up. After all, the same nacht as the day he'd seen her at the produce stand would have been too soon. Too obvious. He would wait. Give her time to let her guard down.

Caleb doubted she would do that.

Still, the bishop had answered the summons to kum visit with Edward and Daed. They were talking now, somewhere near the almost closed double doors of the barn. Lydia's older brothers, James and Kenan, as well as her younger brother, Omar, were doing some of the evening chores.

Both of Lydia's older brothers had taken care to hide the buggies so that it wouldn't appear the Hershberger family still had visitors. Hopefully, that bit of information hadn't leaked when the word had gone out about Lydia's coming home. Or, if it had, maybe the rumor would get around that they'd already left. It seemed not everyone was as committed as Daed to telling the truth, the whole truth, and nothing but the truth, at all times. Daed didn't ever want to be caught in anything even remotely resembling a lie.

Caleb wanted that same commitment for himself.

That would necessitate admitting his sins to Lydia. He'd acknowledged the necessity all along, but....

He swallowed the bile that rose in his throat.

Lydia—the woman of his dreams, the possessor of his heart—was seated on the porch swing. All day, she had been surrounded by other women—her sisters, her mamm, an aenti or two, several female cousins, and her grossmammi. But as the afternoon had passed, the visitors had left, and darkness had descended over the haus as if all the family were asleep.

They weren't. Most of them wouldn't sleep at all. Not until *he* showed up again. Or until weariness overtook them. *Lord, please, if it be Your will, let this end to-nacht.*

Caleb had nein idea what Daed and Edward were discussing with the bishop. Maybe they were hashing out the "agreement of the extent of Lydia's shunning"—which, so it seemed, nobody in Sugarcreek was aware of yet. It seemed as though the bishop wasn't fully convinced of Lydia's guilt, even if he had agreed to announce her shunning for the sake of his brother's reputation. Of course, the men might be discussing other church business relating to the Amish as a whole. Caleb didn't care. Just so long as the conversation remained quiet, the men remained hidden, and nobody knew they were lying in wait.

Time stretched on until a bright moon and countless stars lit the sky.

Caleb repressed a yawn as he finished the work, then went to eavesdrop on the conversation with the bishop. Omar had headed inside to bed. James had gone home to his frau. And Kenan had said he was going to lurk in the cellar, just beneath the porch, where Lydia still sat, swinging and sipping lemonade. She had an air of apparent nonchalance, but Caleb knew how stressed she really was. She'd scarcely picked at her dinner, having spent more time rearranging the food on her plate than eating it.

The bishop had just announced his imminent leave-taking when Caleb heard a male voice outside.

⌒

Lydia's fingers tightened around the glass, wet with condensation because it was still full of lemonade. She hadn't been thirsty to begin with.

Her stomach churned as she recalled the heated stares from Uzzah Graber at the roadside stand two days earlier. His lecherous gaze had been focused on her seventeen-year-old sister, Mariah, until Lydia had entered the building through the back door.

At least that horrible man had torn his eyes away from her sister's assets. Lydia felt a boost of courage and motivation to somehow this man before he went after her sister, or any of the other young maidals in the area. She'd wanted to fight off his advances, but with her sister's virtue at stake, she'd endured them.

But now...now....

"I knew you'd be waiting for me, Lydia," he said, in a voice that sounded like a hiss. "You couldn't stay away. I knew you'd be back. I'm still prepared to hire you as a mamm's helper. You'd like that, wouldn't you? You'd have your own room. Privacy, Lydia." He grinned vilely. "But you've been a very naughty girl, running away as you did. I may have to punish you a bit for your bad behavior."

Her breath froze in the back of her throat. She couldn't get enough oxygen. Where was everybody? The barn door didn't open. Kenan didn't appear around the side of the haus. Maybe none of them realized Uzzah had kum. Couldn't they hear him? She could reply to him in a loud voice, but that might give something away. Maybe she should take a chance. She opened her mouth to greet him, but cringed and remained silent when she remembered the sensation of his large hand fondling her bottom.

"I might be prepared to forgive you, for a kiss." Uzzah stepped up on the porch and approached the swing.

A kiss? The glass threatened to slip from her hand, so she tightened her grip on it. A scream rose in her throat, but she fought to keep it contained. There had to be a quieter way of cooling him down. Unless it only made him angry.

Should she encourage him to stay in order to give the men time to notice his presence and take action?

A splash of lemonade sloshed over the rim of the glass, splattering her fingers and her dress.

Uzzah lowered himself onto the swing beside her, one hand reaching for her lemonade glass. She opened her mouth and sucked in a breath, preparing to scream, but his other hand clamped over her mouth and nose so tightly that her cheeks would likely be bruised. She should've screamed when she'd had the chance. Maybe she could bash him on the head with the lemonade glass, but he took it from her, even as the thought formed in her head. She couldn't look away from the evil gleam in his eyes. It transfixed and terrified her in the same way as the massasauga rattlesnake she'd seen once.

Nobody had believed her then, either. Everybody told her the rattler was endangered, and the snake she'd seen was probably just a nonvenomous milksnake.

Milksnakes didn't have rattles. And gut men didn't threaten.

She twisted to escape from him, even as he forced one of her arms behind her back with enough force to make her shoulder hurt. "Don't fight me, Lydia. The pain will be so much worse. Your shunning will be just the beginning. I'll hurt your family. Ruin their farm and reputation. You don't want that, do you? All you have to do is admit that you feel for me the same way I feel for you, and kum live with me. My frau won't mind. She knows the way we feel about each other."

Lydia imagined that his frau would mind. Then again, this was Uzzah Graber. Maybe she wouldn't.

He lowered his head toward hers and released her arm so that his hand could clasp the neckline of her dress. He jerked the fabric tightly, pulling it upward and pressing his fist against her throat. She clawed at his hand that still covered her mouth. Dug her fingernails into his skin. She needed air. She couldn't afford to faint. If she did, she'd be at his mercy. As if she wasn't already.

"You are going to be a gut girl now, Lydia, ain't so?"

A whimper was all that escaped from behind the bruising hand. Lydia tried to shake her head but ended up shoving her hand against his chest, instead.

"Gut. Tomorrow, you'll tell your father that I've hired you as a helper, as a token of my goodwill and forgiveness for the lies you spread about me. You'll kum home with me then."

Where were her rescuers? Where was Caleb? Had Uzzah harmed her loved ones already? Her hope faded. *Gott? Are You there? A little help, please…?*

She didn't dare look away from Uzzah. Couldn't find the strength to either nod or shake her head. He tightened his grip on her dress, and Lydia heard a ripping sound. She grabbed at his hand. Hopefully, she could preserve her modesty.

"Gut girl. I knew you'd see things my way. And not one word to anybody, or else."

Or else…what? She didn't know.

But….

"Uzzah Graber? What are you doing here?" Bishop Thomas stood on the porch.

How had he managed to get there without anyone noticing?

Uzzah released her, jumped to his feet, and stammered something Lydia didn't comprehend.

She grabbed the glass of lemonade from its perch on the porch railing and flung the contents toward Uzzah, soaking the side of his face—and the bishop's, as well.

32

*C*aleb stood beside Daed at the foot of the porch stairs. His fingers curled into fists, and his muscles ached to pummel this man—this despicable liar—to a pulp. Hardly a gut Amish response. *Forgive, as Gott has forgiven you.*

Lydia's daed had ascended the steps and now stood beside Bishop Thomas. His hands were also fisted, and his arms hung stiffly at his sides. Kenan was positioned at the other end of the porch, where he'd landed after vaulting over the railing.

Waiting, as they all were, for a reaction—either from the bishop or from Uzzah Graber.

Bishop Thomas mopped his face with his sleeve and turned to look at Lydia.

"Oops." She bowed her head. "I didn't mean…well, I did mean…." Her voice caught. Hitched, as if she were stifling a giggle. She sprang to her feet. "Never mind."

"The maidal asked me to kum," Uzzah insisted. "When I stopped by the roadside stand earlier to buy a few plants, she asked me to kum over to-nacht. She begged me to leave my dear frau and to marry her, instead. When I explained that divorce is frowned upon among the Amish, she asked if she could kum work as a mamm's helper and be my mistress. I'm appalled by maidals these days." He glared at Edward. "You should be ashamed, raising a dochter like this Jezebel."

He was so appalled that he'd kum here to see her? Caleb dug his fingernails into his palms. His hands shook as Daed took a step forward. Edward stiffened. Kenan grunted. Still, they all waited, in a silent acknowledgment of Bishop Thomas's leadership—for the moment.

Though that leadership was precarious, at best.

"Interesting," the bishop said. "That's not at all what we heard."

"What you heard?" Uzzah tugged at his straggly beard. "Then you must've heard wrong. I was here. You were not."

"Nein, but I was there." Bishop Thomas pointed in the direction of the barn. "And your comments were heard loud and clear. Edward, Kenan, Preacher Zeke from Missouri, and his sohn, Caleb, were all present, as well. The Bible puts great emphasis on a crowd of witnesses."

Daed cleared his throat. Twice. "Actually, it's a *cloud* of witnesses, but I don't think that's the verse you want." He stepped forward again, this time continuing up the stairs to the porch. "It's Deuteronomy nineteen, verse fifteen: '*One witness shall not rise against a man concerning any iniquity or any sin that he commits; by the mouth of two or three witnesses the matter shall be established.*'"

Pride, wrongful or not, swelled inside Caleb. Someday, Gott willing, he'd know the Scriptures forward and backward, like Daed did.

"What does that mean?" Uzzah blustered, throwing his hands in the air. "It makes nein sense."

"Seems rather obvious to me," Bishop Thomas responded. "Go home, brother, and leave the maidals alone. We will have further discussions with the preachers." He blew out a breath and sent Uzzah a look of disgust.

Uzzah straightened, firmed his shoulders, and marched off the porch. Caleb stepped aside to let him pass. A gut ten paces away from the haus, Uzzah turned around. "You will regret this. All of you. The girl lies."

"The girl" hadn't said a word since apologizing for splashing the bishop. But nobody corrected Uzzah. They all stood in silence, waiting for him to disappear.

"And you," the bishop said, pointing to Lydia. He scratched his head. "You're no longer shunned, but you should do what you can to stop tempting the men. We will have further discussions with my brother." He nodded at the other men, then turned, descended the porch steps, and strode away.

"What?" Caleb snorted. "Nein apology for the horrible things either man said? After all, the bishop himself called her a 'Jezebel,' and—"

"Some people believe they are perfect, no matter what." Kenan stepped closer.

Daed glanced at Edward, then looked at Lydia. *"When Jesus had raised Himself up and saw no one but the woman, He said to her, "Woman, where are those accusers of yours? Has no one condemned you?" She said, "No one, Lord." And Jesus said to her, "Neither do I condemn you; go and sin no more."*"

Lydia stared at him. She remained silent for one second, two, before she dropped back into the swing and buried her face in her hands.

Daed patted her on the shoulder and turned away.

This time, his gaze landed on Caleb. He hesitated a long moment, their eyes locked. Then he whispered, *"Neither do I condemn you; go and sin no more."*

$\backsim$

A sensation of soothing, healing warmth flowed into Lydia's soul. Such a beautiful feeling, unlike anything she'd ever experienced. Tears burned her eyes. A lump formed in her throat. *Neither do I condemn you....*

Gott didn't condemn her.

Ach, Jesus, danki. Danki.

She'd heard that Bible story many times before, but never had it meant so much. Now she'd been the one accused. The one condemned. And yet....

Neither do I condemn you.

Wasn't that what Aenti Judith had been saying in the notes she'd left for Lydia? That Gott accepted her in the Beloved? And the verse that Daed had been quoting all this time about not being crushed, in despair, forsaken, or destroyed...Gott had heard. He'd listened.

Daed.

Silence surrounded her. Even the nacht creatures were quiet. Not even a cricket chirped. Where was everyone?

Lydia wiped her eyes and looked up, expecting to see Daed. Kenan. Preacher Zeke. Caleb. Someone. Anyone.

She looked around. There, in the shadows, sat Caleb, on the top step. His head was bowed. Was he praying?

She scooted off the swing and sat beside him. "Gott is gut."

He sighed. "Jah, about that...listen."

Sudden fear knifed through her. Was he about to say he'd been kidding about loving her and wanting to marry her, after all? Now, when she was finally free to acknowledge her love for him?

"What that man Uzzah accused you of? Adultery?" Another sigh. "I'm guilty of it."

She blinked. Stared at his profile in the darkness. Nein wonder he'd been so forgiving of her. He'd actually....

The pain of betrayal rained down blows upon her. She shut her eyes against the force of them.

"It happened long before I met you. Before I started taking Gizelle home from singings. Back when...well, Daed mentioned a red sports car. It was then. It was her car. Not mine."

Lydia licked her lips, which had gone suddenly dry.

Caleb gulped. "I felt so guilty. Knew what I'd done was wrong. And that was when I decided to...well, to quit playing kissing games, because kisses—and hugs—can start a man down that dangerous slope. I became the stick-in-the-mud that Gizelle likes to call me, but I determined never to kiss another girl unless she was the one I intended to marry."

His transgression wasn't recent, and he seemed to truly regret it. He really was a gut man. But...wait. Lydia gulped. What if his reason for wanting to marry her was because she'd tempted him to kiss her, and he'd succumbed?

"By the time you and I kissed, I already intended to marry you." It was as if he'd sensed her silent concern. "You came to Jamesport and claimed my heart. The second I saw you—at Sam and Abigail's wedding—something inside me recognized you." He shook his head. "I fell headlong into love. Jah, you drove me too crazy to resist, but ich liebe dich."

She could hardly breathe. "You...you still want to marry me?"

"If you'll have me, and if you can forgive me. Earlier debts were paid in full when Gott forgave me."

She reached for his hand. "I forgive you, Caleb. I'll still have you, definitely."

He twisted his body to face her. "Will you...I'd be so honored if...Princess, will you marry me?"

"Jah. Ach, jah. Ich liebe dich, Caleb."

He reached for her, pulling her into his arms. "And ich liebe dich. Forever and always."

33

The next day, Caleb waited on the front porch while Daed used his cell phone to secure three return bus tickets to Jamesport for the following day.

When Daed had finished, he handed the cell phone back to Caleb. "Did you get everything worked out with Lydia?"

"Jah. I confessed everything to her, and she forgave me."

Daed smiled. "And?"

"And I still want to marry her." An equation that made sense.

"Something tells me you already asked and were accepted." Daed glanced at the open windows of the haus.

Caleb grinned. "Guilty as charged."

Daed clapped him on the shoulder. "I'll give you permission, then. But Edward wants you both to wait until the Hershbergers move to Jamesport. They want to live under sound biblical preaching, not in a community where the bishop and preachers lack theological wisdom and refuse to protect their dochters."

"Did he say when they would be moving?" Hopefully, it would be soon.

Daed lifted one shoulder in a shrug. "They're listing their farm for sale tomorrow. And I will put the word out at home. Gott will provide. He always does."

"I'd rather marry sooner than later," Caleb muttered.

Daed grinned. "Jah, but Lydia has to manage the shop for Judith and Mark until October. So...but then...well...." He chuckled. "I suppose you could move into their apartment, and her parents could live in our dawdi-haus until they find a farm of their own."

Excitement filled Caleb. Especially when he turned and saw Edward smiling. And behind him, Lydia and her mamm.

Caleb stepped toward them and extended his hand to Lydia. "Walk with me, Princess?"

She slipped her hand into his. "Now and forever."

Gott had multiplied His blessings by adding Lydia to Caleb's family.

The future was sparkly, sunny, and covered in glitter, for sure.

ABOUT THE AUTHOR

A member of the American Christian Fiction Writers, Laura V. Hilton is a professional book reviewer for the Christian market, with more than a thousand reviews published on the Web.

Laura's first series with Whitaker House, The Amish of Seymour, comprises *Patchwork Dreams*, *A Harvest of Hearts*, and *Promised to Another*. In 2012, *A Harvest of Hearts* received a Laurel Award, placing first in the Amish Genre Clash. Her second series, The Amish of Webster County, comprises *Healing Love*, *Surrendered Love*, and *Awakened Love*, followed by a stand-alone title, *A White Christmas in Webster County*. Laura's last series, The Amish of Jamesport, included *The Snow Globe*, *The Postcard*, and *The Birdhouse*. Prior to *Love By the Numbers*, she published *The Amish Firefighter* and *The Amish Wanderer*.

Previously, Laura published two novels with Treble Heart Books, *Hot Chocolate* and *Shadows of the Past*, as well as several devotionals.

Laura and her husband, Steve, have five children, whom Laura homeschools. The family makes their home in Arkansas. To learn more about Laura, read her reviews, and find out about her upcoming releases, readers may visit her blog at http://lighthouse-academy.blogspot.com/.